BACKFIRE

A JOHN TYLER THRILLER

THE JOHN TYLER THRILLERS
BOOK 7

TOM FOWLER

WideningGyreMedia

Editing by Chase Nottingham

Cover Design by Stuart Bache

Published by Widening Gyre Media. Silver Spring, MD

For Lisa and Isabel

1

"Do you have any proof I was even in the house?"

John Tyler leaned back and waited for an answer. He knew what it would be. From one of the similar chairs on the opposite side of the large desk, his daughter Lexi arched a dark brown eyebrow. As usual, she wore her auburn hair tied back in a ponytail. She was dressed for mid-fall in jeans and a *Fear the Turtle* hoodie Tyler paid way too much for at a University of Maryland campus shop.

"We got three men saw you outside," the North Carolina cop on the phone said in an accent indicating he'd spent his whole life in the state.

"Not my question," Tyler said. "I specifically mentioned the interior of the house."

"You subdued a man in there. Left him tied to the goddamn refrigerator."

"I understand this is your theory. Want to hear mine?"

"Not really."

"It's worth about the same as yours," Tyler pointed out.

The cop sighed. "Fine."

"I'm sure an important man like Mister White would have

used a security system." Tyler paused, and the detective didn't fill the silence. "Maybe something with cameras? You know .. . actual proof I did what you're trying to pin on me." Tyler had done it, in fact. Thanks to Lexi, the alarm system in Ramseur County Executive Con White's house went offline. Tyler had tried to persuade the man to see reason, but he wouldn't budge. In the end, Tyler tossed a hair dryer into White's bathtub, let electricity do its job, and left the mansion.

"No video," the other man said. "Seems the system malfunctioned . . . but I guess you wouldn't know anything about it."

"I'm a simple mechanic, Detective. I don't know much about fancy alarm systems."

"I never let on it was fancy."

"They all are when you're ignorant about how they work," Tyler said. Lexi smiled, and Tyler gave her a thumbs up. When the cop sighed again, Tyler muted the line.

"You're poking the bear a little," Lexi told him.

"It's not like they have anything."

"Still. I already had to visit you in a North Carolina jail once. I'd rather not do it again."

"You won't have to." After getting thrown in the slammer for a phony vehicular violation, Tyler and three other inmates escaped and exposed the county's exploitation of a nearby Indian reservation.

"Like I told you," the detective said, "we got you outside. Three men saw you."

Tyler unmuted his phone and sent the call to speaker so Lexi could hear both sides of the conversation. "A few days after all this happened, your state police cleared me of charges. What changed?"

"I guess you might say we've reopened the investigation."

"Feds cleared me, too," Tyler said, "so I doubt you're

getting any help there." Again, no reply came. "We're back to my original question. Did any of the men outside see me go in?"

It took a couple of seconds for the other man to answer. Tyler imagined the response caused him pain. "No."

"So you're saying you have me dead to rights on trespassing." Silence from the other end again. "You've had something like six weeks to reopen this mess and go over everything, and the best you've got is me being someplace I shouldn't have been. I'm going to guess trespassing is a misdemeanor. If you want to extradite me from Maryland over something so trivial, I don't think it'll go well for you, your boss, or whatever idiot district attorney makes the decision."

"Now, listen here—"

"I would offer to pay the fine, but it didn't exactly clear things up for anyone involved the last time I did. My lawyer works for the Judge Advocate General on Fort Meade. I'm sure he'd enjoy ripping a couple out-of-state knuckleheads some new assholes over a trespassing charge."

"You saying you don't have the skills to get into White's house?" the cop wanted to know.

"Come on, Detective. Fort Bragg is a few hours to the east. I trained there. You could find a thousand men inside those walls who could have made it past the guys outside."

"We didn't see none of them on the premises."

"And you didn't see me inside, apparently."

"You were there."

"You told me one man ended up tied to the fridge."

"Yup. Same way the others were trussed outside."

"Did he happen to spot me?"

"No," the cop admitted. "You apparently got the drop on him."

"Something else a thousand men from Fort Bragg could

have done. Doesn't sound like it was very difficult anyway. Are we almost done here? I'd like to stop wasting my time and get back to work." Smitty and Ortiz, the two employees of Tyler's classic car shop, worked on vehicles in the service bays, and a couple other vintage models waited for someone to pull them in.

"You killed a man," the cop insisted.

"Prove it," Tyler said. "Otherwise, reopened investigation or not, piss off and leave me alone."

"We're gonna keep digging," the detective said.

"It's gone really well for you so far."

"You're kind of a prick, you know?"

"I do. Maybe you can try to add it to your slim list of charges against me."

"You don't get to murder the executive of Ramseur County and get away with it."

"I'm pretty sure things are better off with Con White out of the way," Tyler said. "He was running an illegal operation and paying the Sappony tribe pennies on the dollar for gold taken from their reservation. I follow the news, Detective. I know his successor went back to the table, negotiated a fairer deal, and is now sharing the profits more broadly across the state."

"So?"

"It means people beyond the borders of Ramseur County get to benefit from the money now," Tyler said in a tone suggesting he was explaining the basics of math to a child. "Millions more people will see their lives affected for the better. Sounds to me like I'm something of a hero down there. Now, you might find twelve people who thought the sun rose and set in an asshole like Con White. There's no accounting for taste, but whoever greenlights the case would be taking a pretty big risk. Your DAs are elected, right?"

"Screw you," the cop said and hung up.

"Something I said?" Tyler wondered to the empty line.

Lexi chuckled. "You enjoy tweaking the cops."

Tyler shrugged. "When they're fishing, sure."

"What are you going to do if they decide to charge you?" she asked.

"Call Lowery." Major Kevin Lowery was Tyler's attorney. So far, he'd only needed to make one quick in-person appearance and another over Zoom in the year or so they'd been acquainted. Representing Tyler in another state would be very different, and he didn't know if Lowery would do it or punt it to someone else in the office. Either way, the threat of a JAG lawyer who happened to be an O-4 would force a DA to think twice about bringing charges with anything less than an airtight case—something Tyler knew they would never assemble.

"I should get back to my apartment before traffic gets worse." Tyler glanced at his wall clock. There were few good times to drive on the Capital Beltway, and most of them came well after sundown. It was almost four in the afternoon. Lexi would hit a fair bit of congestion on her drive back to College Park, but at least she wouldn't need to be on I-495 long.

"Thanks for coming by," Tyler said. "I couldn't do some of this without you."

She smiled. "I know, Dad. I'm happy to help. Even happier when you pay me for it."

"Learn to rebuild an engine, and I can give you even more hours."

"I'll pass, thanks." She shrugged back into her jacket. "See you later. Try to stay out of trouble."

Tyler nodded. "I'll do my best."

2

Malachi Golan sat in a Land Rover by the side of the road and waited.

He was patient. His superiors in both Mossad and Shin Bet told him it was one of his best attributes. Wait long enough, and the other guy will make a mistake or show you something he shouldn't. Today, he observed a man named Carl Bendix go through his unexciting daily routine. From an early morning run to a trip for groceries to a brief stop at a co-working space, Malachi tailed Bendix. For someone who had once been an elite American soldier, the guy didn't seem to have good situational awareness anymore.

Maybe getting married years ago made him soft. Malachi carefully avoided personal entanglements in Israel. Sure, he indulged in the pleasures of the flesh from time to time but never with the same woman more than a few occasions. Anything further risked dulling the edge he'd spent years honing.

This is what happened to Carl Bendix, and it would be his undoing.

The basic Android phone on the leather seat beside him

buzzed. It was a new burner—the second from the case he bought—so no name appeared, but he knew the number. "Hello."

"You are watching the American?" Pazir Khayal asked. His English was good, but a noticeable Afghani accent remained.

"Of course."

"And?"

"And I am glad I made different choices in my life. He is soft now. This will be easy."

"Do you expect to stay in California much longer?"

"I doubt it," Malachi said.

"Good. Perhaps you could avoid ordering room service twice a day until you leave."

"I need to eat."

"The country is lousy with McDonald's. Just follow a bunch of fat Americans, and you will find it."

Malachi snorted. "Real work requires real food." He'd always enjoyed a good meal—doubly so on someone else's dime. Pazir certainly had the money to afford steak dinners even at room service prices. "If you wanted to pinch pennies, you could have hired someone else. Instead, you wanted the best, so you came to me despite our philosophical differences. I said yes because your money is good and only because your money is good." Malachi wondered if Pazir would pick up on the implicit threat. The trafficker was the type of man Malachi would have taken out in his Mossad days. Only the promise of rich paychecks kept him from turning a pistol on his benefactor.

"All right, all right," Pazir said. Malachi smiled at the slight tremble the older man probably wasn't even aware had crept into his voice. "Tell me what you have seen so far and what you plan to do."

"He's married. No kids. Works from home for the most

part though he also goes to some coworking space from time to time."

"When do you plan to kill this man?"

"A day or two," Malachi said. "I drove his running route earlier. He passes through an area with no cameras."

"Not even on other buildings?"

"No. It's a dead zone. I got out and checked with the scanner you paid for."

"Excellent. I will wait to hear of your success, then."

"From here, I'll head east. There are still a few good targets before I make it to Maryland."

"Do what you think is best," Pazir said. "I don't care how many of these men you kill. Remember the goal is to make John Tyler suffer."

"I have plenty of ways in mind to ensure he is a broken man before he begs me for death."

"Music to my ears, my friend."

Malachi ended the call before he needed to remind Pazir they were not—and would never be—friends. They were unusual business partners brought together by the union of purpose and money. Malachi was good at killing people and enjoyed it, and Pazir had the bankroll to make it happen. If a few retired American Green Berets died, Malachi would shed no tears. The Israeli held no grudge against them, but he funded his lifestyle by getting paid.

He expected to live the high life for a while after this.

Lexi stretched and threw the covers off her.

She silenced her phone alarm. Emily and Kim, her two roommates, both got up around the same time she did. The trio arranged their schedules to be as similar as possible, and it worked well most days. No one needed to wake up way earlier than anybody else. Lexi took a quick shower, put on jeans and another of her Maryland hoodies, and joined her two friends in the dining room.

Kim, a beautiful half-Asian girl with jet black hair, poured herself a cup of coffee. The machine made two full pots each morning, and judging by the amount remaining, Lexi would need to make the second. "Good morning, sunshine," Kim said. She still wore bangs to cover a faint scar on her forehead from an on-campus shooting a few months ago—an event Lexi knew more about than she told her friend.

"It'll be good once I have some of this magic juice." Lexi poured the last cup from the pot, added some milk, and then set the machine up to brew another round. Past the aroma of java, she smelled toast and eggs.

"I cooked," Emily said. "I was up early." She sat at the table already. Emily was pretty and bore some resemblance to Lexi, especially when it came to their hair colors and preferred style. Lexi stood two inches taller at five-eight. She joined her friend at the table. It seated the three of them easily, four with a fair degree of comfort, and struggled with any gathering of five or more. Their apartment was open concept, and the friends arranged the living room to take up a good bit of the available space.

"Thanks." Lexi spooned some eggs onto her plate and plucked two pieces of wheat toast from the pile. "I guess it's my turn to make breakfast one of these mornings?"

"I think it's been your turn for like a week," Emily said with a grin.

"Great. Oatmeal for everyone tomorrow morning."

Kim shrugged. "It doesn't need to be fancy." She grabbed the chair across from Lexi. "Does your dad cook?"

"Some," Lexi said. "He never really learned how, and I doubt army barracks were the best places to pick it up." She didn't mention her mother. Rachel was acceptable in the kitchen, but she'd never put much effort into it and didn't pass any pearls of wisdom to her daughter. The woman spent the last two years and change enjoying prison food. Lexi doubted her mother would have any gourmet advice to share once she was released.

"Oatmeal's fine," Emily said. "You can put what you want in it. Make it your own."

Lexi spread her hands. "I'm providing you a culinary canvas."

Her friends giggled. "How's your class load today?" Kim asked.

"Not bad," Lexi said after a bite of egg. They needed a little salt and a lot of pepper, but she was grateful someone else took the time to cook this morning.

"You any closer to picking a major?"

"Nope." Like a lot of sophomores, Lexi packed her schedule with general requirements she would need to graduate regardless of what she eventually chose as her major. Emily and Kim declared theirs right away—mass communications and business administration respectively—but Lexi didn't know what she wanted to do once she graduated. Her dad had been career Army, and while she respected his service, she had no desire to enlist. Rachel was a longtime criminal and con woman. Neither parent provided anything useful in terms of picking a career. Lexi acquired a proficiency with computers over the years, and even helped her father on some of his more interesting exploits. Maybe she could find something in that arena. "I'm having fun with you two," she said. "I can figure the rest out later."

"Roommates forever," Emily said. "Or at least until we're done here."

"Or Kim gets married," Lexi added.

Kim blushed. She was the only one of the trio with a boyfriend at the moment, though she and Xavier seemed a long way from shopping for rings. "I don't think we need to worry about that anytime soon."

Emily grinned. "Like I said . . . roomies forever." The girls bumped fists on it. Lexi finished her breakfast. She was happy with her living arrangements—a condition which hadn't always been true over the past few years. The last several months with her mom were fraught with tension, and then she went to live with her dad at a moment's notice. They ended up in a good place, but it took several weeks to get there. Things with Emily and Kim were easy.

Lexi hoped nothing would happen to change that.

3

MALACHI NEVER ENJOYED GETTING UP EARLY.

He would do it when the job called for it, however, as this one did. Bendix, probably owing to his time in the Army, woke up before dawn each day. He hit the streets just after four-thirty for about a forty-minute run. Malachi had seen this unfold the last two days. He'd needed naps in the afternoon, but gathering the intel proved worth it. Bendix ran the same route on days one and two. No reason to presume he would vary it on the third day.

Another example of going soft in his post-military life.

To this day, Malachi varied his routines. He didn't want anyone to find him predictable. If the enemy knew where you would be and when you would get there, the results were rarely good. Malachi waited in a stolen twenty-year-old Ford Explorer. It was big and black, so it would blend in on the SUV-crowded roads of America. Another perk was its lack of both an alarm system and onboard GPS. Popping the lock and driving it away took a minute combined. The owner and her neighbors remained oblivious.

Now, Malachi bided his time in the camera dead zone he

told Pazir about the previous day. Bendix's route took him from one neighborhood to another before looping back. In the half-mile or so of unimproved space, no electric eyes watched the surroundings. It was still dark, so the presence of another vehicle—very unlikely based on the past two days—would be easy enough to spot.

A few minutes later, Bendix rounded a curve and entered Malachi's field of vision. The Explorer sat on the opposite side of the street with its lights and engine off. Malachi slouched in the driver's seat. A street light revealed the earbuds Bendix listened to. Malachi shook his head. The man was making this too easy. He didn't mind a simple job here and there, but on the whole, he preferred being challenged. Showing an adversary you were better demoralized him in his final moments. One last insult.

When Bendix jogged about fifty yards along, Malachi touched the loose wires together again and fired up the Explorer. It was a V6 model, so the exhaust didn't rumble as loudly as the V8. He U-turned, passed the American, and kept going. When he came to a cross street two hundred yards further, he swung the SUV around again. His headlights now illuminated Bendix in the distance. Malachi steered away from the curb to act like he was giving the runner space.

He could have plowed Bendix down from behind. They were both soldiers, however, and he could give the American this final courtesy. As the vehicle approached, Malachi pressed harder on the accelerator and nudged the wheel to the right. The Explorer struck the surprised Bendix, whose head slammed into the hood when his body folded in half on impact. It then flew about fifteen feet, landing in an awkward heap. Malachi drove on about fifty feet before stopping and checking the rearview.

Bendix lay with both legs at odd angles and blood

pooling around his head. He was probably dead already. If not, the vultures would be circling soon. Still, from one soldier to another, there was no reason to prolong his suffering. Malachi put the Ford into reverse and stepped on the gas. The Explorer rocked a couple of times as he backed over Bendix. The grisly scene on the asphalt left no doubt about the man's demise now.

Malachi reversed near a curb, pulled a 180, and drove away. A package of cleaning wipes sat on the passenger's seat. He would remove any traces of himself before ditching the vehicle far enough away both from where he stole it and from the Bendix scene to delay suspicion. Later, he would give Pazir the details.

The first man on the list was dead. John Tyler's suffering had begun.

VERONICA FITZGERALD CROSSED the border into Maryland.

She'd assembled a long story about Tyler in North Carolina. It got a lot of clicks and engagement. She'd been a reporter just long enough to remember when subscription numbers and articles read online mattered. Now, it was all about satisfying some mysterious algorithm standing between the publication and the readers. The depth and popularity of the article led her to write a few follow-up pieces as the fates of the major North Carolina players grew clearer.

In her stories, she avoided mentioning Tyler by name. Instead, she referred to him as a "retired Green Beret," an accurate description which did not make him remarkable in the state housing Fort Liberty (formerly known as Bragg). However, she got a hold of Tyler's military record. The public version was sparse, but he'd clearly been a skilled operator who survived four combat deployments in Afghanistan.

She intended to do a real story on Tyler. There should be enough regional interest in North Carolina and Maryland, and the story could get legs nationally. A sizable segment of the population liked vigilantes who did things the police couldn't. Over the past few weeks, Veronica wrote more pieces than normal to get some extra money in the bank. She took a leave of absence to drive to Maryland and write her *magnum opus* about John Tyler.

Veronica drove up from the southern end of the state. She fiddled with the radio in her car, eventually finding a station playing acceptable pop music. Her suitcase rattled around in the trunk. Beside her on the passenger's seat, her backpack held her laptop and the compilation of all her notes about her subject. Once Tyler retired from the Army about a decade ago, he spent eight years working for a private security company. She couldn't find much about what he did. The organization touted its executive protection capabilities.

Tyler's departure from the private firm is when his life really became interesting. None of his exploits were explicitly spelled out in news coverage. Veronica cast a wide net for stories, blogs, and columns, and spent countless hours reading between the lines and making connections no one else seemed to care about. As far as she could tell, Tyler killed his former commander who got out of Leavenworth years earlier than expected, along with a bunch of the man's cronies.

From there, he took on a Mexican drug cartel, saw his former boss's business burned to the ground, took out a major trafficker who abducted popular singer Alex Anne, opened his own classic car shop, rescued a young woman (and fellow reporter) who'd been kidnapped by a local politician, eliminated a militia in West Virginia, and thrown Ramseur County into chaos.

She didn't doubt Tyler meant well. The people he went up against were the worst of the worst. Still, she wasn't comfortable with one man playing judge, jury, and executioner. Some of her readers would be. Veronica would keep her own biases out of the story. There would be enough content for her audience to draw their own conclusions.

While she could have continued working on the article in North Carolina, Veronica hoped to talk to Tyler and his daughter Lexi. The girl brought her in when it was clear Con White and his lackeys were exploiting the Sappony people. Now, with her dad in the investigative crosshairs, she wondered if Lexi would have anything to say. Tyler would probably stonewall her. Everything she'd learned about him indicated he didn't chase personal glory and was a man of few words.

The part she hadn't worked out was keeping Tyler out of trouble. Law enforcement agencies either didn't connect him to what happened or didn't care. On some level, she understood. Tyler eliminating a cartel's Maryland expansion saved the Harford County Sheriff's Office a lot of work. Why put a ton of manpower into investigating someone who made your life easier? By exposing what he'd done, Veronica would be opening Tyler up to new scrutiny. Maybe even prosecution. North Carolina officials reopened their inquiry after initially clearing him, and while she didn't expect them to find anything, other agencies might dig deeper or better.

She'd even hired some of her own help. Two Maryland private investigators with prior military experience were going to follow Tyler. Veronica told them it wouldn't be easy. He remained alert and skilled—and maybe a little paranoid. Both men assured her they had training in keeping tabs on people like Tyler. They came recommended and well reviewed, so she took them at their word.

Even though he operated in a brutal and extrajudicial fashion, Tyler helped people who needed it. Veronica changed the channel. Frivolous pop songs no longer matched her mood, and she stopped when she came to a hard rock station. For the thousandth time, she wondered how she could write a complete and accurate article while somehow not landing her subject in jail.

She would have time to work on the balance.

$$4$$

TYLER GRIMACED AT THE CHOICES.

"Is there another menu?" he asked his girlfriend. Sara Morrison lived in Columbia—about a half-hour from Baltimore in the direction of D.C.—and took him to a bistro in the posh city. The word *Bistro* being in the restaurant's name should have been the first clue. Tyler hadn't seen Sara in a few weeks, however, so he was happy to take a long lunch break from the shop to meet her.

"Why?" she asked with a smile. Sara was forty-eight and looked at least a decade younger. Today, she wore jeans and a sweater, but in the right outfit, she could turn heads from twenty to eighty. Her black hair hung past her shoulders, and even from across the table, the fruity perfume of her shampoo filled Tyler's nostrils. "Too much avocado for you?"

"And pancetta," he said. "Fancy bacon at twice the price."

"We *are* in Columbia," Sara pointed out.

"The waiter's man bun made it obvious." Tyler found a burger and fries, winced at the price, but figured it was the most normal thing on the list. He set the laminated paper down. "I know you can't tell me much about it, but how was your trip?"

"In a word . . . good."

"How about in a longer word?"

"Interesting." Sara worked as a high-ranking official in the US Department of Defense. She enjoyed a nice office at the Pentagon. Her official title changed occasionally, but she sometimes needed to travel overseas. When she did, the job took her to parts of the world unfriendly to women, Americans, and especially American women. This excursion left her halfway around the world for almost two weeks before she returned last night. While Sara always looked lovely, her makeup didn't quite hide the bags under her eyes.

"Good or bad interesting?" Tyler asked. He'd used the word a lot himself over the years.

"Somewhere in the middle," Sara said. "I'm fine," she added before Tyler could press her. "Nothing bad happened to me over there. Just a long trip." She stifled a yawn. As a prominent official, Sara would travel with a security detail. The odds of something happening to her were long but not impossible.

The waiter popped over for their order. Sara ordered some sandwich with pancetta, and Tyler opted for the pricey burger and fries. When the server walked away again, Tyler said, "It's good to see you."

"You, too," she said with a smile. "How's the business going?"

"Steady. I think we've managed to get a lot of the folks who used to go to Smitty's."

"And the knight errant business?"

Tyler grinned and lowered his voice. "Quiet. The North Carolina cops seem to think they might be able to pin something on me. So far, all they have for sure is trespassing."

"The FBI has still cleared you, right?"

He nodded. "I don't think it'll turn into anything. Some-one's just salty because a crooked politician who was lining the right people's pockets died."

"Sounds like what I've heard," Sara said. "The feds are taking the lead thanks to things crossing state lines. The Sappony have asked for recognition, too. Plenty of moving parts and men with three-letter agency windbreakers walking around, but it'll all get sorted out. You do good work, Tyler. I don't think you go about it the way I would . . . or the way many folks would recommend . . . but the right people get help in the end."

"It's in the knight errant handbook," Tyler said.

"I'll take your word for it."

"You want to take some time off coming up? I really haven't had a vacation in a while. Might be nice to go some-where for a couple days."

"I'd like that," Sara said with a smile. "It would be nice to pack my bags for a personal trip for a change. I've gotten tired of some soldier picking up my suitcase."

"How about a retired one?"

Sara chuckled. "I guess I can make an exception for you."

The waiter returned with their food. The man bun situa-tion remained unchanged. Tyler plucked a few fries and added a little salt. Sara's fancy bacon sandwich came with some side salad full of greens Tyler couldn't identify and wouldn't want to eat. He guessed one was kale. His limited experience with the vegetable convinced him incinerating it was far better than trying to choke it down.

"Any idea where you might want to go?" Sara asked when they'd each eaten some of their meals.

Tyler shrugged. "I figured I would defer to you."

"You just want to use my government hotel rate."

"It's about time you figured out I love you for the travel perks."

Sara laughed around a mouthful of her dreadful salad. "I'll pick a nice destination, then. Your job is to be sure you're not going to be playing knight errant at the time."

"I don't think I will be for a while," Tyler said.

~

MALACHI STEPPED off the small plane and onto the tarmac.

The pilot thanked him for flying, but Malachi ignored him and headed toward the doors leading to the interior of Astro Airfield. He stopped before crossing the threshold and called Pazir. "I'm in Texas," he said when the other man picked up.

"You made good time. An advantage of the expensive charter flight you booked."

"I wanted to get here quickly and without American police taking notice."

"They're still calling the California incident an accident," Pazir said. "Are you going to rent a Maserati and make me spend even more?"

"For a rich man who wants a very specific job done," Malachi said, "you love to count your pennies and nickels."

"How do you think I got to be rich?"

By selling opium and girls, Malachi thought. Instead, he took the diplomatic route and said, "I suppose you're right."

"Let me know how this one goes," Pazir said and ended the call. Malachi grunted, put his phone away, and walked into the small terminal building. One of the perks of a chartered flight was avoiding a large airport. Hundreds and often thousands of people milled about. The food choices were dreadful and meant for commoners. What passed for transportation outside was foreign men in taxis who needed their GPS apps to get around.

Malachi passed almost no one as he walked out the other

side of the terminal less than a minute later. No taxis idled, but the Uber X he booked awaited. It was an Audi Q7 SUV. The driver, a wiry white American in a suit jacket and sunglasses, greeted his passenger and put two bags in the trunk. Malachi kept a messenger bag and carried it into the back seat. The man already knew the destination, so other than a brief exchange of pleasantries many Americans favored, Malachi didn't need to speak to him. Instead, he took out a file folder and opened it.

Carl Burns was a Green beret whose career overlapped with John Tyler. They went on two combat deployments together, with Burns doing his third after Tyler retired and their former commander landed in prison. Burns retired from the Army a few years ago, was now 48 years old, and lived alone about thirty minutes from Astro Airfield. Pazir's people assembled a detailed file, and Malachi appreciated how thorough they were. The man clearly employed a few people who knew how to get information by illicit means. Israel had long been good at the cyber arts, and Malachi came to respect it as a means of supporting soldiers and organizations like the ones he worked for.

The extended dossier told a story of a man struggling to re-adjust to civilian life. Burns bounced between jobs which should have been beneath him and was currently unemployed. He lived in a house he inherited from his late father or else he might have been homeless. The file also mentioned he sought therapy for post-traumatic stress disorder, a common problem for warfighters. Pazir's team even managed to obtain some of the records from the therapist who worked under the Veterans Administration.

Malachi didn't read the psychiatrist's notes. He'd seen plenty of good, strong men have trouble when they left the service. Before going into intelligence, Malachi spent eight years in the Israeli Defense Force. He'd seen combat. Been forced to shoot people if he wanted to wake up the next day. Some people could handle it and keep going. Others needed help, and he didn't fault them for it. Pazir probably saw it as a sign of weakness. Malachi resolved to keep the expenses high while he worked on this little revenge campaign.

Skipping past the therapy notes, Malachi came to the section detailing Carl Burns's activity. He belonged to a gym and went for at least an hour every day. Without a job, he performed some repairs on his house and even did a little work for others nearby. His social life consisted of drinking in bars, usually alone, though the report did not suggest the man had a problem with alcohol.

Malachi knew he would need a plan. He couldn't take Burns lightly. The man served with distinction in the 5th Special Forces Group with counterterrorism and counterinsurgency missions. Even if he were retired and mentally compromised in some way, his extensive training would kick in if he were in danger. The instincts never really left you as Malachi understood all too well. Burns would also enjoy the advantage of reach as he stood six-seven. As the Uber neared his hotel, Malachi continued reading, spending several minutes on Burns's house and the surrounding area. He wouldn't be able to replicate the method he used to kill Bendix.

Just as well. A fresh challenge called for fresh thinking.

5

TYLER WAS IN THE SHOP GOING OVER THE WORK FOR THE WEEK when his cell phone buzzed.

Musa Sadozai's name and number appeared on the screen. They'd served together in the Army and did three overseas tours under former Colonel Leo Braxton. Musa and Tyler had kept in touch since they both retired, but neither was the type to make social calls. Tyler wondered what was wrong as he answered the phone.

"It's Gumby," Musa said.

"What?"

"Bendix. He's dead."

"Shit." Tyler blew out a deep breath. Alan Bendix had been a good soldier and a better man. He and Tyler went into many houses, compounds, and sketchy facilities overseas and always made it out alive. The man even accepted the nickname Gumby with good humor despite hating the old cartoon and toys. Everyone eventually accepted their monikers just like Tyler had to do with Tippy. They were badges of respect.

"Yeah," Musa said. "First man we've lost since we've been home. Probably had a run of good luck there for a while."

"Where did he end up?"

"California."

"Where he was from," Tyler said. "Do you know what happened?"

"Car accident."

Something in his friend's tone made Tyler frown. Musa was an Afghan-born Muslim whose family came to the US when he was an infant. He took a lot of crap for it in the Army, did his job very well, and came out the other side. He didn't really have an accent, but Tyler didn't like something in what he said. "He was driving?"

"No. Hit and run while he was out on his morning jog."

"I guess whoever ran him down fled the scene?"

"Far as I know, yes."

Bendix probably chose a good route. Close to his house. Well lit enough even in the morning to see a car coming. He would have run on the left side of any roads so oncoming traffic would be in front of him. "Does this smell fishy to you?" Tyler wanted to know.

"A little. I don't have many details yet, but I've asked." Musa settled in as a cop with the Delaware State Police after retiring. He would have contacts in law enforcement who could share information with him. "We'll see what I get."

"Maybe I'm overreacting because Gumby is the first one of us to go, but this just doesn't shake out right."

"Maybe," Musa acknowledged. "I learned your instincts are pretty good. If you think this is fishy, there's a good chance it is."

"What do you want to do about it?"

"I was about to ask you."

"I want to find the son of a bitch and put his head on a pike," Tyler said.

"What if it really was an accident?" Musa asked.

Tyler shrugged. "Then we let the locals handle it, and the driver goes to jail. If it was something malicious, though . . . we deal with it. Our way."

"I was already thinking of flying out there for his widow and family. You in?"

Tyler grimaced. He didn't care for flying, and long flights only made the feeling worse. He'd chosen the Army over the Navy to his father's eternal chagrin because Tyler got seasick. The same unease gripped him when he flew, though not as strongly. He could usually manage with some Dramamine, deep breaths, and white-knuckle grips on the armrests. Still, this was Gumby. Their first unit mate to die since the war. The man had a family, and his friends should show up for them. "Yeah," he said after a moment. "I'm in."

"Good. I'm going to try and get a flight tomorrow. You want me to buy you a ticket, too? You can always pay me back. I know you're good for it."

"Sure. Thanks. Text me the details, and I'll see you at the airport."

"You got it, Tippy." Musa hung up. Tyler set his phone down. He stared from his office into the service bays without really seeing what went on. A memory played in his head. The team breached a large stone house. They dispatched a few hostiles near the front and moved through. Tyler and Bendix on the wings of the formation both spotted a tripwire a scant few seconds before someone was about to walk into it. A couple minutes later, Bendix took care of things, and they kept going, taking out everyone inside while sustaining no casualties.

It could have been a lot worse. Alan Bendix made sure it wasn't. He'd saved ten lives by using his eyes and his wits, and now, he'd never get to save anyone else again. Tyler knew he would need to spend some time at the easel later. His therapeutic painting program helped a lot over the last few years. For now, however, he needed to pack for a California trip he never wanted to take.

∼

Malachi sat and observed.

He'd needed to move the car already. A nosy neighbor paid too much attention to the Range Rover sitting on the street and not moving. Malachi rented the vehicle from a local using an app. He chose one with tinted windows. The older man in the house couldn't see inside, and the engine remained off. Still, the guy proved persistent, and Malachi didn't want to attract attention.

He moved the SUV, kept watch a short while longer, and then left the neighborhood. Taking out Carl Burns would be considerably different than Alan Bendix. On some level, jobs always had their differences. The remoteness of Bendix's area, however, was not replicated here. Burns and others on the surrounding streets lived on plots of about an acre each. Pretty good size, nice yard, and Malachi figured some association made sure the grass stayed manicured. He'd read about the petty power of homeowners' associations.

While an acre made for a decent piece of property, it also left neighbors a reasonable distance away. Burns lived around the middle of his street, so houses continued in both directions. The nosy fellow lived across the road one dwelling down. If he kept trying to see what was going on, Malachi would take him out first. He wouldn't even charge Pazir for it. Nuisance control was free.

Malachi proceeded slowly down the street and stopped past Burns's house. He could keep an eye on things using the mirrors. Since going to the gym earlier this morning, Burns hadn't left. Despite a one-car garage attachment, he parked his half-ton pickup in the driveway. Typical American. Packing the house so full the garage needed to become storage. So many people in this county never could have made it in Israel.

At least the fellow from the other residence didn't make a return appearance. No one bothered Malachi as the day wore on. He needed to turn the engine on and run the air conditioning a few times, but he never did it for more than three minutes at once. He'd endured far worse than the warm interior of a luxury SUV completing missions in the past.

After a few hours, it became clear Burns had become a homebody since leaving the Army. Maybe losing his job compounded this. He might have seen himself as lacking purpose. Malachi contemplated how it would look if he needed to kill the retired soldier inside his own house. Staging a scene to look like a home invasion would be child's play. He'd done his first almost twenty years ago. The complication would be getting out of the house—and the neighborhood—unseen.

A Land Rover didn't exactly help.

If he needed to come back, he would have to use a far less conspicuous vehicle. The Explorer worked well in California. This area may require a pickup. There should be plenty of inventory for the taking. Another hour passed with nothing but the occasional bursts of cold air. Malachi started the Land Rover and guided it down the street. He made a right at the first intersection and drove around.

The community formed a rough rectangle with roads running both north-south and east-west. Considering the size of the properties, the units were consistently spaced. Not too far from the neighbors but also not too close. Anyone on either side would hear a gunshot but not some raised voices, a brief fight, and a stabbing. So long as Malachi dispatched Burns with a minimum of noise, no one would hear him.

He drove each street twice more. Some houses sat closer to the street. Over half the yards were fenced, and the majority of those bore a *Beware of dog* sign. The place on Burns's left featured a fence, but the one on the right did not. The home behind it also had an open yard. Malachi wouldn't need to park on the same street. Police would question anyone in nearby houses first, and they would never see whatever vehicle he arrived in.

As Malachi drove back to his hotel, Pazir called. "The next one is finished?" he demanded as soon as Malachi accepted the call.

"Not yet, no."

"When?"

"If things go well, I should be done with him tomorrow?"

"And in the meantime," Pazir said, "you will enjoy another expensive hotel stay and car rental."

"I told you what I needed when I accepted this job," Malachi reminded him. "If you offer cut-rate pay, you get cut-rate work."

"Mind your tone, Israeli. You are a means to an end. You would do well to remember this." Pazir rang off before Malachi could answer.

"Bastard," he muttered. Pazir offered a flexible timeline and generous compensation so long as Malachi met the objectives. He did, and he would continue to. Still, Malachi harbored no illusions about the man whose money he accepted. Pazir's death would be a net positive for the world.

When he'd finished the work he agreed to, Malachi resolved to make the world a slightly better place for free.

6

The flight was miserable.

Dramamine could help Tyler handle a normal trip in the air. He expected occasional bouts of turbulence. Their jaunt to California, however, shook and bounced so often it felt constant. He spent most of the time gripping the armrests hard enough to rip them free and hoping he wouldn't need to reach for the air sickness bag. For his part, Musa slept much of the way, and even the most turbulent moments didn't rouse him. Tyler managed to keep his breakfast down for the duration, though his legs felt a little wobbly once the crew gave the all-clear to stand.

"You look a little green, Tippy," Musa said.

"I feel bad enough to be a bright emerald," Tyler grumbled as he opened the overhead compartment and pulled out a black roller bag.

"I caught up on my rest."

"You get more word on Gumby from anyone you know?"

"No," Musa said as they filed toward the door. A perky blonde stewardess cheerfully thanked everyone, though her expression wavered when she saw Tyler.

"I guess we'll see what his widow has to say."

"Tiffany."

"Was he married when he left?" Tyler said.

"I think they were dating at the time." Inside the terminal, Tyler and Musa found the rental car desks. They got in line at the Hertz counter, and after a ten-minute wait, the clerk handed Tyler the keys to a Dodge Charger. He clung to the vain hope it would be a Hemi model, but when they reached the lot, he saw it was the V6. Still, it would be about a hundred times better than the generic four-cylinder econoboxes so many commuters piled into.

They reached their hotel about twenty minutes later. It was too early for check-in—even Musa's charm failed, and Tyler knew better than to try—so they left their bags and headed to Bendix's house. "Nice area," Musa said when they neared their destination. The homes were average in size, but large, shallow lots left them spaced pretty far apart. Most featured garages and looked new or at least recently renovated. The Bendix house was near the top of a hill. Tyler curbed the Charger in front and killed the engine. Musa ran a hand over his short beard. A little gray had crept into the black, though the hair on his head remained unchanged. They both climbed out.

It had been years since Tyler needed to visit the home of someone killed in action. As a warrant officer, he rarely made those house calls. Usually, a sergeant would do it. Sometimes a lieutenant. He'd gone along on a couple and dreaded both. This felt much the same. At least Tiffany already knew her husband's fate. He wouldn't need to watch horror dawn in her eyes and color drain from her face. When she opened the door, she looked back at Tyler and Musa with joyless eyes left red and puffy from crying. "We served with your husband," Tyler said.

When Tiffany made no response, Musa added, "John Tyler and Musa Sadozai."

She nodded and beckoned them inside. "Thanks for coming. I'm turning some folks away. Only letting in the names I remember him mentioning over the years." Tiffany was a petite redhead. The roots of her hair had gone gray. She wore jeans and an unadorned light sweatshirt.

"We're very sorry to hear about Gumby," Tyler said. "Alan."

A faint smile played on Tiffany's lips. "He complained about that damn nickname now and then." She led them into the living room. White carpet covered the floor, and it matched the walls and crown molding. The large sectional and two recliners were a light tan. Tyler and Musa both took seats on the sofa. Tiffany dropped into a chair and sighed. Her eyes landed on Musa. "You're a cop, right?"

"Delaware state police," he said.

"You heard much about what happened?"

"No. I'm not acquainted with many folks out here, so I only know what's been reported."

"I'll tell you this." Tiffany leaned forward but didn't lower her voice. "This was no goddamn accident. Someone wanted Alan dead bad enough to run him down and then back over him to make sure they finished the job." She closed her eyes, and a tear slid down each cheek. "The police haven't come to that conclusion yet, but it's probably inevitable. One of them gave me the details. Otherwise, I'd be in the dark."

"No cameras caught what happened?" Tyler said.

Tiffany shook her head, and her red curls wagged. "Alan went for a run every morning . . . weather permitting. He did about four miles. Two out and two back. Along the way, he must have passed through an area with no cameras."

Tyler and Musa exchanged a quick glance. Whoever ran their friend down chose the spot deliberately. Alan established a routine, and his killer studied him long enough to capitalize on it. This was a premeditated murder. Musa asked the inevitable question. "Do you know anyone who would have wanted to do this?"

"No. I told the police the same thing."

"We're not the cops," Tyler said. "We don't have to make a convincing argument to a prosecutor. No judge and jury."

"I can skip right to executioner?" Tiffany said. "I don't think Alan would want that. I'm sure your group had to do all manners of things overseas, but he was very law-and-order here."

"Fair enough. We want to stay for his funeral. If there's anything you need, please let us know."

"I will. Alan kept your numbers on his Rolodex, so I can call you." She chuckled. "I always made fun of him for using it. Silly old thing."

Tyler and Musa left a few minutes later. With Tyler's stomach no longer doing somersaults, they stopped for lunch at a halal deli. "You think we're going to learn much here?" Tyler asked Musa once they were en route back to the hotel.

"Depends who we ask," he said. "I doubt it. Our best hope is to find a local cop who's ex-Army, too. Still, not sure what he would tell us."

"I'd hate to fly all this way just to leave empty-handed."

"You just had a very nice lunch."

Tyler grinned. "True. You know what I mean, though."

"I do," Musa said, "and I feel the same way."

"What does your religion say about revenge?"

"*Qisas.*" When Tyler remained quiet, Musa added, "You could translate it as, 'retribution in kind.'"

"I like your translation," Tyler said.

LEXI'S PHONE rang after dinner. She got up and headed into her bedroom to answer it. Her dad was out on the west coast, so it would be the middle of the afternoon for him. Maybe he'd even gotten over the flight out there by now. "How's California?" she asked.

"Warmer than Maryland," Tyler said. "I didn't even need the jacket I brought."

"I meant your friend."

"I know." Tyler blew out a deep breath, and it hissed in Lexi's ear. "It's sad. His widow doesn't think it was an accident."

"Isn't that a pretty common belief?"

"It is, but one of the cops working the case gave her some information. Whoever hit Gumby ran him over and then threw his vehicle into reverse to do it again."

"Gumby?" Lexi said.

"His last name was Bendix. You never heard of Gumby and Pokey?"

"I feel like I missed them by a couple generations."

"Gumby was very bendy," Tyler said. "Hence the nickname."

"Wait . . . do they call you Tippy for some ridiculous reason, too?"

"Most monikers come from the ridiculous."

"You have to tell me now."

He chuckled, and Lexi smiled. Her dad probably wanted to take his mind off Bendix and the widow for a few minutes. "You may remember from your history class this country had a president named John Tyler. Back in the eighteen forties."

"Kind of hard to ignore when he shares a name with your dad," Lexi said. She remembered learning about this period. Once everyone in the class knew her dad had the same name as a former president, they didn't shut up about it for days.

"He originally was on the ballot as the VP for William

Henry Harrison, who was hailed as the hero of the Battle of Tippecanoe. When their campaign kicked off, someone made a song called 'Tippecanoe and Tyler Too.'"

Lexi had a vague recollection of this from some time in middle school. "So Tippecanoe actually refers to the other guy?"

"William Henry Harrison, yes."

"But Tippy is *your* nickname?"

"I told you these things were often ridiculous," Tyler pointed out.

"You did," Lexi said. "There's one mystery solved, at least. What are you and Musa going to do about Bendix?"

"For now, we're going to the funeral."

"Come on, Dad. I don't know Musa well, but if he's anything like you, he's already thinking about the people he might have to shoot."

"We may have discussed the possibility of an independent inquiry," Tyler said.

"Uh-huh. What if the cops make an arrest?"

"Then they have a good case for a murder charge. We let it play out."

"You might already be a wanted man in North Carolina," Lexi said. "You'll ruin my rep here on campus if you're on the lam from another state."

"Well, we can't have you suffer undue embarrassment."

"No, we can't."

"Seriously, though," Tyler said. "It's likely someone targeted Gumby and ran him down deliberately. We don't know why yet. Could be a thousand reasons, but you know the way I think by now. I get the feeling it has something to do with our Army days. If it does—"

"Bendix may not be the only target," Lexi broke in.

"Right."

"Was he a Braxton guy?"

"No." Growing up, Lexi heard snippets about her dad's commanding officer. The contingent of men most loyal to the disgraced colonel joined his ill-fated attempt to start a black-ops security company upon his unexpected release from Leavenworth. A couple of them kidnapped Lexi, and her dad —with a little assist from his daughter—put them all in the ground.

"Let me know what you find out, then."

"I will. If this is some sort of blowback from a dozen or more years ago, I want you to be careful. Anyone who might come after me can easily find out about you. I know your building is secure, but a determined adversary could still devise a way in."

"I'm your daughter, Dad," Lexi said. "Mom's, too. Being careful is in my DNA." He might bristle at the mention of her mother, but too bad. Lexi inherited things from both of them and not just in the sense of genes. Rachel's criminal tendencies led her to be very cautious. Lexi considered herself to be her father's daughter first and foremost, but she couldn't ignore her mother.

"Good. Make sure you are. I'll talk to you soon." They hung up, and Lexi rejoined her friends. Emily and Kim were scrolling through Netflix on one of their schoolwork breaks.

"Everything good?" Emily wanted to know.

"Yeah." Lexi smiled. "Everything's fine."

7

MALACHI ALWAYS THOUGHT OF HIMSELF AS A CAUTIOUS MAN.

He'd earned the reputation in the IDF, Mossad, and Shin Bet. People sometimes underestimated him, interpreting his tendency to observe and learn as passivity. He never gave them the chance to make the mistake twice. If killing Burns took an extra day, then it took an extra day. Pazir never gave him a strict timeline—and Malachi would have ignored it if he did. California police remained stumped as to the identity of the hit-and-run driver. The approach worked.

He canceled the second day of the Range Rover's reservation. No refund was possible, so his benefactor would just need to be angry about it. This was not an operation designed for penny pinching. Malachi instead rented a more conventional vehicle. In America, the Honda CR-V and Toyota RAV4, both crossover SUVs, were the most popular "cars" on the road. He reserved the former.

Many people would probably consider it a fine vehicle. Cloth seats. Minimal leather. A four-cylinder engine. Malachi felt like a peasant driving the thing. He was forced to admit it was comfortable and quiet, and it would have swallowed a bunch of cargo if he needed its hauling capabilities. Most importantly, the Honda allowed him to blend in on Burns's street. Not many people parked luxury cars in their driveways here. The Range Rover stood out.

Standing out went against the principle of being cautious.

Malachi spent an uneventful day in the CR-V. Burns emerged from his house to go the gym and followed it with a quick trip to a nearby supermarket. Otherwise, the man spent another day at home. This must be what it was like to have no job and feel adrift. Burns's skills should have qualified him for any number of jobs. He could even do the same kind of work Malachi did. Why, then, did the retired soldier spend most of his time indoors?

This second day of observation convinced Malachi he could do the job soon. The neighbors wouldn't be an issue. A more pedestrian car didn't compel the nosy fellow of the previous day to see what went on. Burns's trips to the gym came in a predictable window. In the evening, he would be vulnerable in his house. Pazir called a couple times. Malachi didn't answer, instead responding via text about his plans to take care of Burns the following day.

The Israeli woke up the next morning, used the treadmill in the hotel's fitness center, and enjoyed a hot breakfast. He didn't need to get to Burns's street early. The man's routine wouldn't change. Malachi returned the rental car and then took a taxi to a neighborhood about a mile from Burns'. The area was more developed. A parking garage sat at the end of a row of buildings in various states of disrepair. No cameras at the entrance or exit.

This would be easy.

Malachi first found a pickup at least two decades old. He got inside, hotwired it, and drove it away. It would be his second getaway car. He parked it alongside a minor road about three miles from his target's residence. Another cab ride back to the area near the parking garage gave him more vehicles to choose from.

This time, Malachi picked a Toyota Camry sedan. He chose it because the car was still pretty common, and its badging indicated it had a V6 under the hood. Anything was better than a basic four-cylinder for trying to make a quick exit.

When Malachi reached the man's street, Burns was gone. This would be his workout time. Sure enough, he arrived home thirty minutes later. Malachi ate a quick lunch in the car, then drove through for a fast food dinner and a couple necessary errands. He'd enjoyed a nice breakfast, and he couldn't risk someone seeing him in a restaurant—or the stolen car in the parking lot.

When the sun made its descent, Malachi drove around the corner to walk through the neighbor's unfenced yard and then Burns'. He slipped on a pair of thin black gloves and stuffed a balaclava in his pocket. For this job, he went armed with a knife and a snap gun to get past any locked doors.

With dusk for cover, the black-clad Malachi slipped across both expanses of grass. A small concrete patio hung off the back of Burns's house. Two doors—one normal and the other of the sliding glass variety—led to the inside. Malachi chose the conventional one. He jiggled the knob enough to know it was locked. The snap gun would make a little noise, but it would also get him past the tumblers quickly.

When it did, he padded off the patio, crouched against the house, and waited. Burns didn't investigate. Malachi went back to the door, opened it, and crept inside. He entered into a kitchen. The room was dark, but light from nearby gave him enough illumination to see. Voices came from the other room. Did Burns have company? No. It was a commercial. Malachi exited the kitchen and peeked around the corner.

Burns sat in a recliner watching a show. The carpet and

furniture looked old and mismatched. The screen was by far the nicest and most valuable thing in the room. Burns was at Malachi's ten o'clock. The soldier showed no signs he knew anyone was in his house. When Malachi dashed into the room, Burns spun off the chair and turned to face the intruder. "Who the hell are you?" he asked in a Texas drawl.

"Does it matter?"

"Not really."

"I promise to kill you quickly," Malachi said. "This isn't personal."

"Who sent you here?"

Malachi answered by rushing forward. Time away from the service hadn't dulled Burns's reflexes. He turned away every strike. Malachi avoided a punch, but his adversary's long legs allowed a side kick to find the mark. "You might want to start talking while you can," Burns said.

Malachi offered no reply. He'd learned a few things about his taller enemy. Long limbs tended not to be the quickest. Malachi fired off several fast jabs. He focused on the body to bring Burns's arms in, then nailed him under each triceps. It would slow the man down even more. The intended victim's eyes flashed. He knew the tactic, and he also knew how to try and get out of it. Malachi avoided the kick, however, and drew the knife as he slipped behind the larger man. A stab under the ribs elicited a soft grunt.

When Burns wobbled, Malachi drove the knife home several more times. The man was dead before his body slumped to the blood-stained floor. Malachi thought American Green Berets were overrated. Not a single one could cut it in Mossad. Maybe John Tyler would offer more of a challenge. The Israeli wiped the blade on the deceased soldier's shirt before returning it to his pocket. He would dispose of it later. For now, he rummaged around the house, knocked a few things over, and tried to make it look like he'd come to rob the place.

Malachi exited via the rear door, made it back to the Camry, and drove away. He didn't attract any attention. Reaching the truck, he wiped down any surface he might have touched in the Toyota. Then, Malachi grabbed a change of clothes from the pickup and walked into the trees to put them on. Some blood inevitably got on his others. He tossed them and the knife into the Camry, emptied one of the vodka bottles he picked up after dinner around the interior, and lit a match. While the car burned, he drove away in the truck.

Several miles farther, about a twenty-minute walk from a bus station, Malachi did the same thing again. He didn't relish riding with so many people, but this was part of being cautious. The police might check flights out of Bendix's area, and if they were really industrious, they would also look into charters. Establishing a pattern violated the principle of caution.

Malachi walked away from the blazing truck. He fished a blond costume wig out of his bag, made sure he grabbed one of the IDs Pazir's team prepared for him, and headed toward the bus station.

8

____

Tyler answered the insistent pounding on his hotel room door.

Musa stood on the other side. He wore his black suit jacket and pants with a white shirt, but a gray tie remained undone around his neck. His mustache and beard were short and trimmed to the point not a single hair was out of place. "It's not time to leave for the funeral yet," Tyler said. Musa's somber expression didn't change. "What now?"

"We might have another one to go to." Musa walked in without waiting for an invitation. Tyler closed the door while his friend dropped onto the chair near a small desk. Tyler sat on the edge of the bed. "It's Burns."

"Stretch?"

"Yes," Musa confirmed.

Tyler remembered working with Carl Burns. The man had been a good and diligent soldier. He struggled letting loose, and only indulged in games like basketball after a lot of prodding and cajoling. Burns shot a Taliban sniper from about 700 yards away early in their second combat tour together. It turned the tide of what ended up being a brief skirmish but could have been much longer and worse. "How?"

"Cops are calling it a home invasion."

Tyler snorted. "Easy to fake. We were already suspicious with Bendix, but this is number two. With one, maybe he pissed the wrong person off. Now, we have to presume someone is coming for us."

"I know."

"I presume you talked to local cops?"

"From Texas, yes."

"Did you mention this?"

"Not their problem," Musa said. "They're interested in comparing notes with the investigators out here, but I don't know how far we'll get. Very different MO the second time. Stretch got stabbed to death. House was ransacked, though the cops don't know if whoever killed him took anything."

"I would guess not," Tyler said. "Rummage around a little, and you've set the scene enough. Besides, Stretch never struck me as the type to keep a lot of valuables."

"He was between jobs. Probably didn't have many to begin with."

"Any family?"

"Don't think so," Musa said. "Wasn't married, and he didn't have any close relatives left. I think next of kin is a cousin who lives a few states away." Musa crossed his arms and frowned. "If it's the same killer, they were careful to make this look completely different than Gumby. What do you want to do?"

"Why are you asking me?"

"You're the warrant."

"Ten years ago, Sergeant," Tyler said. He thought about recent events. If someone came gunning for the old unit, it would need to be a capable enemy they made a decade or more ago. Or maybe a descendant of some asshole opium lord who was funneling money to the Taliban. Either way, figuring out the antagonist's identity would be a challenge. Anyone who watched for routines could have taken out Bendix. Killing Stretch in his own home required a skilled operator—someone who could get in and out unseen. Not leave an evidence trail. Those were just as important as being able to get the advantage long enough to drive a blade home. "I think we need to work this out."

"Agreed," Musa said.

"We can't do it from here. Too many unknowns. We go to Gumby's funeral, and then we head home. You can keep working your law enforcement contacts. I'll see what I can dig up."

Musa grinned. "You suddenly become computer literate?"

"I can turn it off and on without any help. My daughter does a lot of the rest."

"How is Lexi?"

"Good. Living in an off-campus apartment this year."

"You must be concerned," Musa said.

"Always," Tyler said. "Recent events only make it worse. I told her about Bendix. She'll be cautious . . . and right now, we have no evidence our mystery killer is going after family members."

"What are we going to do about Stretch?"

Tyler shrugged. "We'll come back when this is all done. Get a bunch of us together and give him a proper send-off. I think we have something larger at play here, and I think Stretch would want us to take care of it."

"All right." Musa stood and whipped his tie into a nice knot in about fifteen seconds. Tyler, who never liked wearing the blasted things, felt a little jealous. "Meet you downstairs." He left, and Tyler finished getting dressed. He slipped into his white shirt, put on a red tie—which took him three tries to get right—and shrugged into a black jacket matching his pants. Both he and Musa considered bringing their old dress uniforms but decided against it. Especially considering the recent murder of Carl Burns, blending in was definitely the way to go.

~

MALACHI FELT delighted to breathe the open air again.

The bus ride had been torture. Sitting in a metal chamber with so many poor and middle-class people was not an experience he wanted to repeat. Making matters worse, the fellow in the next seat was a talker. He wanted to chat even when Malachi made his preference for quiet obvious. Finally, the man got tired and fell asleep. If there were fewer people around, Malachi might have strangled him.

He walked away from the station in Louisiana as fast as he could. It was just as hot here as in Texas, and while the air felt humid, he would gladly take it over a tin capsule on wheels. Malachi wondered if he needed to be so cautious in his transportation. Texas was a long way from California, and police wouldn't connect two murders carried out in such radically different fashions. Perhaps he needed to watch fewer *NCIS* reruns. Leroy Jethro Gibbs wasn't coming to question him.

Once he'd walked about a half mile, Malachi bought a bottle of iced tea from a convenience store. He drank half, leaned against the far side of the building, and slipped his phone out. Pazir called earlier and followed up with two texts wanting an update. Malachi wanted the job finished for many reasons. Most of them were financial, but he also relished the idea of watching Pazir die. "It is about time," the older man said.

"I left Texas," Malachi said. "Your accountant will be pleased to know I took a bus."

"You?" Pazir chuckled.

"Don't get used to it. It was awful. I'll either drive or fly from here on out."

"You crossed a second name off the list. I don't mind paying for results."

"Let's talk names," Malachi said. "Getting to them all would require me to criss-cross the country."

"Not necessary. Remember, our goal is to make John Tyler suffer before you kill him. Three or four of his old friends getting killed should do it."

"I was thinking the same thing. You have an idea for the next target?"

"Do you?"

"He's some distance away," Malachi said, "but I was looking at Musa Sadozai. The files say he and Tyler were close back then. They might still be." Musa was also an Afghan-born Muslim, which made him an inviting target for Malachi. His units in Mossad and Shin Bet didn't wait to be targeted by the enemies surrounding their tiny country. They took the fight to them. He didn't divulge this reason, of course. No need to anger and offend his benefactor.

Yet.

"Very well," Pazir said. "If they've remained friends in the years since, so much the better for us. He's a policeman, though. You're not sneaking up on a vagabond this time."

"I know."

"And the entire force will be looking for whoever killed him."

"I'm well aware," Malachi said. "You don't need to explain these obvious things to me."

Pazir chuckled. "Fine. I suppose you're smarter than most of the people I surround myself with."

Another mark against you, Malachi thought. Instead, he said, "It is settled, then. Musa will be next."

"When do you think I should come to America?" Pazir said.

"Do you have a schedule in mind?"

"I was planning to fly over when the third man was eliminated. My arrangements are tentatively in place."

"Whenever you want, then. It will take me a day or two to get to Musa ... plus the time I need to observe him."

"Very well." Pazir ended the call without another word. Malachi stuffed his phone back into his pocket. Tomorrow, he would replace the current one with another burner. In the meantime, he considered his options for getting to Delaware.

9

MALACHI CHECKED HIS PHONE AS HE ATE LUNCH.

He treated himself—with Pazir's money, of course—to a nice meal. Steamed shrimp, crayfish, dirty rice, and french fries. He didn't expect to eat it all, but someone else paid for it, so why not indulge a little? The bus ride had left him hungry and thirsty, and he ate more of the food than he expected. While working on his second bottle of water, he checked Texas news outlets to see if any picked up the murder of Carl Burns.

A few did. He found one online paper which ran a short but solid article covering the major details.

LIBERTY, TX.—Local resident Carl Burns, 49, was found stabbed to death in his home on Yellow Rose Street last night in what police believe was a violent home invasion.

Burns's body was discovered by a neighbor who saw him lying prone from the front window. The neighbor called 911. Police entered the home to find Burns died of multiple stab wounds.

Police spokesperson Lt. Amanda Cole said it appears the perpetrator broke into Burns's home sometime the prior evening. "At this time, we believe Mr. Burns was attacked by an unknown intruder or intruders upon entering his home," Lt. Cole said. "Officers noticed some damage to a lock at the back of the residence. There were signs of a brief struggle and ransacking of the home."

It is unclear if anything was taken during the incident. Lt. Cole said investigators are still cataloguing items and assessing if anything of value may be missing. She noted the violent nature of the attack indicates robbery may have been a motive.

No suspects have been identified so far, and police are seeking information from anyone who may have noticed suspicious activity near the victim's home during the timeframe of the incident. "We encourage anyone with any details that may be relevant to come forward," Lt. Cole stated.

Burns served twenty years in the US Army, retiring as a staff sergeant in the Green Berets. He served three combat deployments. Since retiring, Burns did not keep a steady job. Neighbors described him as quiet but friendly. He lived alone in the Yellow Rose Street home and police say he has no known enemies who may have targeted him.

The homicide remains under active investigation. Police are urging residents to be vigilant and report any suspicious or criminal activity.

Malachi smiled. The home invasion was an easy sell. Police around the world fell for it. He'd lost track of how many countries he'd staged the same type of death in. The continent count still stood at five. Maybe he'd get to ply this particular trade in Australia, but Antarctica was a pipe dream. Occasionally, a neighbor would remember seeing someone, but neither Malachi nor the teams he worked on ever came under suspicion no matter the locale. He celebrated his record remaining intact by eating the last shrimp and downing the rest of his water.

After his late lunch, Malachi moved on. He waited a while, puttering around in shops and bookstores until the sun went down. Then, he looked for a car to steal. He favored reliable older models which appeared well-maintained. They wouldn't have GPS units built in, owners were unlikely to install an alarm, and the engines wouldn't break down. It took a couple streets to find a good candidate, but he happened upon a black Lexus sedan sitting on a parking pad in an alley.

The houses here were close together. Most still had lights on inside. Malachi checked for cameras and didn't notice any. To be extra cautious, he slipped the balaclava over his head. The Lexus hailed from the early aughts, and its model number indicated a V8 under the hood. No blinking red dot from the interior. Malachi was about to take out his tools when he wondered if someone left the car unlocked. He tried the handle, and the door opened.

"The hell you doin'?" a harsh whisper came from behind him.

Malachi turned slowly. A tall man, slight of frame except for a paunch, stared at him. A cigarette dangled from his mouth, and he pointed a large revolver at Malachi. This was exactly the kind of gun he would expect someone from the southern United States to brandish. At least the fellow maintained good trigger discipline. An aroma of alcohol emanated from him. The Israeli put up his hands. There would be a chance to get the weapon, and he would take it. For lack of anything else to say, Malachi offered, "Nice car."

"She is. Maybe I oughta keep her locked." He reached into the pocket of his shorts for the keys. When the man glanced down, Malachi stepped to the side and then surged forward. He disarmed his surprised assailant, reversed his grip on the weapon, and clobbered the owner with the butt. The guy crumbled to the concrete. Malachi took the keys and put them in his own pocket. A groan came from near his feet. Leaving a witness would be a disaster. Malachi beat the man with the butt of the pistol until his skull cracked in two places.

He kept the gun and climbed into the sedan. Using the owner's keys, he started the car and drove away. The neighborhood seemed quiet. The engine firing up had been the loudest sound. Still, Malachi couldn't count on the man's body going undiscovered for long. He eased the car up to ninety on the highway. A road sign heralded a rest stop with a scenic overlook ten miles ahead. Malachi exited when he saw the ramp. Tractor trailers lined the shoulder of the roads. Truckers were already asleep for the night.

Malachi parked the Lexus away from other cars and SUVs. He opened his bag, took out a wipe, and cleaned the gun thoroughly. The scenic overlook proved to be a lie. It afforded a decent view of trees but wasn't worth a sign on the highway. Still, it was a great platform from which to throw a gun into the void. Malachi watched for activity in the parking lot, saw none, and used his knife to remove the license plate on the Lexus. It only had one in the rear, and he swapped tags with a shopworn Dodge Durango.

In the Lexus, Malachi reviewed the file on John Tyler's old unit. Musa Sadozai made a fine target. If Malachi continued driving northeast from Texas, however, he could stop and take out another retired soldier on the way. He decided this was the best course of action. Pazir would approve. In the unlikely event he didn't, it provided one more reason for Malachi to kill him when he'd finished the mission.

Tyler and Musa landed at BWI Airport.

It was ten-oh-five at night when their plane taxied to the gate. Tyler yawned, the last of the Dramamine still making him a little sleepy. "You good to drive?" Musa asked.

"I'll get a coffee inside."

"Shops might be closed."

Tyler shrugged. "Plenty of places a mile or two away. I'll be fine." At least this flight had been smooth. Once they were back in the terminal, Tyler discovered Musa was right. All the eateries were closed for the night, and while a book and magazine shop remained open, it didn't sell hot food or drinks. They exited the building and walked across the road to the hourly garage.

"Two of us dead," Musa said as the elevator doors closed. "We should be careful. Someone could be waiting here for us."

"I've already thought about it," Tyler told him.

When they got off on the third level, each walked in opposite directions without discussing it first. Both men fell back into old patterns instinctively. Tyler worked the left side, looking in all the stairwells and checking around and behind each parked vehicle. A few minutes later, he and Musa met in the middle at the far end. "All clear," Tyler said.

Musa nodded. "Same. I got the word out to the guys I'm still in contact with. I think we'll cover everyone who's still alive."

"Good."

"How many are you still in touch with?"

"Well, there's you," Tyler said. "Leon Sharpe." Sharpe, now a captain with the Baltimore Police, left the unit after Tyler's first deployment. He'd be unlikely to land on a target list but still deserved a heads-up. "And … uh … you."

Musa chuckled. "Seriously?"

"I was at the heart of the Braxton fallout. Didn't exactly get a great deal of support." Because of Tyler's evidence and testimony, the Army brought charges of war crimes against their former colonel. Braxton had been successful according to the metrics the brass cared about—namely dead terrorists

—so the man seen as leading the charge against him got a frosty reception. It made Tyler's decision to retire an easy one. "I mostly wanted to put everything behind me and move on."

"You still do the painting?" Musa said.

"Yeah. I didn't back then. Wouldn't meet the right shrink for at least five years, so you could probably say I wasn't great at processing things."

"It's all good, Tippy. I'm just busting your balls."

Tyler grinned. "I know." They shook hands. "Take care of yourself. Let's keep in touch about this."

Musa bobbed his head. "Yeah. And let's hope we don't have to go to any more funerals."

Tyler climbed into his vintage Oldsmobile 442. The dark green muscle car rumbled to life when he turned the key. He'd restored it over a period of a few years following his exit from the Army. Many of the parts remained original. The biggest change came when Tyler retrofitted a newer six-speed automatic several years prior, replacing the original four-gear model the Olds rolled off the assembly line with. The extra two gears enabled the car to access its considerable power in a more modern—and much better—way.

When he was on the highway, Tyler dialed Leon Sharpe. "Not worried," he said when apprised of the situation.

"I think you're unlikely to make a kill list," Tyler admitted, "but I wanted to warn you anyway."

"I appreciate it. I'd like to think working at HQ makes me a hard target."

"Probably does."

"You find your ass in a sling, you call me. Understand?"

"Sure. Take care, Leon."

Next, Tyler called his dad. He wondered if the old man would complain about the late hour and didn't have to wait long for an answer. "Can't be good if you're calling this late."

"Did I interrupt bingo?" Tyler asked. His father moved

into an active adult community a couple years before. The minimum age to get in was fifty-five. Zeke Tyler was seventy-seven and basically had the run of the place. He was still mentally sharp and physically active, and the outgoing nature which helped him in the Navy worked just as well at Evergreen Acres. Tyler felt some residents really stretched the idea of being active adults, but his father liked the place, so he kept his objections to himself.

"Bingo's tomorrow. What's going on?"

"I think my old unit has attracted the wrong kind of attention."

"Reporters? CID?"

"No," Tyler said. "Two of them are dead recently. Musa and I are pretty sure someone killed them both."

"Where?" Zeke wanted to know.

"One in California and the other in Texas."

"Far enough apart to be a coincidence. At least the cops are going to think this way."

"Right," Tyler said. "Which is why we can't."

"You have any idea who'd be coming after you?"

"Not offhand. We made a pretty long list of enemies. Most of them are dead, but there could be a brother, son, cousin, or something looking for revenge."

"You calling to give me a heads up?" his father asked.

"Yeah. I know you're always on the lookout, but make extra sure now. People who can find me can find you. It's happened before."

"Let them come. I got enough guns for everyone on my floor."

"Tell your friends which end to point at the bad guys, then." Tyler and his dad said their goodbyes and ended the call. He didn't need to worry about his father, but he still did. If this mystery assassin made it to Maryland, someone in the Tyler family would put him in the ground.

10

"What's going on, boss?"

David Ortiz stood in Tyler's office. They both watched two men install an upgraded security system at Special Operations Classic Car Repair. The building came with a basic setup from its time as a gas station, and Tyler continued to use it. Now, with two of his friends murdered by an unknown killer, he needed something better.

"I'm kinda wondering, too," Smitty added from the doorway. He was Tyler's first hire and former boss until a cartel burned his shop to the ground. Smitty felt some understandable resentment for a while but agreed to come on when Tyler opened his business. The man was a really good mechanic and much better at dealing with the public than Tyler. Smitty was thin and wiry, about ten years older than his boss, and his hair was mostly gray.

"Shut the door," Tyler said. Smitty did. Tyler blew out a deep breath. "I know there are occasional . . . extracurricular activities when it comes to working here." Smitty's lips turned down. "Two of the men in my old unit are dead. I'm pretty sure they didn't go accidentally."

"You think someone might be coming after you?" Smitty asked.

"Me in particular? No idea. Our unit, yes. The first one was in California and the second in Texas. Two's not much of a pattern, but whoever it is seems to be heading east."

"And you want to be prepared," Ortiz said. It wasn't a question.

"Can't you do a lot of this yourself?" Smitty asked, waving a hand in the direction of the two men working.

"Sure." When the cartel was gunning for him, Tyler wired two cameras on his road into the street lights. "The basic work is easy enough. I want to make sure we have cloud backup, encryption, and a whole bunch of other shit I don't really understand . . . so I called in the professionals. Even paid a little extra for same-day service."

"You're sure this guy is coming after you?" Ortiz wanted to know.

"I'm not hard to find," Tyler said. "If he does come here, it's not just me I need to keep safe."

"I'm tearing up over here, boss." Ortiz rubbed his cheek under his eye for emphasis.

"Consider this your upcoming Christmas bonus, then."

"Now, it ain't so funny," Ortiz said, but a lopsided grin belied his words. "You know we could take this guy out."

"I'm not sure it's one person," Tyler said. "Details are in short supply, and the crime scenes being half a country apart doesn't help. We could be looking at two guys or even a team."

"You've certainly made your share of enemies."

"I've made your share, too."

Ortiz agreed. He and Smitty left the office to return to the service bays. Tyler reviewed the itemized invoice from the security company. His eyes watered anew at the final price, but this was a necessary step. In addition to taking the old components out, the workers were installing four cameras inside, six infrared-capable models around the exterior, a control panel, desktop PC and monitor to keep an eye on things, a large uninterruptible power supply to keep things running, and cloud storage to hold backups. Plastic domes would encase the electric eyes to offer a degree of tamper resistance. Tyler chose the most aggressive backup interval to ensure his files made it online as quickly as possible.

If the worst happened, he wanted Lexi and the police to see what went down.

He left the office and worked on a brake job in one of the bays while the men continued with the install. Once they announced completion, Tyler walked around the inside and outside of the shop to check their work. Everything looked good. Cameras were visible but hard to reach, and a potential burglar or killer couldn't access the wires to cut power. The company charged a high rate—especially for a rush job—but they did well. The technicians spent about an hour showing Tyler how to operate the system from the PC. They needed to cover a few features twice. "My daughter will understand all this," he told them. The older of the two—probably ten years Tyler's junior—offered a sympathetic smile.

When they left, Tyler got back to work with Smitty and Ortiz.

∼

Veronica Fitzgerald left her hotel room.

She'd compiled a great deal of background information on John Tyler. The public version of his service record remained heavily redacted. She met with a contact in the Army. The man flatly refused to fill in certain details, but he was able to shed a little light on some things. Tyler and his unit mates had been "serious ass-kickers" in Afghanistan, to use her contact's term. They enforced the Bush Doctrine of going after the terrorists—the Taliban in this case—and those who supported them with equal force and determination.

Such activities would lead to a long list of enemies. As far as Veronica could tell, most of them were dead. The ones who remained alive were no longer in positions to fund revenge campaigns halfway around the world. Like any good reporter, Veronica set up alerts for the men who overlapped with Tyler. She chose those who shared at least two combat tours with him. People often didn't want to be sources while still in the middle of activities, but a decade or so on, attitudes changed. She hoped to reach out to some of the men and learn a few new things.

She never expected to hear two of them died.

The second seemed like a clear home invasion. The first man, Bendix, got run over on an early-morning run. Tragic, but accidents like this happened every day somewhere in America. Veronica hopped into her rented Hyundai Tucson and left her Towson hotel for the drive to Tyler's shop. It sat in the city but maybe a mile from the Baltimore County line, and waiting until after rush hour made her trek on the Beltway easy. The business stood at a major intersection—Harford Road and Northern Parkway.

Many places offered decent vantage points, but Veronica chose one where she was unlikely to be disturbed. A store on the opposite side a little farther along Harford Road was closed for renovations. The lot sat empty, so she pulled in and oriented the SUV to get a good look at Special Operations Classic Car Repair. It was a squat building. The main area wasn't very large as the three service bays consumed most of the square footage. Two men—an older white man and a wiry Latino—worked on cars. Tyler popped in and out.

A van belonging to Prime Security of Maryland sat next

to Tyler's muscle car. Two men in company uniforms worked on the exterior of the shop, making occasional trips to their vehicle for parts. It looked like Tyler hired them to install or upgrade the business's security system. Did he feel threatened by the deaths of two men he knew? Veronica wondered if there was more to those stories than she first thought. A man like Tyler didn't do things on whims. He also would never open a shop without some kind of alarm system, so Prime Security was there to make it better.

She'd avoided following Tyler herself because he struck her as the type to sniff out a tail in a matter of minutes. His record spoke of PTSD and several failed VA therapy programs before he found one that worked. She wasn't privy to the details and didn't push for them. Unlike many of her fellow journalists, Veronica felt people enjoyed basic privacy rights especially when it came to matters like their medical records. Tyler wasn't a public figure, so no one but he and his doctor needed to know the contents of his file.

Over her years of reporting, she'd known other former soldiers with PTSD and even did a story on a couple. The men looked for threats everywhere. They were hyper aware of their surroundings, exits, choke points, and potential vulnerabilities. Even after managing their conditions, those behaviors remained. If Tyler was the same, he must have seen his shop as a potential weakness. Two former colleagues dying and a security system upgrade a couple days later were not coincidental events in Veronica's mind.

She took out her notebook, jotted a few things down, and settled in to observe the shop.

11

LEXI PUT HER RIGHT THUMB ONTO THE SMALL READER, AND THE lock disengaged.

Security was one of the major selling points for her—and especially her dad—when deciding on her off-campus apartment. Plato's Parlor took two thumbprints from each resident. One got them into the building. The other did, too, but also summoned the police. It was a countermeasure against someone being forced to open the door and let an intruder in. Two levels of redundant power kept the system running in the event of an electrical failure.

Inside, Lexi opened the door to the apartment. Here, the building used a conventional lock and key system. She'd finished her last class of the day. Macroeconomics was a yawner, but it also made a nice way to conclude things. She could come back, drink some much-needed coffee, and get on with the rest of being a college sophomore. For her, this mostly consisted of homework, hanging out with her roommates, and working part-time at her dad's shop.

She called him to see how the day was going. Getting

some admin hours this weekend would help her budget. "Probably best you stay away for now," her dad said.

"Why? What's going on?"

"We lost a second guy from the unit."

"Sorry, Dad," she said. "Was this also suspicious?"

"Supposedly a home invasion."

"You don't think it was?"

"I think it's easy to get into someone's house, shoot them, and then stage a scene for the cops." Lexi didn't ask how he knew this. He and his team probably had to do things like this in Afghanistan.

"Where was this one?" she asked.

"Texas."

"They could be unrelated."

"They could," he admitted. "I could also sprout wings and start flying."

Lexi chuckled. "It would make you more efficient at the shop."

"I guess it would. Look . . . I'm probably being a little too cautious, but I'd rather you not be here in case someone's out there gunning for my old unit. I already upgraded the security system today."

"Wow. Probably wasn't easy."

"For the price I paid, I hope it was goddamn difficult."

"All right, Dad," Lexi said. "I won't come around this weekend."

"Thanks," he said. "Make sure you're on alert, too. I don't know what's going on yet, but someone who could find me could also find you. Get a rape whistle if you don't already have one."

She didn't, and Lexi made a mental note to buy one. It was a good idea even if some maniac wasn't crossing the country killing retired Green Berets. She also resolved to visit the gun range this coming weekend. Lexi tried to establish a biweekly cadence, but some of the other demands on her time caused her to slack off a little there. She was also due for a kickboxing class to keep her skills sharp.

Even without working at the shop, her schedule was looking crowded.

"I will, Dad. Let me know if you need anything."

"Roger. Be safe. Love you."

"Love you, too." Lexi ended the call. By the time she finished making coffee, Emily and Kim walked in. They took a different Econ class and seemed to like their professor. Lexi wished she'd signed up with them, but she tried to finish her course load without any long breaks each day.

Once everyone had a cup, Kim asked, "You working this weekend, Lexi?"

"No," she said. "Things are a little slow at the shop right now. There's not enough for me to do."

"Hopefully, it'll pick up soon. Everything good with your dad?"

"Yeah." Lexi smiled. "You know him. He's fine."

MALACHI CHANGED cars in South Carolina.

This one came without incident. No one saw him. He didn't need to bludgeon anyone to death. He snagged a vintage Cadillac Coupe de Ville and borrowed the plates from a Honda Civic. Both came from an apartment complex with a sprawling parking lot too big for the cameras mounted on the building. The Caddy still had a tape deck in the dash, and the owner kept a case of cassettes under the passenger's seat. The music showed eclectic tastes with a mix of hard rock, hip-hop, and jazz.

Malachi wanted something to keep him awake on the drive, so he went with the hard rock. Def Leppard played through the so-so stereo. He rolled the window down and turned the volume up a couple clicks. "Rock! Rock! (Till You Drop)" provided a good start. Malachi drummed the fingers of his left hand on the steering wheel. He needed to change the tape a few more times and even pulled into a rest area for a few hours' nap.

He made southern Virginia the next morning. Most importantly, he arrived in time to see Giovanni Orlando leave his house and head to his job. Malachi hung back in the Cadillac to avoid suspicion. Orlando owned a remote place in a wooded area a short drive north of Marion, Virginia. He drove a Ford pickup into the city and turned into the gated lot at Teleperformance Marion. Malachi kept driving. He continued along Main Street for another quarter mile before turning around.

Teleperformance Marion featured a gate which slid back when a keycard activated it. It remained open long enough for Malachi to piggyback inside, but he would then run into a second layer of security: a guard in a small building who checked IDs when workers entered. Orlando's truck settled into a spot around the middle of the lot, and the man walked into the building a moment later.

Malachi drove back out of town and returned to the man's home. He lived on a long street. Houses stood far from each other. Thick trees surrounded Orlando's house on all sides. They cleared enough to form a small front and rear yard— the latter with a fence—and a driveway. Getting through the forest would be a challenge. Malachi left the Caddy a short jaunt down the street and doubled back to Orlando's property.

He realized the challenge immediately.

A camera sat mounted into a tree a few feet along the driveway. A power cord ran down to the ground where it likely connected in the nearby log shed. The Israeli reversed course and moved into the woods. About fifty feet in, he spotted another electric eye. If Orlando placed them in the forest out front, he would have done the same in the rear. Even if Malachi planned a middle-of-the-night assault, Orlando's alarm system might alert him to the presence of an intruder.

Even presuming a successful foray through the trees, the house was easy to defend. It was made of logs big enough to have been the stumps for massive trees. Bullets would have a hard time making it through. The home also sat at a slight elevation compared to the surrounding property. Orlando chose the place well and ensured he could defend it. For the first time, Malachi felt challenged taking on these retired special operators.

He would need to change his tactics. First, however, he wanted to rest, so he got back into the Cadillac and headed to a Comfort Inn about nine miles away just before the town of Atkins. Malachi checked in under an assumed name and paid cash for a room and paper map of the area. He ordered delivery of the nicest meal he could find for lunch, which turned out to be an above-average steak, mediocre baked potato, and asparagus he needed to reheat in the small microwave.

Malachi checked the map and made a few plans. He would need some additional equipment, but Giovanni Orlando would be dead tomorrow, and the mission could continue.

12

Tyler enjoyed a Saturday off.

As a business owner, he was used to pulling odd shifts—especially on weekends—to make sure everything hummed along. A backlog of repair jobs was the most common cause, but Tyler also liked to catch up on admin work when no one else would be there to disturb him. Today, he stayed home and dug an old photo book out of his foot locker in the basement.

The Braxton mess consumed the end of his twenty-four years in the Army. It tainted Tyler's memories of his service and even his opinion of the armed forces as a whole. Braxton's friends—who wore stars on their shoulders today if they remained active—tried to go after Tyler for turning in the disgraced colonel. It didn't work, but he'd avoided a lot of get-togethers and similar events over the years. Connecting with people one-on-one was fine, but Tyler didn't have any use for a large gathering.

The first photo made him smile. Their unit posed in front of the burning compound which had been owned and operated by an opium distributor until a few minutes before the picture. The man and his trusted employees refused to flee even in the face of imminent defeat, so their bodies joined the blaze inside. Alan Bendix lay on the ground, head propped on his elbow, wearing a ridiculous grin. Carl Burns, a head taller than anyone else, gave Tyler bunny ears from the back row.

Tyler never fancied himself as the sentimental type, but flipping through the photos made him wonder what connections he'd missed out on over the years. He had his family, a few friends, and Sara. It was enough. But would it always be? He was fifty-two now. A decade removed from active duty. Those ten years had seen a lot of tumult in his life. He'd begun a private security job, gotten divorced, suddenly gained custody of a teenaged daughter, quit the security gig, gone to work for Smitty, opened his own shop, and shot a bunch of people along the way.

Maybe widening his circle would have been a good move.

"Bah," Tyler said to the empty room. The psychiatrist who got him into a therapeutic painting program told him he couldn't change the past. He could only process it and not allow it to define the present. After a few more minutes spent reminiscing with old pictures, Tyler climbed the staircase to the studio he maintained in an extra bedroom. He set up a fresh piece of paper, pictured what he wanted to paint, and chose his colors.

At some point, his phone vibrated. Sara. He ignored the call and kept working. The husk of a building took shape, and red-orange flames rose from its surface. Dark gray smoke filled the top of the page. Sara called again. Tyler again declined the call and kept working. The skeleton of a vehicle arose from his brush strokes at the bottom, and he filled it out into the world's worst-looking Hummer. Long ago, Tyler learned not to be self-critical of the quality of his output. Getting things out of his head was the priority.

When Sara called a third time, he answered. "Hard at work?" she asked.

"In a manner of speaking."

When Tyler didn't elaborate, Sara filled in the conversational gap. She'd gotten better at doing it during their two years of dating. "Meaning what?"

"Painting," Tyler said. "I was in the zone."

"I did a little work from home today. You want to get dinner later?"

"I don't know. I'd like to see you, but I'm also not sure I'd be great company tonight."

"Why not?"

"Two guys from my old unit are dead."

"Oh, gosh. Tyler, I'm sorry."

"Thanks."

"Judging by your tone, I'm going to guess you're suspicious."

"I don't think they were accidental or coincidental," Tyler said.

Sara sighed. "What does it mean for you?"

"No idea, but I have to presume someone's coming after all of us. Maybe multiple someones."

"Sounds like you need some company," Sara said.

"I'm not sure I—"

"Tyler, I'm coming over. I'll even cook you dinner."

He chuckled. "You might want to stop at the store first. I haven't exactly been shopping a ton with Lexi living in College Park."

"Fine. I'll pick up supplies on the way. See you in an hour."

Tyler went back to his painting and finished the Hummer. He quickly added three figures—himself, Bendix, and Burns—though he drew them all standing. Tyler put his brushes down and looked at the photo again. He wondered who might be next. His eyes settled on a man in the back row. Fred Flanker was the CIA operative embedded with them for a few years. As far as Tyler knew, he remained with the agency. If things got worse, Flanker would be a good man to call.

MALACHI ENJOYED a nice breakfast in the Cadillac.

He probably should have ditched the car by now. Keeping it represented a risk. Had he been staying in a larger town, he would have. In his limited exposure to southern Virginia, people kept to themselves. He'd only seen one police car on the road. Once he took care of Orlando, he would need to find a new set of wheels.

Yesterday evening, Malachi bought a rifle from a military surplus store. Americans had a lot of hangups about pistols and automatic weapons, but he could pay cash for a bolt-action M24 in good condition, and walk out with it the same day. The Army stopped using the rifle over a decade ago, phasing it out for semiautomatic models capable of firing much faster. Malachi planned to kill Orlando with a single shot, so the greater rate didn't appeal to him. The shop owner was also happy to sell him a box of 7.62X51mm NATO cartridges. Malachi test fired the weapon in the woods last night and made a few small adjustments to the scope.

He finished his breakfast, which included a couple extra delicious biscuits. Now, he cleaned his hands, grabbed the bag holding the loaded M24, and climbed out of the Coupe de Ville. It was a cool Saturday morning, and cloud cover kept the sun at bay. This worked to Malachi's advantage. He knelt on a small rise across the road from Orlando's house. Trees on the target's property made line of sight inconsistent, but this was the best he would get. Depending on where Orlando stood, Malachi enjoyed some good sight lines.

Of course, if the man never emerged from his house, Malachi would need to come up with an alternate plan. It was autumn in rural America, however. Leaves covered the grass. Some bushes looked a little unruly. The notes Pazir's team assembled could only get so detailed, but Orlando struck Malachi as the type who would want to keep his property looking nice. All the neighbors did. One fellow bagged leaves when Malachi drove along the road.

Lights went on inside. Orlando was awake and moving around. Malachi checked the rifle for at least the third time. He felt confident taking the shot from his current position. He knelt about 400 meters from Orlando's front door, well within the range of the M24. The nearest fence lay a good hundred meters away. As far as Malachi knew, he was on common ground not part of any person's property. About a half-hour later, Orlando appeared behind the house. He carried a rake and several folded brown paper bags around from the shed.

Americans and their yard work. Predictable.

In the end, Orlando fell into a pattern the same way Bendix and Burns did. The exact nature was different every time. Bendix forgot his OPSEC training and ran the same route each morning. Burns retreated into himself and rarely left the house for any length of time. Now, Orlando would rake and bag piles of leaves because his neighbors created the expectation. Malachi plucked a few blades of grass from the dirt and tossed them into the air. A slight breeze blew them from his left to right.

The Israeli watched the retired Green Beret walk around the yard. His movements were free and loose. Even an untrained observer would know Orlando was a man who could handle himself. Malachi put his left shoulder against a nearby tree. Branches and overgrowth obscured his position from across the way, and the lack of sunlight would prevent the telltale glint off the rifle or scope. This was almost too easy. It felt a little unfair not to give a fellow soldier a fighting chance.

Too bad. Pazir didn't hire Malachi out of a belief in fairness.

When Orlando emerged from the cover of a maple, Malachi lined him up in the crosshairs, making a minor adjustment for the slight wind. He wished the store carried a suppressor. The report would tell people something happened. Still, this was a rural area. People fired guns with some regularity. Orlando bent slightly to work the rake. He collected a bunch of leaves in a small pile and then moved to his left to do it all again.

When the man stood straight, Malachi fired.

By the time the crack of the shot pierced the quiet morning, the bullet entered the side of Orlando's head just below the ear and blew his jaw clean off. The body slumped to the grass like a puppet whose strings someone had pulled taut and then suddenly cut. Malachi scampered to the Cadillac, tossed the rifle onto the backseat, and covered it with the blanket from his hotel room.

He drove away at a moderate pace to avoid attracting attention. On the road, he would need to find a new vehicle and ditch the Caddy. Musa Sadozai was next on the target list, and if Malachi made good time, he could reach Delaware tonight.

13

———————

Tyler's eyes fluttered open at the noise.

His phone vibrated on the nightstand. Narrow strips of sunlight came through the blinds. He noticed the other half of the bed was empty and felt around on the nightstand. The screen told him two things: it was almost 10 AM, and Smitty called. "Tyler."

"You coming in, boss?"

"Isn't it Sunday?"

"You signed yourself up for today. Jake, too, but I'm covering for him, so he'll take one of my shifts later this week." Smitty's son Jake, who also worked at the original shop owned by his father, put in two shifts a week at Special Operations Classic Car Repair. He was a good mechanic if a little unreliable.

"Crap," Tyler said. He must have drawn up the roster more than a week ago. In general, the shop opened one Sunday a month to catch up on projects. "I'll be in shortly."

"Lexi's here, too," Smitty said, amusement in his voice. "She thinks you only would have overslept like this if your girlfriend came by last night."

"Did you get your hair braided before you started gossiping with my daughter?"

The older man chuckled. "I'm going to give her a wrench if you're not here soon."

"I'll take my time, then," Tyler said and ended the call. Lexi was supposed to avoid the shop this weekend. Why was she there? Tyler tended to his morning duties and headed downstairs. Sure enough, Sara sat at the kitchen table drinking coffee from a plain white mug. She smiled as Tyler walked in.

"You must have been tired."

"I was."

"I guess I wore you out, then." She grinned.

"Too many carbs at dinner gets me every time," Tyler said. Sara came by with a bag of frozen meatballs, fresh pasta, sauce, and garlic knots. It turned out to be an excellent meal, though the volume of carbs wasn't the only reason Tyler slept well. He poured himself a cup and took a sip.

"A likely excuse," Sara said. "You all right?"

"Sure. I actually need to get to the shop. Apparently, I signed myself up to come in today."

"You need to learn to delegate better."

"I'll work on it once I take care of whoever killed two of my friends."

Sara squeezed Tyler's hand. "There's oatmeal in the fridge. You'll need to add some liquid, but it'll heat up well."

"I didn't even know I had any in the house."

"Thank Lexi, then." Sara slid off the chair and kissed Tyler. "I need to get going, anyway. You're not the only one who has a little work to do today."

"I thought you senior Pentagon types were good at delegating," Tyler said, "especially to unsuspecting men in uniform."

"Some things I can't fob off." Sara headed upstairs. Tyler

added milk and cinnamon to the oatmeal, heated it up for a minute, and ate it warm. By the time he was ready to get dressed, Sara returned to the the first floor. "You ever think about not being a knight-errant?"

"I guess you could say it's a calling."

"Because you can't walk away from certain things," Sara said. Tyler nodded. "I do love a man with a code."

"Someone needs to pay, and I'll find out who it is." Tyler was a planner and door kicker, not a trained investigator, so he expected Musa would help here.

"Take care of yourself, Tyler. Make sure you stay on the good side of the grass." She gave him a lingering kiss good-bye. "Let me know how things are going."

"I will," he said. When Sara left, Tyler got dressed. He spent an extra few seconds scanning the outside of the house before walking to the 442. The Sig Sauer in a holster on the door provided some comfort as he fired up the engine and headed to the shop.

It was Sunday, so Veronica Fitzgerald got off to a late start.

She allowed herself to indulge in room service. For the prices the Sheraton charged, she probably wouldn't do it again. Unless she had some reason to celebrate later . . . like finishing and selling a story about John Tyler. After she ate and changed clothes, Veronica climbed into her rental and headed from Towson toward the city-county line. It was an easy jaunt around the Beltway and a straight shot down Harford Road.

This time, she stopped in a different lot. Her vantage point remained across the street but about fifty feet closer. The shop was open on a Sunday, though it didn't look like Tyler had made it in yet. The older guy worked on a car.

Veronica noticed a Honda Accord coupe in the lot. It didn't seem like the kind of vehicle Tyler's shop would work on. They focused on domestic muscle cars but would generally take on anything at least two decades old.

Lexi Tyler appeared in one of the windows. Veronica remembered getting an email from her a couple months back. It started her interest in the girl's father. On some level, the current story almost felt like a betrayal. Lexi got the word out regarding the shady deal Ramseur County made with the Sappony along with a few details about the gold mining operation. Veronica used the information—and uncovered plenty more of her own—to write a few hard-hitting exposés on local officials, the city of Beauregard, the county, and the history of the bad contract. The death of Con White—which Veronica still thought Tyler had a hand in—only fanned the flames.

Veronica owed it all to Lexi's tip.

A tip she made in good faith. Was this any way to repay her? "Thanks for giving me the biggest story of my career," she said to the otherwise empty interior. "In return, I'm going to blow up your dad's life."

It sounded really shitty when she said it out loud.

Veronica rapped her fingers on the Tucson's steering wheel. Could she still chase down leads and write the story without tossing a grenade into everything Tyler spent years building? What if she left his name out of it? He could simply be a nameless and faceless retired Green Beret whose training and sense of duty didn't allow him to walk away from trouble. "No," she decided.

The public had a right to know what went on. From the port of Baltimore to a swanky Bel Air neighborhood to rural North Carolina, John Tyler used the skills he learned in the Army on a freelance basis. He didn't take any money as far as she could tell, and he acted on the side of the good guys. Still, one man playing judge, jury, and interstate executioner was a story no matter how noble his intentions.

Lexi passed in front of the window again. She looked toward Veronica's SUV. It made the reporter slide down a little in her seat. "I'm sorry, Lexi," she whispered. "You didn't ask for this, and I'm sure you don't deserve it, but I need to do my job." A rumble from the shop's lot announced the arrival of Tyler's classic Olds. Veronica remained low and peeked over the dash. One of the PIs she'd hired zoomed past a moment later. Tyler climbed out of the muscle car, took in his surroundings, and headed inside.

He had no idea what was coming.

14

———————

Tyler was about to close up for the day when Musa called.

Smitty left a few minutes before. Lexi rolled out a couple hours ago. Tyler doubted the call would be about anything good, but he answered anyway. "We lost another," Musa told him.

"Goddammit." Tyler's fist slammed the desktop. "I had a feeling this was why you called. Who?"

"Disney."

Giovanni Orlando. A stereotypically loud and good-natured Italian who turned into a stone-cold killer when it was go time. Tyler ran into him three years ago, but they'd always been bad about staying in touch despite only living a state apart from one another. "Southern Virginia," Tyler said. "Whoever's doing this is heading our direction."

"I know. Either of us could be next, but you're closer geographically. Watch your back, Tippy."

"I am." Tyler paused. "When did he die?"

"Yesterday. Disney was working in his front yard. Someone shot him in the head."

"No witnesses?"

"A couple people heard the report," Musa said. "He lives in a pretty rural area, though. Some farms not far away. Gunshots happen sometimes, and when they do, no one really thinks about them."

"So no real witnesses?" Tyler wanted to know.

"No."

"How does this son of a bitch keep getting in and out unseen? Even if Disney lived in a remote area, whoever killed him needs to drive there. No one saw a suspicious car?"

"You realize this isn't my investigation, right?"

"You realize one of us on this call is a cop, and it isn't me?"

"Locals mentioned a Cadillac driving out of the area sometime after the shot. Could be nothing. No one got a plate or a good look at the driver."

"How do you always manage to hear about these things?"

"I've kept in touch with most of the guys over the years," Musa said. "I know some of them gave me crap. I moved on, and so did they. And like you mentioned, one of us is a cop, and police tend to share information with their brethren."

"You're gonna need to keep your eyes open, too," Tyler said. "Nothing says this asshole can't skip over Maryland and go after you."

"I know. I'm back to work tomorrow. I'm going to let my commander know what's going on." Before Tyler could ask, Musa added, "Yes, I trust him."

"All right. Be safe."

"You too, Tippy." Musa broke the connection. Tyler needed to make another call, but he would have to do it from his house. He checked the new security monitor. All quiet outside. Of course, someone could have taken a rifle and climbed onto a roof across the street. Tyler refused to live in fear. He locked up the shop, checked for threats, found none, and drove home. Looking at pictures yesterday—one in particular—kicked up all kinds of memories.

The killer after his friends needed to be an experienced operator. It could have been more than one person. Tyler put the likelihood of it being an American pretty low. Some people would turn coat for the right amount of money, but someone skilled enough to take out three former Green Berets would have a high sticker price. The better bet was someone from overseas. Lots of foreigners had axes to grind against Tyler's old unit.

One man might be able to help him get answers.

Inside his house, Tyler flipped through his Rolodex. Every time he used it, Lexi mocked it as a dusty old relic. Maybe it was, but it still held a business card for Fred Flanker's cover company. Tyler got the card a long time ago. He didn't know if the business remained open, or if the CIA moved Flanker to a different phony operation. The phone rang when he dialed the number. "Stansfield Printing," a young woman said.

"Oh. I guess I didn't expect you to be open on Sunday."

"We're here seven days a week, sir. Can I help you?"

"I'm trying to reach Mister Flanker," Tyler said. "Is he in today?"

"No, I'm afraid he's not. Could I take a message?"

"Sure. Tell him Tippy called."

"Is there a last name?" the receptionist asked.

"I think I'm the only Tippy he knows. Does your phone show my number?"

"Yes, sir."

"Good. This is the best way for him to reach me. Thank you." Tyler ended the call. He wondered how much the girl knew about her boss. He also wondered when Flanker would get back to him. As someone who joined the unit for a pair of two-year deployments, his neck was potentially in the noose, too.

Tyler always found self-interest to be a strong motivator.

~

DESPITE WANTING to have a relaxing Sunday, Sara Morrison headed to her office at the Pentagon.

During the week, she left early enough in the morning to make her commute only mildly bad. On the weekends, it was easy. She unlocked her office, walked past the reception area, and settled in at her desk. Her large L-shaped workspace held both an unclassified desktop and a laptop accredited to process sensitive compartmented information. She would need both for this.

First, she searched news articles for stories of former soldiers killed recently. Cross-checking the Army registries for the years Tyler spent on active duty, she came up with three: Alan Bendix in California, Carl Burns in Texas, and Giovanni Orlando in Virginia. All died within a few days of one another. It was certainly possible for one man to be behind all three, but doing so required an aggressive travel docket and some financial backing.

Police departments would start to talk to one another. They'd monitor airports, commercial flights, and trains. A single killer would need to fly charter, ride the bus, or drive a car. It sounded like Tyler presumed a lone operator came gunning for his old unit mates. Sara would need her SCI laptop to pull a list of likely targets. She was making the assumption that some foreign interest bankrolled the killer. The gunman himself might have been an American, but she hoped not.

Tyler's unit, under the command of disgraced—and deceased—Colonel Leo Braxton, cut a swath through the

Taliban and their supporters. They made a lot of rich and powerful enemies, many of whom died violently before Tyler retired. A few remained alive, though Sara's research revealed men who chased glory because they couldn't afford their old lifestyles. Unless one of them found a skilled assassin to work for peanuts, none of the men would be responsible.

Who else could it be? Sara sighed as she pondered the possibility of an inside job. Tyler got a handle on his PTSD. Not everyone did. A unit member in the throes of mental illness could go after his former friends. It would explain the lack of resistance. Police reports said Alan Bendix made no attempt to dodge the vehicle that ran him over, Carl Burns died after a brief struggle, and Giovanni Orlando got sniped by someone he didn't see—or didn't perceive as a threat.

"That's a stupid idea," Sara said, sweeping it into her mental dustbin. She returned to her list of Taliban members and major backers. It didn't seem likely one of the survivors could be involved. What about friends of family of the many dead men? She eliminated those whose assets wound up in the US government's hands. It still left a decent number, and adding known criminal associates ballooned the list.

It was too much for Sara to tackle alone. She could delegate the work—she smiled at the memory of telling Tyler he needed to do it more—but would lack a good answer if anyone asked her why they needed to look into the friends and family of old Afghan warlords. No, she couldn't ask any of her civilian staff to do this. Sara saved the list, added a few notes, and sent it to some of the military folks she worked with. They could divide it up and figure things out, and they wouldn't ask questions.

She attached an explanation just in case.

ALCON,

Three retired Green Berets across the country died under suspicious circumstances.

I've compiled a list of people who might have a vendetta from their Afghanistan days.

Let's not treat this list as exhaustive, though. Do what you do.

Also, uncomfortable as it may be, I want you to reach out to the special investigators in your service. We need to know if, for instance, a SEAL with an ax to grind might do something like this.

These men gave their all. We owe them our best.

V/R,

Sara

Considering the timeline of when the three men died, Sara didn't know how long she had to come up with something. A killer could already be stalking his next victim—even Tyler. Still, she had to try.

15

Malachi made it to Delaware late Sunday night.

After ditching the Cadillac, he checked into the nicest hotel he could find. The Hyatt would have to do. Places like this didn't take phony names and wink-wink cash payments. He used the second of four ID and credit card combos Pazir provided him at the outset of the mission. He slept well in a plush king bed and ordered a decadent room service feast for breakfast. His benefactor would probably complain again.

Once he'd eaten, exercised, and showered, Malachi left the hotel. He needed another vehicle. Rentals were out. Agencies always kept newer cars, and Malachi didn't want a GPS chip to betray his movements. An apartment parking lot a ten-minute walk from the Hyatt offered several opportunities. He cased the area and waited for a few people to leave before making his move. A couple minutes later, he drove away in a black Camaro which wore the plates of the Chevy Equinox parked beside it.

Today, he would begin his observation of Musa Sadozai.

He'd need to be careful and opportunistic. The first three men let their skills atrophy and their sharpness grow dull.

Musa left the service and began working as a cop almost right away. Driving a police cruiser around Delaware was a far cry from riding in a Hummer through the explosive-riddled wasteland of Afghanistan. Malachi understood firsthand. Sadozai's performance evaluations—another win for Pazir's computer guys—showed a man who still knew how to get things done. The cop promised to be his toughest challenge yet.

Part of it came from the job. While Sadozai was the lone occupant of his car today, this may not always be the case. Police, like wolves and women, tended to travel in packs. If one rolled up to the scene of something amiss, a bunch more would follow. If Sadozai grew suspicious of a certain black Camaro in his rear view, he could radio for reinforcements. Malachi would be none the wiser until a phalanx of patrol vehicles insisted he pull over.

So he hung back, keeping at least two cars and one lane of traffic between himself and Musa whenever he could. When it became obvious the cop drove his beat on a long stretch of road, Malachi would find a parallel street and covertly tail him from there. The lieutenant—a rank the man never achieved in the Army—answered a couple calls to people's houses but spent a lot of time behind the wheel. At one point, Malachi guessed his target pulled over to pray in the cruiser.

When Musa stopped his state-issued sedan at a halal deli for lunch, Malachi parked nearby. He donned a cap, pulled it low over his eyes, added a pair of glasses with no prescription. and entered the deli a few minutes after his target. This was definitely a risk. In a two-man operation, Malachi's partner would have done this part of the operation. One on the target and the other in the car in case things went sideways. He didn't have such a luxury anymore. Besides, halal meat was also kosher, and he was hungry.

Malachi spotted Sadozai sitting at a table by himself with

his back to the far wall. The Israeli approached the counter, ordered a pastrami sandwich combo with chips, filled the paper cup with iced tea, and sat on the opposite side of the restaurant. This didn't put a lot of distance between him and Sadozai. The deli featured a counter with six stools and about fifteen tables spread out around the tiled floor. Framed photos on the walls showed famous buildings from throughout the Middle East including the Burj Khalifa, Church of the Holy Sepulchre, the al-Asqa Mosque, and the Princess Tower. Malachi had seen them all. The collection made him wonder if the owners even visited the Middle East. It reminded him of pizzerias displaying pictures of Italy when the proprietors were Greek.

Sadozai got his food—a sandwich and chips like Malachi. The cop scanned the room. His eyes lingered on Malachi for a second before moving on to someone else. Malachi came in armed with only a knife. He didn't expect to have a shot to kill Sadozai in here, but the blade would let him do it if the opportunity somehow presented itself. When the skinny fellow behind the counter called his order number, Malachi retrieved his food. It sat on a basic paper tray. He fought the urge to wrinkle his nose. Here, he was a man who ate deli food served on paper plates amid photos of landmarks the owners likely never saw.

The pastrami was good, at least. It tasted fresh and peppery. Even the chips were crisp and salted just right. For his part, Sadozai ate in silence, glancing occasionally at his phone but keeping his eyes up most of the time. Malachi clenched and unclenched his left fist under the table. Only two other patrons ate in the restaurant. He'd seen two work- ers. There was probably a third in the kitchen. Five people plus the target. It would be messy and too big a risk. For John Tyler—the final name on the list—he might take the chance.

Not for Musa Sadozai.

If the Afghan cop went to relieve himself, all bets would be off. Malachi would follow him and let him bleed out in the bathroom on a floor tainted by urine. Kevlar did little against a knife, and the vest always stopped a couple inches above the waist anyway. The chance never materialized, however. Sadozai finished his lunch, dumped out his tray, and set it on a metal shelf atop the trash can. Malachi waited for an opening, but the trooper mumbled something into his radio, scanned the interior again, and headed for his car. Malachi wolfed down the rest of his food. Sadozai's car remained in the lot.

When it pulled out, Malachi left and headed for the Camaro. He would find another opportunity to kill Musa Sadozai. For now, the chase was back on.

TYLER'S CELL phone buzzed while he stood under an old Jeep.

He didn't recognize the number and let it go to voicemail. A couple minutes later, the same call came in again. He stepped away to answer it this time. "It's a good thing you're the only Tippy I know," Fred Flanker said.

"I guess it is. How are you?"

"Impressed you kept my business card all these years."

"I'm old enough to keep a Rolodex," Tyler said. "Turns out they're still useful."

Flanker chuckled. "I think we're the same age. I understand." He paused. "I have to say . . . I didn't really expect to hear from you again. Can't imagine you called for a recruiting pitch."

"Definitely not."

"What's going on?"

"You want to talk over an open line?"

"Call is secure on my end," Flanker said. "I know you're on a burner. I think we're all right."

"Good. I'm still getting the permits to build a SCIF in my basement."

"I always liked your dry wit, Tippy."

"I hope you also liked the way I tend to get down to business. Three men dead. Bendix, Burns, and Orlando."

"Yeah," Flanker said with a sigh. "I heard. Terrible stuff."

"Suspicious, too."

"I agree, but I'm not exactly in law enforcement."

"No, but you *are* in a bunch of photos from the unit," Tyler said. "If whoever's doing this can find Orlando in the sticks of southern Virginia, they can find you."

"What do you want from me, Tyler?"

"I expect you to act in your own interests. It's what your people do best, after all. In this case, I think your interests line up with everyone's. You may not be in law enforcement, but let's not pretend you don't have access to considerable information."

"All right," Flanker said. "I won't quibble with your evaluation. Let's meet today."

"Yes. Let's."

"You know where Casey's Coffee is?"

"Pretty sure I can find it," Tyler said.

"You know how to use a GPS?"

"My daughter taught me. When?"

"How about fifteen hundred?"

"See you then," Tyler said and ended the call. He remembered a conversation with Lexi a few years ago. Tyler told her he didn't have any friends in intelligence. This was true. Flanker would be the closest thing. Tyler's issue with most CIA operatives was the way they played fast and loose. He didn't always like everyone in the unit, but he knew they all fought for the same side. This was less clear with the Agency's men. Flanker had his own agenda sometimes, but he always seemed to be on the right side.

Tyler hoped he remained there.

16

Tyler found Casey's Coffee easily enough,

It stood on Eastern Avenue in an area he used to know as Greektown. The building was large and squat, like it served as a restaurant in a past life, with a massive front window and flat roof. Only two other cars sat in the lot, and Tyler parked the 442 away from them. He walked inside to find two baristas. Fred Flanker raised a paper cup from his seat at a small table. He looked much the same as Tyler remembered, though an extra ten pounds changed his formerly lean silhouette. The goatee was gone now, also. Probably too gray. Tyler empathized. The suit-clad CIA man was the only patron inside.

Tyler ordered a black coffee, declined several times to add something to it or make it into a latte, and joined Flanker at the table. "Quiet place," he said as he dropped onto the dark wooden chair. It allowed him to keep the front door in sight, and he wondered if Flanker chose the opposite seat knowing this. The color fit the interior motif. Even with overheads and natural light coming in the front window, the dark gray paint lent the place a bleak vibe. A few pictures hung scattered throughout the shop. All were photos of recognizable DC landmarks. "How many people are aware the CIA owns it?"

Flanker grinned. "Not many. I'm not surprised you picked up on it. Did the name help?"

"No." Tyler gestured to the interior. "Just . . . everything taken in concert."

"William Casey was Ronald Reagan's CIA director for six years."

"I was nine when Reagan took office," Tyler said. "I don't think I remember most of the people in his cabinet." A long cheap-looking counter demarcated the area where the baristas currently stood and lallygagged. A wooden door stood in the corner beyond. "You got a SCIF back there?"

"Close," Flanker said. It couldn't be a proper sensitive compartmented information facility. The building lacked perimeter fencing, full-time security, and the locks on its doors were all wrong. "We can't store anything in there, but we can go in and have conversations the public shouldn't overhear."

"Speaking of the public, any of them ever wander in?"

"Yes. It's a real shop. I don't know if it turns a profit. We don't need it to, of course, but many people pop in for their morning or afternoon caffeine fix." Tyler scanned the items in the glass display case. Flanker caught his eyes. "Delivered from a local bakery. None of the workers know."

"How do you explain using the back room, then?"

"Membership card."

"Seriously?"

"Seriously." Flanker sipped his drink which smelled sweet even from across the table. Tyler took a pull of his coffee. It was a smooth medium roast. "They think the owner sells memberships. It beats knowing the truth."

"You gonna flash your card?"

"Might as well." Both men stood. Flanker slipped a minimalist wallet out of his front pocket. He found a laminated card and showed it to the baristas. One of them came around and unlocked the door. Flanker and Tyler entered, and the former closed and locked up behind them. The space here was more colorful, at least. The center of the floor was empty. Two chairs and a couch sat clustered at each end of the wide but shallow area. There were no windows, but soft lights overhead provided plenty of wattage.

Flanker sat in one of the chairs on the right. Tyler eased onto the sofa, positioning himself to keep the door in his field of vision. "Like I told you, three men are dead, and none of them went accidentally."

"I did a little digging," Flanker said. "Agencies share information better now. I remember when we had to dump things in FinCEN because we *couldn't* share it." Tyler recalled hearing a few stories of the Financial Crimes Enforcement Network and figured this was the context. "FBI doesn't have much yet. Locals are handling it, but with a little federal encouragement, they're all talking to one another." Flanker paused when Tyler didn't say anything. His usual tactic of silence wouldn't work on someone trained in interrogations and counterintelligence, but old habits died hard. "You're still concerned," the Agency man added.

"I am. The order indicates someone moving across the country. We have to presume he's smart enough not to book a ticket and fly coach."

"You think it's one person?"

"Could be. More operatives potentially complicate things, especially when you're moving three thousand miles. One guy could have done all this."

"A skilled guy, sure," Flanker said.

"This is where you come in. Maybe he's some foreign

intelligence operator. I don't know. What I do know is we're all in the crosshairs . . . including you."

"I'm not sure I agree on the last point, but you could be right." Flanker bobbed his head. "Okay. I've kicked the tires on this already. I'll keep looking into it. If you hear anything, you let me know."

"Same for you."

"I will," Flanker said.

The two shook hands, and Tyler left the secret back room. He downed the rest of his coffee, checked out the large window to see if anyone took an interest in his trip here, and exited the shop. It was a strange place, but oddities abounded when intelligence agencies were involved. Now, Tyler needed to hope his lone acquaintance from Langley came through.

LEXI'S last class got canceled, so she headed to a local gun range.

Her dad texted to say a third member of his old unit turned up dead. Shot in the head by an unknown killer. Lexi heard the tension in her father's voice even if he didn't talk about it. This had him spooked—a condition in which he rarely found himself. The whole mess made her nervous by extension. She remembered being anxious about making some cheer squad in sixth grade the first time her dad took her to the range.

The pistol leaped and barked in her hand, and all her concerns faded away.

She was a terrible shot back then, sometimes missing the paper target completely even from fifteen yards. Now, she could pepper them from twenty-five and still do well at fifty. Lexi steadied sight alignment on a target shaped and styled like a burglar with the stereotypical striped shirt and mask over the eyes. She blew out the breath in her lungs and squeezed off four rounds. All struck her two-dimensional victim in the torso. Any of them could prove fatal.

Lexi knew why her dad was spooked. Someone who really wanted to come after him might first go looking for her. After it happened with Braxton's men, she resolved never to be a liability like that again. Ever since, she made sure to go to kickboxing on schedule and find time for the range. Most of her friends were into yoga and hiking, in part because both paired well with drinking wine afterward. Lexi had nothing against either activity—and even went along sometimes—but neither helped her not be a victim.

When she finished after about an hour, Lexi packed her pistol back into its case and drove into College Park. She arrived at the apartment a few minutes before Emily and Kim returned from their final classes. Lexi lay on her bed, her laptop open to an assignment and headphones playing an Alex Anne album. Listening to her friend's music also helped with stress. Kim knocked on the door, and Lexi paused the music. "You're back early."

"My last class got canceled. I'm looking at the assignment for it."

"Want to get some lunch?" Kim asked. "Emily and I are hungry."

Lexi smiled. "Me, too. Let's go."

As a university town, College Park offered lots of options. Most were geared toward speed and budget. Lexi recalled an anecdote her dad told her about cars. "They can be cheap, fast, or reliable. Pick two. You never get all three." His logic didn't extend to local eateries. Some were better than others, but none of them served bad food. The best of the bunch were consistently good.

No one wanted to be out for long, so they ended up at Potbelly. Lexi was hungrier than she realized, easily polishing off a small meatball sub and a bag of chips. Emily and Kim each got large subs and nibbled at them. They took more than half to go. As Kim pulled her Corolla into the lot, Lexi spotted a man standing between their building and the neighboring one. She'd never seen him before. Tall and thin in a long coat, his head was on a swivel looking around.

The hairs on her arms stood up.

Emily and Kim got out of the car. Lexi remained inside. "You coming?" Kim asked, her face a mix of mirth and what-the-hell-are-you-doing.

"Yeah." Lexi got out, the car chirped when Kim locked it, and the trio walked toward their building. The strange man remained. "You want to walk off our lunch? I could stand to stretch my legs." Lexi's roommates stopped. "It's a quarter of a mile around the whole complex." She let out a nervous chuckle. "Ask me how I know."

"I'd rather get started on my homework," Kim said.

"Me, too," Emily added. "I have a project due in two days, and I've done like nothing for it."

The man approached them. Lexi instinctively reached behind herself, but the pistol remained in its case in her bedroom. If he pulled a weapon, she'd have to resort to her kickboxing training and get her friends out of the area. "Y'all got something to eat?" he asked. When he was closer, Lexi could see a couple of his teeth were missing, and both his general appearance and odor conveyed his need for a shower.

"Sure," Emily said, handing the stranger her leftovers from Potbelly. "Enjoy."

"Thank you, miss. Y'all have a blessed day now." He shuffled away, and Lexi exhaled.

"What's up with you?" Kim said, frowning. "You're really on edge, Lexi. What's going on?"

"I guess it's just the grind getting to me a little," she said.

"You good? Everything all right with your dad?"

Lexi nodded and hoped her smile was convincing. Her friends' expressions didn't change. "Yeah. He's fine. I am, too." She'd told her roommates something similar last week. This time, Lexi didn't even believe it herself, and her words really felt like a lie.

17

———

Pazir's team came through again.

They were almost as good at intelligence gathering as his former Israeli agencies. This time, Malachi read a report detailing the kinds of calls Musa Sadozai responded to as well as the geographical hot spots. He didn't work any of the prime real estate like the beaches. Sadozai's patrol generally encompassed the center of the state, west of the shoreline and south of Dover Air Force Base.

It gave Malachi ideas of where to plan an ambush.

Sadozai received awards for his service to the Delaware State Police, but the report showed him doing very little dangerous work. The lone time he'd fired his service weapon came six years ago. It was a long way from a team of Green Berets taking out the Taliban and their strongest supporters. While Malachi didn't doubt Sadozai put his time in at the range, he also knew it didn't replace being in a firefight. Fearing for your life.

Today, Malachi sat behind the wheel of an old Toyota SUV. Sadozai drove his cruiser on all manners of roads. When he made a traffic stop, Malachi kept going and waited by a convenience store about a quarter-mile up the road. Sure enough, the Charger with its ugly light bars mounted on the roof breezed by a few minutes later. Malachi let another car go ahead of him before pulling out again.

Another traffic stop followed in short order. This time, Malachi drove on for about a half-mile and turned into a lot. He pulled out a map of the state and compared it with the data Pazir's team compiled on Sadozai's calls. One area showed promise. Malachi needed an uncrowded spot to try and take out Sadozai. He'd managed to avoid notice so far. There was always an element of luck to these operations, but careful planning played a large part, too.

Malachi tapped his finger on Lums Pond State Park. While fall might attract hikers looking to give their boots a few more uses for the season, not many would be there late morning on a Tuesday. The map showed entrances and exits, the pond the park was named for, and provided rough information about elevation. Malachi keyed the new destination into his phone's GPS and headed off.

Twenty minutes later, he pulled into the main entrance. Another would have been closer to where he wanted to go, but this allowed him to see how many people visited the park today. Only two other cars sat on the lot. Malachi backed into a spot so he could make a faster exit, took out his phone, and dialed 9-1-1. An operator came on the line quickly. "Nine-one-one, what's your emergency?" a woman asked.

"I need the police, please."

"What's going on, sir?"

"I think I saw a man with a gun at Lums Pond State Park," Malachi said.

"You think?"

"I didn't stick around to find out. I'm in the parking lot now. It's not crowded, but if he does have a gun, a few people are going to be in danger."

"We'll send an officer to investigate," the operator said. "Can you stay on the line?"

Malachi broke the connection. He grabbed a rifle bag from the backseat. Once he exited the car, he popped the battery out of his phone and deposited the components in separate trash cans. Then, he entered the park and looked for a good spot to set up.

MUSA FINISHED his third traffic stop when the radio on his chest crackled.

"All units, report of a possible man with a gun at Lums Pond State Park," the female dispatcher said. "Caller isn't certain, and he left the area."

Musa pressed the talk button. "This is unit eighteen. I'll check it out."

Another voice came on the line. It sounded like Officer Hawkins. "Eighteen, you need backup?"

"I'll let you know when I get there." Musa climbed back into his car. The young idiot in the Subaru WRX pulled away at a reasonable pace. It was probably the first time all day he didn't push his foot to the floor. Musa figured the kid would go back to driving like a jerk soon enough, but at least the ticket, fine, and points on his license might give him pause. Traffic was light, and Musa got his Charger back onto the road, made a U-turn at the first opportunity, and headed for the park.

He'd been here several times before, both as an officer responding to calls and as a citizen enjoying a respite. The area was quite scenic, and Musa came here sometimes to pray. He felt connected to nature and the divine in places like this. Every time he visited, it confirmed his decision to leave the Army years ago. He made a few friends there, but a bunch of soldiers didn't like having an Afghan-born Muslim in their ranks while they pursued men who were mostly Afghan-born Muslims. Moving to Delaware had been good for Musa's mental state and his faith.

Only three cars sat in the main lot when Musa pulled in. He left his lights and siren off. If some maniac really were here with a gun, spooking the man—they were always men—wouldn't do any good. Musa exited the Charger and spoke into his radio again. "Unit eighteen on scene at Lums Pond State Park. Will advise if I need backup." He looked to the sky. Clouds covered the sun, and trees would surround him, so he folded his sunglasses and slipped them into his shirt pocket.

"Roger, eighteen," the dispatcher replied.

Musa stepped onto the main trail. It began as stone and then changed between wood and natural grass as the terrain allowed. The pond which gave the park its name sat in the center of a massive cluster of trees featuring some scenic overlooks and also sudden drops. He knew the terrain, so Musa kept up a good pace as he veered to the left when the trail split. From here, it formed a long loop around the water.

The call didn't specify a location for the man who might have a gun, so Musa kept an eye out. Tree coverage grew heavy on the left. A hill sat back in the forest, and another entrance led to a popular hiking trail up to its apex. When he'd walked another hundred yards or so, the cloud cover parted, and rays of sun streamed through the canopy.

The telltale glint of a rifle flared in his vision.

Musa spun, but the bullet clipped him above the left hip. It raised a line of blood and went numb after a flash of pressure, but it wasn't a serious injury. He ducked and ran farther along. Two more loud cracks split the serenity of the venue, and two more shells kicked up dirt and grass behind him. Musa came here a lot. He knew the terrain better than anyone else on the force. His assailant would be working off a map and maybe a day on the trails.

Here was a chance to find and take out the man stalking his former unit. Musa envisioned doing this with John Tyler and a few other guys, but he couldn't be picky. On the trails, he could put himself in a good position to turn the tide on the mystery man who'd traveled the country. Delaware would be his final stop.

Musa cut a hard right into the woods, ducking under a branch and maintaining his pace. Here, he could get ahead of his pursuer and maybe even set a trap for him. He also didn't need to do it alone. "Eighteen to dispatch," he said as he ran along, "assailant confirmed at Lums Pond. Shots fired at the police. I repeat, shots fired at the police."

18

TYLER SAT AT HIS DESK WHILE SMITTY AND ORTIZ WORKED ON A couple cars.

He'd been out there with them until a few minutes ago. The mess with his old unit distracted him, and he'd needed to redo his work a couple times already. Tyler brought his Rolodex in with him today. He needed to get the word out. Even if their assailant remained unknown, everyone else needed to know the situation. If they were prepared, the mystery shooter's next stop could be his last.

Tyler flipped through names, frowning when he came to the ones already dead. He dialed Harvey Lee, and the man picked up. "Tippy? Been a long time."

"It has, Oswald. I wish I called under better circumstances."

"Yeah." Lee sighed. "I heard about Bendix. Felt bad I couldn't make it out there."

"It wasn't only him," Tyler said. "Stretch and Disney, too."

"Jesus Christ. What's going on?"

"I wish I knew. Musa and I are looking into it. He has

contacts in law enforcement, and I . . . well, I like kicking doors in and shooting assholes."

"You all need some help?" Lee asked.

"Not yet. I wanted to be sure you knew what was going on."

"You haven't given me a lot of details yet, Tippy."

"True. Stretch got stabbed in a house. Cops are calling it a home invasion, but we know how easy they are to stage."

"We do indeed."

"Disney was working in his front yard when someone sniped him," Tyler said. "He never had a chance. California, Texas, and then Virginia. Whoever this bastard is, he's coming this way."

"We need more than you and Musa trying to run this down. No offense."

"None taken. Remember Flanker?"

Lee snorted. "Yeah. Not too bad as far as agency men go."

"He's poking around, too. I managed to convince him he could also be on a target list. Whoever our killer is, he's very skilled. Could be someone from a foreign army or intelligence service with a grudge. He'll be good for pulling those details."

"I guess. This doesn't strike me as a problem we solve with spies, though. You, me, and Musa can take out the son of a bitch. Let him come for one of us and bam! We get him."

It sounded like Lee suggested using someone as bait. Tyler didn't care for the idea. "Right now, we're trying to gather information," he said in the interests of being diplomatic.

"I think we can do more."

"We breached a lot of compounds. Took out a lot of people. Crossed a bunch of names off wanted lists."

"What's your point?" Lee wanted to know.

"We didn't do any of it without gathering intel first. Three men are dead already. I want to feed whoever's doing this into a wood chipper feet first, but I think we need to know more up front. No point in adding any names to his kill list."

Lee remained silent a few seconds before answering. "Fine. You're right. I'm pissed, and I'm letting it get to me."

"I understand. Keep your eyes open. Carry wherever you go."

"Already do."

Tyler grinned. "I figured. Just be careful, Oswald. I've been to enough funerals for old friends this year."

"You got it, Tippy," he said and ended the call. Ortiz appeared in the doorway a few seconds after.

"I know," Tyler said, "I need to get back to work."

"It's your shop, boss. You seem a little distracted. Still have the same problem as before?"

"It's gotten worse . . . but yes."

Ortiz offered a solemn nod. "I don't know if the prick is coming after you or not, but if you need me, I'm down."

"I know." Ortiz helped Tyler take out a militia in West Virginia several months back. He was a good man and a better shot. Ortiz's Army career ended when an IED took off part of his leg, but he was a solid worker and happy to help with some of the extracurriculars Tyler valued. "It's still early in the operation. I'll let you know."

Ortiz nodded. "You got it, boss." He returned to the service bay. The other cars out there wouldn't fix themselves, so Tyler got back to work, too. He hoped Flanker and Musa were gathering useful intel.

~

MALACHI HAD another shot lined up when Sadozai turned hard into the trees.

"Shit," the Israeli muttered. He scampered down from his

perch. The first round clipped his target thanks to the sun coming out and giving his position away. Still, even a minor wound would have an effect, bleed, and slow someone down in a chase. Thanks to using the rifle, Malachi spotted Sadozai a head start of about four hundred yards. Even managing a long gun, however, he wasn't injured, so he expected to close the distance.

His quadriceps burned as he hustled up a hill. Tree cover made the target hard to spot. Sadozai was still a skilled operator. He would enjoy the additional advantage of knowing the terrain. It all made for a good challenge. The man was also a Muslim who abandoned his faith to hunt his own people for the US Army. Malachi didn't care much for Afghan Muslims, but he at least respected those who honored their faith and convictions. Malachi slowed and studied the ground. He could make out footsteps in the dirt and grass, but the most telling things he saw were occasional drops of blood.

Even if Sadozai managed to cover or hide his tracks later, the injury would give him away.

A flash of movement appeared in Malachi's vision about two hundred yards ahead. Sadozai cut across the trail. Malachi put the rifle to his shoulder, made his best guess where the target would be, and fired. The bullet tore into a tree, sending splinters of wood into the grass. He ran ahead, but no body lay on the ground. "I'll find you," he called to the woods.

"Backup is coming," Sadozai hollered back. "You might want to hurry."

The closest police station was a fifteen-minute drive away, and this figure presumed officers remained in the building ready to roll when a call came in. Malachi still had at least ten minutes, and the vastness of the area would allow him to evade simple American cops. He dashed off in pursuit and crested a hill. The descent down the other side was long and gradual, and Musa Sadozai jogged at the bottom.

Malachi paused, raised the rifle, and fired, but his haste made him miss high. Sadozai ducked and sprinted off to the right, clutching his side as he did. The man was already slowing. His four-hundred-yard head start was down to half the original figure, and every minute brought Malachi closer. It was only a matter of time, and an operator like Sadozai would realize it.

It might make him desperate.

Malachi slung the rifle over his shoulder, drew a pistol, and continued his pursuit. He would be cautious of tricks. The M24 remained at easy access if he needed it again. For now, the 9MM would suffice. Malachi enjoyed the element of time. The cops would need to find Sadozai even if they knew his location, and the injury would further sap his strength, stamina, and speed by then.

Sometimes, winning was a matter of being able to wait longer than the other guy. Malachi would take the victories any way he could. Each one brought him closer to eliminating John Tyler and then going after Pazir himself.

19

Musa paused against a tree and took a deep breath.

It made his side hurt. The wound wasn't bad, but adding stress and exertion on top of it did not make for a winning combination. He knew the area well, but the bleeding injury was starting to slow him down. For the first time, he wondered if he would be able to survive the encounter—to think nothing of coming out on top. Three of his friends were dead already. He didn't want to join them.

The mystery pursuer crested a hill and hurried a shot. It shredded the air about a foot above Musa's head. "Lucky," he muttered through gritted teeth as he dashed away. He guessed his assailant carried an M24, and he'd been well within range. With another second for his adversary to prepare, Musa would probably be dead.

He thought about the lay of the land. The head start he enjoyed at the beginning would continue to ebb as his injury slowed him. He wouldn't be able to make it out of the area. Backup remained several minutes away, and even once they arrived, officers would need to find him in here. Musa quieted his radio and stayed off comms to minimize the chance of his pursuer hearing a crackle and knowing his location.

If he couldn't win the encounter, he needed to survive it and be useful later.

He paused again, bent at the waist, and sucked in a few lungfuls of air. An idea formed in his head. It would require him to do his parts exactly right and then get a bit lucky. As much as soldiers and special operators tried to deny it, luck played a role in many successes and failures. Musa changed direction and headed toward the water. He knew of a cliff ahead, and he could fool his adversary there.

If God really smiled on him, the bastard chasing him would slip and fall.

Musa ran as fast as his legs would allow. They burned with exertion as the wound in his side flared. Near the edge, Musa identified a path down the almost sheer drop. It was about a hundred feet to the bottom. He took out his phone, set it to record a video, and propped it against a nearby oak. There had been no sign of his adversary for a few minutes now.

Might as well give the son of a bitch a hint.

Musa moved down the narrow path. Gravity would turn his walk into a run and then a fall soon, so he kicked his feet out and slid on the dirt. He screamed for effect, making sure to let out a long and loud one. Once he reached the bottom, Musa dashed to his right about ten steps, sprawled out on the grass, and tried to position his arm and leg at weird angles to make it look like he fell. He cranked his head to the side as much as he could.

If the man chasing him found him—and if he were any good, he would—he'd see a target who fell to his death in the effort of getting away. So long as he didn't spot the phone, Musa would have him on video. If he survived the next few minutes, he, Tyler, and the rest could gain some key intelligence. Musa turned the volume on his radio up. He keyed the mic and whispered. "This is eighteen. I'm near the pond at the southeast side. Tango nearby. Give me your twenty if you're responding and be loud about it."

Musa heard footsteps from above. Lying down for the past few minutes made things easier, so he focused on taking shallow breaths. This was where the luck component came in, and he said a silent prayer to help.

THE SCREAM DREW Malachi's attention.

Maybe Sadozai didn't know this area so well after all. Or maybe pain and the growing weakness from loss of blood made him careless. Either way, the pursuit would end soon. Malachi headed off in the direction of the distressed cry. He walked through a cluster of trees whose unruly branches intruded on the dirt path. Ahead, the trees abruptly ended, and it looked like the ground fell away.

Did Sadozai tumble off a cliff?

Malachi allowed himself a smile at the thought. The man might have taken himself out of the fight if the fall were long enough. As the forest thinned, Malachi approached cautiously. He scanned nearby to make sure Sadozai didn't lie in wait to push him over. The Israeli leaned forward enough to see down the sheer drop.

The body of Musa Sadozai lay at the bottom. His left arm and leg lay at odd angles, and the position of his head could have indicated a broken neck. "You killed yourself, you idiot," Malachi said, gathering phlegm and spitting on the corpse. He raised his pistol, put a round in the dead cop's back, and started away from the edge. Before he'd gone far, a radio sounded from below. "Eighteen, this is twenty," a deep male voice said. "I'm five minutes out . . . over."

"Unit fourteen also responding," a woman called. "ETA is six minutes."

Malachi leaned over the cliff again and hocked another loogie onto the dead Muslim. "Your friends are too late." He put the pistol away, stepped a safe distance from the edge, and took out his phone. "Musa Sadozai is dead," Malachi said when Pazir picked up. "Your dossier helped me pick the location."

"Did he suffer?"

"From his own stupidity, yes. I put a round in him for good measure. He won't trouble us again. The plan can continue. John Tyler is next."

"Excellent," Pazir said. "You are ahead of schedule. Take your time with Tyler. He has been a thorn in our sides for over a decade. Study him. Find his weaknesses."

"This is not my first time hunting a man," Malachi said.

"I know, but Tyler is not any man. He is a man who must feel despair like none other before he dies. Exploit every vulnerability you can. I want to know how badly he suffers. If it's safe to do so, I want to watch him beg for death as the light leaves his eyes."

"Leave Tyler to me. I'll let you know about the rest." Musa ended the call and slipped his phone away. A siren rang out in the distance. He had time to get away. Even if the cops pulled into the lot in sixty seconds, it would take them several minutes to find the body of their friend. By then, Malachi would be gone.

There was no easy way nearby to get back to the top, so he ran to the west. There, about six hundred yards away, a dirt trail zig-zagged up a shallower hill. Malachi scanned it for footprints but didn't see any. Musa Sadozai really fell over the edge in a place he knew well. Blood loss worked wonders sometimes. Malachi made it to the top and moved into the trees. He made sure to stay a safe distance from the trail as he picked his way back toward the entrance. The police would be in the area soon, and while they all searched for their fallen friend, he could make his escape.

The next stop was Maryland.

20

—————

Tyler's phone buzzed with an unknown number in the middle of the afternoon.

"It's Musa," his friend said.

"You all right? You sound kinda weak."

"Son of a bitch came after me, Tippy."

Tyler had been standing and now dropped onto a chair. "At least you're alive."

"I am. Some good planning and a little luck. This guy is good. Real good. He almost got me."

"What happened?"

"I answered a call at a park. I know now it was a setup, but we got a report of a man with a gun. I was checking the area out when the sun broke free of the clouds. Spotted the glint you never want to see. I had enough time to move a little bit. The shot winged me. I ran. I was hoping to turn the tables on the prick, but I was losing blood. He almost took my head off a few minutes later."

"How'd you get away?" Tyler wanted to know.

"Basically played dead at the bottom of a cliff. Made him think I fell. Jackass put a round in the Kevlar on my back anyway. Got a couple cracked ribs. I'm on light duty for a while, and my captain wants me to take some leave considering what's been going on."

"And this asshole thinks he killed you."

"He does," Musa said. "I haven't told you the best part yet."

"What is it?"

"I had a head start, so I set my phone up to record at the top of the cliff. Our techies are analyzing it, but they're going to give it back to me . . . along with cleaned-up versions of the video and audio . . . when they finish."

"Great work, Musa," Tyler said. "Fast thinking. We might finally learn something about who this guy is and maybe who's footing the bill."

"You think this isn't a lone wolf?"

"I don't know at this point." Tyler paused. "We made a lot of enemies. None in the last decade, really. Any who've survived will probably be our age peers or older. If they held on to even some of their money, they could pay someone to come to the States and hunt our unit down. At the end of the day, none of us are impossible to find."

"Makes sense," Musa said. "I hope to get something from my people tonight or tomorrow."

"You still in the hospital?"

"Yeah, but they're not going to keep me. Got some stitches in my side. They don't do anything for grapefruit-sized bruises or cracked ribs." Musa chuckled. "Hell, the doctor won't even prescribe me anything for the pain. Good thing I have Advil at home, I guess."

"You up for a little hunting if we can figure out who's coming after us?"

"You know it," Musa said. "If you're right, though, I want everyone involved. The shooter, the money man, the guy who stapled the papers in whatever files they have on us . . . all of them."

"I agree," Tyler said. "Our own little Bush Doctrine."

"You can even call it the Tyler Doctrine."

"I don't need my name on anything official."

"You know anyone else who could lend a hand if we need it?"

Tyler thought of Ortiz. He was always willing to join a just cause. Flanker would probably help, too, and he might even get some intel before Musa's police friends did. "I have a couple folks in mind. You rest up. Let me know what info you end up with."

"You got it, Warrant." Musa hung up.

Tyler needed to make another call.

TYLER DIALED Fred Flanker and got his assistant at the print shop. "I'm still the only Tippy he knows," he told the young woman when she pressed him for a surname. After asking to place him on a brief hold—Tyler found "brief" often did a lot of heavy lifting in these situations—she came back on to say she would transfer his call.

"Miss me so much?" Flanker asked.

"I think I need some coffee. How about you?"

"Little late in the afternoon for me."

"You're not hearing me," Tyler said. "We need to talk over a hot beverage. Got a place in mind?"

"I do. When can you get there?"

"Give me a half-hour," Tyler said and pressed the red button to end the call. He told Smitty he needed to head out early, got in the 442, and drove to the CIA's java shop. Flanker already sat at the same table as before. This time, a man and a woman occupied a spot nearby. Tyler's eyes flicked to them. Flanker offered a fractional shake of his head.

The baristas weren't busy. Tyler ordered a black coffee and a danish. Flanker eyed up the pastry as Tyler pulled out a chair and sat across from him. "How's the printing business?"

"Oh, you know." Flanker shrugged. "It has its ups and downs. I don't have many irons in the fire at the moment."

"I might be able to help you out, then," Tyler said. "I need some custom work done."

"We can handle it." The other couple stood, tossed their cups in the trash, and left.

"Goddamn civilians," Flanker muttered.

"You're a goddamn civilian," Tyler pointed out.

"You know what I mean. Besides, so are you." Flanker showed his membership card, and the two of them adjourned to the private meeting room. "What's so urgent?"

"Whoever's coming after us took a shot at Musa today."

Flanker frowned. "He all right?"

"He'll live. Got clipped by a round and another almost punched his ticket."

"I hadn't heard."

"Maybe you should be coming to me for help. I seem to be ahead of your analysts on this one."

"It's not like I can take an entire team, pull them off whatever else they're doing, and have them run this down," Flanker said. "We're still crunching everything. You have any theories?"

"I think we're looking at two men," Tyler said. "One's the shooter. The other is older and has the checkbook. He might also have a few people working behind the scenes. Our killer seems to know a lot about his victims, after all."

"You think a foreign intelligence service is behind it?"

"I don't know. It doesn't need to be very sophisticated. A couple of former red teamers is probably good enough. If you want to chase them down, go ahead. It's a long story, but Musa might have gotten our guy on video. He's waiting for his people to process what he captured."

"Wow." Flanker nodded. "I always thought he was smart. Any images could really help. Even one taken in profile could be enough."

"If I get something from him, I'll pass it on." Tyler ate some of the danish. It was fine but probably should have been sold or tossed a couple hours before. He needed an afternoon pick-me-up, though, so he wouldn't complain. "You seen anyone suspicious?"

"Outside of Langley . . . and you?" Flanker grinned. "No. I know you probably figured you needed to paint me as a potential victim to get me involved. I'm happy to do this even if whoever these people are have no idea I exist. I was embedded with the unit for four years."

"I hope you don't get shot," Tyler said. "If you do, I'll nominate you for sainthood."

"My parents would be so proud," Flanker said. He checked his watch. "I need to get back. I'll let you know if I come up with anything."

"Likewise."

"Whoever this is must be damn good. Three taken out, plus we almost lost Musa."

"The guy thinks Musa is dead. If we get a handle on who's coming after us, he's down to help."

"I am, too. Unofficially, of course."

"Of course," Tyler said.

21

———

Malachi took a seat inside the Chesapeake House.

It was a large rest stop off I-95. He headed south from Delaware in a stolen Hyundai Sonata. It was one of the older models with a V6 under the hood. The car didn't look like much which increased its odds of not attracting attention. Still, Malachi parked it far from the entrance. None of the eateries inside appealed to him, but he was hungry, so he made do with Burger King.

At the appointed time, another man joined him.

The newcomer was large and black, with muscles honed in the gym and a scar on his left cheek which started below the eye and ran almost to his mouth. The man's perpetual scowl exuded hostility. No one would approach him without a good reason and even then in halting steps. He set a tray from a sub shop on the small round table. No one sat near them, and the late evening hour probably combined with this guy's vibe to keep everyone a safe distance away. "You Mal?" he asked in a gruff voice.

"I am."

"Clarence." He thumped his own chest with a meaty fist. "Whose face you need broken?"

"Someone who's caused a number of problems for my associate," Malachi said. He refused to refer to Pazir as his boss. "First, I want to make sure we're clear on the requirements."

"We good," Clarence said. "You want some asshole beat down but not killed, and I gotta get it all on film."

"Digital, but yes." Malachi took a small camera from a bag on the chair beside him. It was a tiny hunk of plastic about half the size of a deck of cards. He'd included a sheet of instructions for setting it up to transmit. "You want to wear it around your neck, set it nearby . . . whatever. I don't care as long as it works."

Clarence grabbed the camera without looking at it, and he slipped it away while his dark eyes remained on Malachi. "It'll work. I might enjoy kicking the shit out of guys, but I know how to use tech."

"Good." Malachi slid another piece of paper across the plastic tabletop. "Here's some info on your target." Clarence's eyes scanned the page. "I want you to go into this with all the information you need. Your target is a skilled man."

'This guy's no joke. No wonder you're paying more than the going rate."

"He's also fifty-two and has been out of the military for a decade," Malachi said. "There's no need to pretend you're facing him in his prime." He paused a beat. "I presume the amount is sufficient?"

"What if it ain't?" Clarence leaned forward. His bulk crowded the table. "What if I look at the file and decide I need a little more?"

"Too bad. I made a good faith overpayment because of the expected quality of your opposition."

"We may differ on the quality, and how much more you need to kick in."

Malachi leaned back in the chair. "I will not give you a penny more."

Clarence shrugged his large shoulders. "I ain't the type to offer refunds."

"And I 'ain't the type' to negotiate against myself. You might tell me Tyler is dangerous. I agree. You'll also say you are, too, and I don't doubt you." The Israeli flashed a thin smile. "You would be a fool to think I'm not. I've killed plenty of people who were bigger, meaner, and even uglier than you." Clarence glared, but Malachi continued. "You can either do the work for the generous amount I paid you, or you can give me my money back."

"Like I said . . . ain't the type to offer refunds." Clarence stood.

Malachi grabbed his wrist, and despite his best efforts, Clarence couldn't shake the hold. "Let's be clear on one thing. Before I leave you to bleed out in a shallow grave, you'll tell me how to get my money back." Malachi dug his thumb into a pressure point on Clarence's wrist. The big man gritted his teeth. "A little more pressure, and a bone in your wrist snaps. It'll hurt, but I promise what I do to you after will be far, far worse." Clarence stared at Malachi for a few seconds but eventually averted his eyes and nodded. Malachi released the hold, and Clarence rubbed the area above his palm.

"All right, man. Jesus. Fine. The amount we agreed to."

"Excellent," Malachi said after waiting for someone carrying a tray to leave the immediate area. "I knew you'd see reason. If you manage to injure this man, I'll pay you a nice bonus for your time and trouble."

"When you want this done?" Clarence asked.

"Tomorrow morning. Make sure the video works."

"It will."

"Good. Now, go eat somewhere else. It's best if not too many people see us together."

"Yeah." Clarence scoffed. "Sure." He carried his tray to a spot on the other end of the dining area. Malachi finished his meal and headed outside. The stolen car hadn't attracted any attention. With Clarence occupying John Tyler tomorrow, he could pursue other avenues for making his quarry suffer.

Tyler's young and pretty daughter provided the best target of all.

TYLER USED a morning run to help clear his head.

The painting did a lot of heavy lifting in this area, too. Few things beat getting out and hitting the pavement, however. Tyler had never been a fast runner, but he always qualified well within the acceptable ranges for every PT test. In the decade since he left the Army, he'd only lost a few seconds compared to his final official two-mile time. Today, he ran on the streets of the Mount Washington area of Baltimore where he lived.

Tyler bought the house from his father shortly after leaving the service. He'd updated the place since, but it still looked a lot like the place his dad had bought some thirty years before. Tyler ran along Northcliff Drive, around the bend where it became Bonnie View, and then picked up Kelly Avenue. He jogged past the Shrine of the Sacred Heart Catholic Church and the Mount Washington school before turning onto Greely Road. He only stayed on it for a block before making another turn to the port side onto Smith Street.

Several roads led off of Smith. Years before, Tyler used a pedometer to figure out the route he needed to take so he could hit two miles. It required doing a loop of the cul-de-sac on Thornbury Road before continuing and weaving his way back to Northcliff. Lexi used a watch and phone to track her steps. Tyler eschewed both. He knew he was getting two miles in, and simple subtraction would tell him how long the run took. On the final turn from Eastcliff, Tyler spotted a large black man in the middle of the sidewalk.

He slowed and assessed the stranger. The guy was tall and broad, and a permanent scowl lent him a very unfriendly appearance. A large scar dominated the left side of his face. He wore loose-fitting gray sweats and a matching hoodie. A car Tyler had never seen before sat on the opposite side of the road about thirty feet farther along. Tyler stopped a few steps away. "Need some advice on the route?"

"You Tyler?"

"I'm pretty sure you know the answer already."

The large man pounded one meaty fist into his open hand. "Always nice to get confirmation while you can still talk."

Tyler glanced around but didn't see anyone else out and about this early. He was giving away five inches and at least fifty pounds to this new enemy. "Who sent you?"

"What?"

"Who sent you?" Tyler repeated, glad for a moment of conversation to catch his breath from the run. "Always nice to get an answer while you can still talk."

The guy scoffed. "I ain't tellin' you shit."

"You will."

A hard cross served as the fellow's sole reply. He had long arms and loaded up for it, so Tyler enjoyed plenty of time to step to the side. His foe kept the defenses up pretty well. Another powerful but slow punch followed, and Tyler avoided this one, as well. His adversary tried a quick side kick to capitalize. Smart. Tyler lowered his left arm to block it. "This your best?" he asked. "I hope you don't charge a lot."

"Screw you, pops," the guy growled.

The attacks came faster following the taunt. Civilians who took their work seriously were easy to provoke, and provocation often led to mistakes. Sure enough, the big man lowered his guard, and after blocking a hard jab, Tyler walloped him in the gut. It forced his enemy to back up a step. Tyler followed with sharp kick to the same area. While his larger foe remained bent over, Tyler elbowed him in the head. It wasn't enough to drop the man, and he managed to avoid a second strike.

His long legs carried him a decent distance away while he regrouped. "No shame in packing it in," Tyler said, standing in place. Again, his foe came at him. Tyler blunted several punches. He used his left elbow to turn away a left cross and leaned in, following it with a hard right which rattled the larger man. Tyler kicked him in the back of the leg, driving him to one knee, and elbowed him again in the head. This time, the guy fell onto his back. Tyler got one stomp on his adversary's midsection before the guy rolled away.

When he came back up to one knee, he held a knife in his right hand. It was a lock-blade model, long and sharp enough to gut someone. "I'll give you one chance to put it down," Tyler said.

"Or what?" the man answered with a sneer.

"Or I'll take it from you, and things won't go well for you from there."

Large shoulders shrugged. "I like my chances."

"Most idiots do."

A long step carried the menacing man to Tyler, who dodged back to avoid a wicked slash. Two more followed, and they cut only air. Just like with his punches, the black guy's long arms and tendency to load up for maximum power meant his attacks were easy to see coming. He enjoyed a large advantage in reach but gave it all away in technique. Tyler caught his foe's wrist after one attempted cut. He couldn't hold it for long but didn't need to. A simple attack against a pressure point opened the man's hand, and Tyler capitalized on his enemy's surprise by bending his fingers back hard. The knuckles snapped with a loud crack, and the guy howled in pain.

He also covered his injured hand with the other. It compromised his defenses. Two kicks, a hard cross, and an elbow later, he lay prostrate on the sidewalk. Tyler stepped on his broken fingers, eliciting a fresh cry of agony. "I don't normally do things like this," Tyler said, "but three of my friends are dead. You didn't do it. You're not good enough. Unless I missed my guess, the guy who killed them hired you . . . probably to see how good I was and maybe even soften me up. Am I right?"

"I ain't got nothin' to say," the guy said through gritted teeth.

Tyler ground his wounded digits into the concrete again. "Double negative. You must know something. Who hired you?"

"I don't know his name."

"What *do* you know?"

"We met . . . at a big rest stop. I do this kind of work for a living—"

"You might want to consider a career change," Tyler broke in. "Or at least better target selection."

"Screw you."

"What did the guy who hired you look like?"

The man shrugged. "Little bigger than you. Sounded foreign, though."

"Foreign like what? Mexican? French? Middle Eastern?"

"I don't know. Shit, do I look like a linguist?"

Tyler had to grin at the comment. "No." He took his foot off the injured hand, which the man immediately covered to protect. Tyler slipped on a black running glove, picked up the knife, and buried it in his antagonist's left leg just above the knee. This brought on an entire round of agonized howls. "You look like a man who took money from someone who killed three of my friends." Tyler jerked his chin toward the Camry across the street. "Your car's an automatic, so you don't need the left leg to drive. Good thing there's a Hopkins facility nearby." He leaned closer but remained out of striking distance. "I'm going to finish the run you rudely interrupted. It'll probably take me about five minutes. If you're still here when I come back, you won't survive to see minute six. Got it?"

"Yeah."

"Good. Now, piss off." Tyler jogged away, adding a little extra distance to his run before doubling back toward his house. As he approached, he noticed the car and its driver were gone.

22

Malachi ignored his ringing phone. He sat across and about a hundred meters farther along the street from Alexis's apartment building. Either the girl understood security, or her father convinced her to live here. Regardless, Malachi was impressed. This wasn't some typical apartment where a stranger could buzz a random unit and get inside. Residents used their thumbs to open the outer door. This required a biometric database which the operators would need to keep secure. They also had to provide redundant power in the event of an outage. Malachi knew he could bypass the main entrance, but it would take some forethought and maybe a little fortunate timing.

The phone rang again with the same unknown number. Malachi had a feeling he knew who called him, and he got his confirmation right away. "The guy hurt me, man."

"I told you not to take him lightly."

"He coulda killed me."

"Did your camera record everything?" Malachi asked.

"What?" the contractor said. "I tell you this guy whooped my ass, and you wanna know about a camera?"

"Yes."

"Yeah, the damn thing recorded."

"Why are you calling me, then? We had an arrangement. Win or lose, you held up your end."

"He stuck a knife in my leg," Clarence said through gritted teeth. "Right above the knee. I can barely move. Hell, I might be a goddamn cripple after today."

"Was it your weapon?"

"Yeah, so what?"

"So the inherent risk of a weapon is someone takes it and uses it against you," Malachi said. "If you'd left the blade in the car, you wouldn't be in this position."

"But I am . . . and now, I think you owe me."

Malachi wondered when they would get to this part of the conversation. At least Clarence didn't keep him waiting long. "I compensated you above your normal rate. Call it hazard pay. If you didn't take the proper precautions, it's not on me."

"A guy getting stabbed above the knee is suspicious." Clarence's voice lowered to just above a whisper. "People gonna wonder."

"Do the staff suspect anything?"

"Naw. I told them I slipped and did it myself. Not sure they believed me, though. Doctors ain't gonna question it for now. 'First, do no harm' and all. Once the Hypocritic oath is done, they might come in with some cops. I ain't gonna lie to them. They ask me what happened, I'll tell them."

Malachi didn't bother correcting Clarence on the Hippocratic oath even though the lack of precision bothered him. "Let me guess. Some extra money would ease your conscience if the cops asked questions, and you felt compelled to tell something other than the truth."

"You catch on quick."

"Where are you?"

"Sinai Hospital," Clarence said. "It was the closest to

Tyler's house. I'm supposed to get moved to a room in a half-hour or so. I'll text you the number."

"Fine." Malachi didn't know where the facility was, but it would be easy enough to find. "I'm in the middle of something. Give me about ninety minutes."

"Don't be late," Clarence said before breaking the connection.

Malachi set his phone down and let out a deep breath. Working with independent contractors always introduced the possibility of complication. Mossad and Shin Bet only hired the best people. In an unfamiliar country, Malachi tried to do the same, but Clarence didn't measure up. The man talking to the cops represented a minor vulnerability. He didn't know enough about Malachi to point a definitive finger at him. Still, the operation didn't need such a nuisance. Not when he was in Maryland and so close to making John Tyler suffer.

Visiting Clarence would cost some time, but Malachi would take care of him and close off the vulnerability. Then, the real work could resume.

Tyler dialed Captain Leon Sharpe and told him what happened.

"You'd never seen the guy before?" his friend asked.

"No. Considering everything else, I think our mystery friend hired him."

"Why?"

"The odds of someone randomly attacking me on a jog are low," Tyler said.

"Maybe not. You're a slow runner. Someone would have plenty of time."

"Very funny. I'll have you know my two-mile time has barely changed since I retired."

"Not like it was ever anything to boast about," Sharpe said.

"Anyway . . . I don't think this was some random incident. The guy was waiting for me. He knew where I lived and what route I might take if I ran on the streets."

"Why send some amateur after you? If it's our guy, he went after everyone else directly."

"I don't know." It was a valid question. Adversaries rarely changed tactics in the middle of a successful operation. As far as the mystery assassin knew, Musa was dead, making him four-for-four. "Let's focus on trying to figure out who this asshole is and maybe where he met the guy he sent. He would have come from Delaware."

"Lots of places along Ninety-five," Sharpe said. "Rest stops. The Chesapeake House."

"You think you can get footage?"

"Sure. Harford County likes me. I'll see what I can get." He hung up. Tyler wanted to talk to Flanker again, but he decided to wait until Sharpe came back with something. In the meantime, he did a brake job on a mid-'80s Camaro in the far service bay. The owner had brought his car since Tyler opened the shop, and after catching up on some work at the beginning, the car only needed regular maintenance now.

Tyler was washing his hands when Sharpe called back. He toweled off and took the call in his office. "I'm sending you a few pictures," the captain said.

"You got something?"

"Not really. Check them out."

Tyler took the phone away from his ear and opened his texts. Sharpe sent five photos. For surveillance cameras, they had pretty good clarity. Unfortunately, the man they were interested in must have known where the electric eyes were. The combination of a hood, hat, and dark glasses meant there were no usable shots of his face. They still needed Musa's footage. "Goddammit."

"I hear you," Sharpe said. "The third one shows him talking to someone. Is he the guy who came after you?"

Tyler spread his fingers and zoomed in. The image grew more pixellated, but a closer look at the face gave him the answer. "He's the one."

"This asshole is singling you out for some reason. He went after everyone else himself. Probably watched them a day or two, then took them out. For you, he meets with this guy and has him take a run first. Why?"

"Damned if I know," Tyler said.

"We all made enemies over there," Sharpe said. "Comes with the job if you do it well. You've spent the last couple years attracting some of the wrong kinds of attention."

"Sara calls me a knight-errant."

"Sara's fool enough to love you. Whoever's paying this prick hates your guts."

"Why go after the others, then?" Tyler demanded. "If someone wants to take a shot at me, he should take the shot. I agree I might have pissed some people off these last couple years, but this doesn't seem like a personal vendetta, Leon. If it were, why are three of our friends dead?"

"I wish I had an answer." Sharpe sighed, and the sound of wind carrying distant thunder filled Tyler's ears. "I'm speculating. It's part of police work. Maybe the other guys died so it wouldn't seem personal."

"Your theory is someone hates me, and to get back at me, he paid some mystery asshole to kill three guys I've barely talked to since I retired?"

"Maybe he thought we were all still tight," Sharpe said. "I know I've lost touch with people over time. I need to get better at it. Maybe the money man doesn't know the ins and outs of your charming personality."

"He's missing out, then," Tyler said. He scrolled through the rest of the photos. "I presume you've already run the car in the last picture?" The unknown man climbed into what looked like an old Toyota RAV4.

"Reported stolen from Delaware. Plates are from a different vehicle. It hasn't turned up on any of the highway cams or toll plazas."

"He's probably found something else. We need to presume this guy is smart, and he would know you only get a day or so out of a stolen car most of the time."

"I need to get back to work," Sharpe said. "Don't go flying off half-cocked just because this bastard is in Maryland. Or was. He might have left again for all we know."

"I won't. Thanks, Leon." Tyler hung up, forwarded the images to Flanker, and dialed his office. The secretary got him on the line once Tyler pretended to be angry about the delays with a print job. "Check your inbox."

"Hello to you, too."

"Hello," Tyler said. "Check your inbox."

Flanker fell silent for a few seconds. "Clever son of a bitch," he said. "He must have known where the cameras were."

"The guy in the third picture came to visit me earlier this morning."

"And?"

"He didn't leave happy."

"What about the SUV in the last photo?"

"Leon said it was reported stolen from Delaware. We should presume he's already in something else. I know none of these are great images, but do you think they'll help you?"

"Can't hurt. I don't have anything official to report yet, but I'll let you know when I do." Flanker paused. "How is Leon Sharpe, anyway?"

"Big, loud, and bossy," Tyler said.

"Pretty much the same, then?"

"Pretty much."

"People don't really change, Tippy. I'll be in touch when I know more. Thanks for sending these." Flanker hung up.

Tyler went back to scrolling through the five images on his phone. "I'm going to find you, you miserable prick," he muttered to the concealed face.

23

LEXI, KIM, AND EMILY NEARED THEIR BUILDING.

They'd all been to lunch together. When their schedules aligned and permitted little trips like this, they tried to take them. Lexi drove this time, and she guided her Accord Coupe along Route 1 in College Park. It was definitely a university town, but plenty of businesses and shops remained open with little patronage from students. The trio went to one of the several diners in a three-mile stretch. The place also served a great brunch on the weekends. None of them could take advantage of the bottomless mimosas yet, but the rest of the menu made the trip worth it.

As she waited at a traffic light near their building, Lexi spotted a car. It sat across the street and maybe a couple hundred feet farther along. A vehicle sitting in a lot wasn't remarkable, but this one stood apart from the others. The driver reversed into the spot, and the angle of the car suggested the space was designed for people to pull in. Someone remained behind the wheel.

The light changed. Lexi put the Accord into first gear and drove to their apartment complex. "You guys see the car across the road?" she asked her friends as she stopped the Accord in one of the spots assigned to their unit. "Looks older."

Kim turned and looked out the rear window. "The black one?"

"Yeah. I think it might be a Mustang."

"So?"

"Someone's sitting in it."

"He could be waiting for his wife," Emily said.

"Maybe. He backed into a spot you're supposed to pull into, which allows him to see our building pretty well."

"You seem a little paranoid," Kim said, turning to face Lexi and frowning in concern. "Everything all right?"

"Yeah." Lexi realized she was lying again. "Maybe you're right. I'm probably making too much out of it."

The trio exited the car, and Lexi locked the doors. Kim pressed her right thumb to a reader beside the entrance. A small LED light flashed green, and the electronic lock disengaged. Emily and Lexi also scanned their thumbs before they walked in. Lexi made sure the door closed behind them before she headed to their apartment. "That was a nice lunch," Emily said. She smiled, but it faded quickly. "Now, I have a paper to write."

"Me, too," Kim said. "TikTok first?"

"Of course." They giggled and walked down the hall together. Lexi needed to do some work, too, but the car across the street bothered her. It was easy to agree with her friends about being paranoid. They didn't know what was going on with her dad. On some level, Lexi may have been reading too much into the situation, but it certainly seemed suspicious. She inched closer to the slider which led to their small balcony. Lexi pulled back the curtain enough to look outside.

The Mustang was gone.

MALACHI NEEDED to break off his observation of the daughter to attend to Clarence.

The girl had just returned with her friends. All of them were pretty. He wondered if he might catch more than one of them in the apartment when he made his move. If so, there were ways other than physical pain to make Alexis Tyler suffer before he killed her. Knowing she'd brought violence and pain to her friends would only make the process more enjoyable. Sexual assaults happened all the time in college towns. American girls strutted around like whores, and the men were little better.

He parked in a visitor's space at Sinai Hospital. The place would have cameras everywhere. They'd been easy to spot in the Chesapeake House. Healthcare facilities took security seriously. Malachi couldn't count on being able to spot all of them. He slipped the blond wig on again and checked his reflection to make sure it sat correctly on his head. Combined with a pair of phony glasses, he would look enough like someone else to avoid suspicion. Malachi left the stolen Mustang and approached the main building.

Once inside, he told the guard he was visiting his niece. The man issued him a pass, advising Malachi to peel it and stick it to his shirt. Malachi said he would. Clarence's recent text provided a room number. Malachi headed into the main wing and took the stairs to the third floor. Doctors offices lined both sides of the corridor before the patient rooms. The first two were locked. The third opened. Malachi peeked inside, found it empty, and grabbed a white lab coat off the coat rack. It was a little short but fit pretty well. An ID badge identified a woman, Doctor Elise Gentry. She was a pretty woman with a short black bob.

Malachi guessed the ID also served as an access card to

the medical supply closet. It did. He knew better than to look for anything strong like morphine. Giving Clarence a fatal overdose would be easy, but hospitals kept controlled substances in a different area. A basic syringe would suffice. Malachi grabbed one, ripped the sterile packaging off, and pulled the plunger back. He slipped the needle into the pocket of the coat.

Cameras in the ceiling captured most of the area. Some were out in the open, and smoky plastic domes covered others. Even with his disguise in place, Malachi avoided looking at them. He found Clarence's room. The whiteboard outside the door indicated no one had been assigned the other bed yet. Malachi walked in and found Clarence alone in the room. He lay in the bed closer to the window.

Clarence frowned and stared as Malachi approached. After a few seconds, he smirked. "Nice hair."

"Thanks."

"You come to settle up?" Clarence wanted to know.

"Eventually." Malachi dropped into the chair beside the bed. Clarence's left leg remained on top of the covers. Thick bandages covered it from the middle of his thigh to below the knee. An IV bag filled with a clear liquid hung from a rack, and a tube ran into the man's left arm. "Looks like he got you pretty good."

"Yeah. Bastard. Once I'm back to full speed, I'm going to pay Tyler another visit."

"I wouldn't," Malachi said.

"Yeah? Why not?"

"What makes you think it'll go better the second time?"

"I'll have a gun."

Malachi knew it wouldn't make a difference, but he didn't belabor the point. "Has anyone besides the staff talked to you?" he asked.

"You mean have the cops come yet?"

"Yes."

"No. They probably will, though. What I tell them depends on you."

"How much?"

"To keep my mouth shut?" Clarence said. "I think I need another five large. I don't like lyin', though. My momma raised me to be honest. You gotta ease my guilty conscience. Let's call it ten total."

"Your guilty conscience is pretty cheap," Malachi said.

Clarence scowled. "You wanna make it fifteen?"

"No." Malachi flashed a quick smile as he stood. "I brought cash with me."

"Thought you might."

Malachi reached into the coat pocket and closed his fingers around the syringe. With his left hand, he covered Clarence's mouth. He stuck the needle into the IV line and injected the air bubble into it. Clarence tried to scream, but only a muted yell sounded in the room. Malachi waited for the numbers on the vitals monitor to change. He pulled his hand away. Clarence stared at him with wide eyes before pain twisted his features. Malachi slipped out of the room. As he left the area and headed for the stairs, he heard a nurse call for a crash cart.

24

Later in the day, Flanker called Tyler back. "I have something," the CIA man said. "Meet me at the coffee shop."

"You guys work quickly."

"Like you said, this one's kind of personal."

"See you soon," Tyler told him. He found Smitty, said he needed to take care of something, and left. Smitty was used to this by now. Even from the days when Tyler worked for him at the prior location, something would happen, and Tyler would need to miss time because of it. Ortiz grew accustomed to it, also. Not for the first time, Tyler wondered what kind of boss his extracurricular activities made him, but neither of his employees complained. Hell, one usually offered to lend a gun and help.

Tyler parked at the coffee shop and went inside. Three customers besides Flanker sat in chairs around the interior. Tyler ordered a black coffee and a donut, found the latter mediocre as he took the first bite, and joined Flanker at the small round table. A backpack sat on the floor, one of its straps looped around Flanker's leg. His gray suit pants were almost the same color as the backpack. "You have a locking bag in there?" Tyler asked in a quiet voice.

"Yup."

"You definitely found something, then." None of the other three patrons seemed to be in a hurry to leave. "Maybe finding a different venue would be a good idea."

"You're not cleared anymore. Haven't been for ages."

"I'm pretty sure you could arrange a visitor's pass."

"This is easier," Flanker said. He fixed a table of two women with a sour look. They must have been here a while. From what Tyler could gather, their paper cups were nearly empty. Each made a muted hollow *thunk* when set down. "In some ways, at least."

A couple minutes later, the women moved along. A portly man around the same age as Flanker and Tyler remained, but he was far more interested in his laptop screen than anything happening around him. Flanker flashed his alleged membership card, and the pair adjourned to the rear room. Once the door was closed and locked, Flanker took the sack from his shoulder and set it down. He pulled out a long canvas bag with a large metal lock at the end. Tyler remembered these. They were designed to be hard to open—both by picking and cutting—if they ever fell into the wrong hands. Flanker's key got him in, and he extracted a manila folder. "This would be more impressive at Langley," he said. "I could put this asshole's picture on a big screen in an operations center."

"Visitor pass," Tyler said.

"Yeah, yeah." Both men sat, and Flanker slid the folder across the table. "Our guy is Malachi Golan. Whoever sent him must really hate us."

Tyler scanned the summary page of the dossier. Golan spending time in the Israeli Defense Force was not significant. The country required military service. The next two lines caught his attention. "Jesus. Mossad *and* Shin Bet? Gotta be a pretty rare double play."

"It is. This asshole is a heavy hitter."

"Why's he available for hire, then?"

"Early retirement. Packed it in at thirty-eight with twenty years counting his time in the IDF." Flanker shrugged. "We both know guys who were counting down the months, weeks, and days until they hit their twenty and moved on."

"Sure," Tyler admitted. "Most of them didn't go on to become contract killers."

"Golan's last couple years in Shin Bet saw a corruption investigation," Flanker said. "No one could ever prove anything."

"So it's possible someone encouraged him to leave."

"Maybe. With some more time, we might learn the answer. We do know he didn't stick around long after the investigation wrapped up. Maybe the whole mess pissed him off, and he decided to walk away. My team's guess is he was dirty, managed to avoid discovery, and got out while the getting was good."

Tyler flipped pages, landing on one which featured a graphical flight plan from Tel Aviv to some small airport in California Tyler had never heard of before. "He landed three days before he killed Bendix."

"Yeah." Flanker sighed. "His movements from there are hard to track. We figure he took private flights and stole some cars. A hit on his photo came from a bus station in Louisiana after Burns died. We only made the match recently. No one named Malachi Golan got on a Greyhound, so he's probably traveling under an alias."

"Burns didn't die," Tyler pointed out. "This bastard killed him in his own home." Tyler kept looking at the flight page. "I'm surprised he flew into the US under his own name."

"He has family here," Flanker said. "Easy enough to explain if someone asks."

"Okay, we know who the killer is." Tyler flipped back to the beginning of the dossier. It must have held about a hundred pages. "I'm not a speed reader. Does your team have any insights as to who's paying the bills?"

"It's a good question. Our unit never encountered Golan or any group he was affiliated with. There's no reason we'd be on his radar unless someone paid to put us there." The Agency man blew out a deep breath. "We made *beaucoup* enemies over the years. The good thing is most of them are dead. The surviving number is pretty small, but then you have people who might want to avenge someone who died. Hell, even you pissed a well-connected trafficker off all by yourself."

"All part of my charm," Tyler said.

"I guess I'm telling you the candidate pool is large enough to make even an educated guess difficult."

"If it's someone from Afghanistan . . . even the trafficker I dealt with last year . . . we're looking at mostly Sunni Muslims."

"Yes."

"Pretty unusual for an Israeli to work for a Sunni. There's nothing in the summary about Golan being a traitor."

"No, he was a patriot," Flanker said. "Probably still is. I doubt he would act against Israel. Money has a way of blurring the lines of loyalty. If someone wrote him a big enough check to go after us, Golan is the type who would say yes."

"How'd you find him?" Tyler wanted to know.

"We started by pulling any known foreign intelligence service personnel who came to the States in the past month. Reasonably long list as you might imagine. Your photos actually helped. We couldn't see the relevant details of Golan's face, but the pictures gave us the overall size and structure. It helped narrow our search."

"All right." Tyler closed the stuffed folder and pushed it back across the desk. "We know who's coming for us, at least. He's in Maryland." He patted the file. "You have a version I can take with me?"

"I'll make sure someone emails you a clean copy," Flanker said. "I presume you want to go after this asshole."

"Hell yes," Tyler said, "but I also want to do it intelligently. If he's using aliases and stealing cars, he's going to be impossible to track. He also thinks Musa is dead, so we have an advantage there. We don't know enough to find him yet, and we're not investigators, so we'll keep gathering intel, use our advantages, and then take him on."

"Sounds like a plan," Flanker said.

Tyler wasn't sure it deserved the title yet, but it was a start.

VERONICA'S HIRED investigators earned their keep.

Their reports said they needed to work in tandem, rotate vehicles, and avoid getting too close, but they were able to keep tabs on Tyler. He didn't go many places—his house, the shop, a local grocery store, and Fort Meade. Recently, he'd made a few trips to a coffee shop neither man had ever heard of. Each time, he met a well-dressed man and disappeared into some back room.

Veronica scanned one report. *The barista informed me the other room was reserved for members. When I inquired about membership, he told me the owner—and only the owner— handled it. The place is weird. I'm positive the back room isn't some members-only club, but I don't know what it could be. My guess is it's an area law enforcement or intelligence uses, and the whole place is an elaborate front.*

She sat at a table across the street and about a hundred feet away from Casey's Coffee. The same PI who filed the report told her the other guy just arrived. Veronica zipped down as quickly as she could, and she'd recently placed an order at the tapas bar nearby. The hostess suggested she try the outdoor seating while the weather remained cooperative, and Veronica smiled and agreed. A throaty rumble announced the arrival of Tyler's car. He parked it in the lot adjacent to the coffee shop and went inside.

Three other patrons sat at tables. Tyler and his mysterious friend in the nice suit chatted over hot drinks for a few minutes. When a pair of women filed out, the other man led the way to the back part of the business. He flashed something from his wallet to gain access. Veronica couldn't see what it was. Membership would be a decent cover for some DC agency. Punting the selection process to the owners—whom Veronica guessed never appeared—kept random people from signing up.

A little while later, Tyler left, and his friend followed him out the door a couple minutes later. He carried a large bag on his back. Veronica used a magazine to cover the digital camera she'd placed on the table, and she snapped a few pictures of the other guy as he exited the building and walked to his car. He climbed into an Audi sedan. Whoever the fellow was, he avoided using obvious government vehicles.

Veronica munched her tapas and transferred the images from her camera to her phone. She picked a couple that offered the clearest look at the other guy's face. A little gray stubble covered his otherwise clean-shaven cheeks. The man looked unremarkable. No one would take notice of him. He looked a little taller than average, wasn't too heavy or thin, and kept himself in shape without being jacked. The kind of man no one's eyes would linger on for long. Perfect for the kinds of work many three-letter agencies did.

It was also a face Veronica had seen before.

She found it in her photo collection of Tyler's old unit. The mystery man wasn't identified in the photo—none of them were—but it was definitely him. He didn't wear a uniform like the others. Who was this guy, and why did Tyler take a few meetings with him at a weird coffee shop? Veronica finished her meal and walked back to her Tucson. The story kept getting more interesting.

25

After classes the next day, Lexi drove to visit her grandfather.

A couple years prior, he moved into an active adult community. Despite being twenty years older than the minimum, he soon took over the place. Lexi always admired her grandfather's outgoing nature when around other people. Those genes definitely didn't make it to her dad, and only a few trickled down to her. She headed through the gates of Evergreen Acres. Groups of people played pickleball on a set of courts along the main drive. Lexi parked her Accord in a guest spot outside her grandfather's building.

The old man smiled when he opened the door. Age caused him to stoop a bit, and his hair grew lighter and thinner, but Zeke Tyler still looked like someone you wouldn't want to go against in a bar fight. Last year, the two of them helped her dad free one of Lexi's friends when a politician abducted her. Despite being seventy-seven, her granddad sniped two guys with a bolt-action rifle from a few hundred yards away. "Lexi. Good to see you."

"You, too." She hugged her grandfather close before

walking into his apartment. As always, the place was spartan and neat. The sofa and recliner sat equidistant from the coffee table. All surfaces were free of dust. The furniture emphasized function over style. Kitchen counters remained spotless. If someone from the Navy came to inspect Zeke Tyler's quarters, the place would pass with flying colors. "How have you been?"

"Fine." He waved a hand. "Everyone here is playing pickleball now. It's like the official sport of old folks."

"Do you play?"

"Here and there." He shrugged. "It beats shuffleboard."

Lexi wondered how often Evergreen Acres put the "active" in "active adult." Many of the residents she'd seen on her trips here were age peers of her grandfather and didn't get around nearly as well. The smell of something burning reached her nostrils. Lexi wondered if Zeke left a pot on the stove until she spotted a single candle across the room. It was a basic tall and thin one. She pointed toward it. "What's up with the candle?"

Her grandfather sighed as he sat on the couch. "Today is a terrible anniversary. Years ago, when I was still a chief, one of my sailors committed suicide."

Lexi frowned. "I'm sorry, Grandpa."

"Be sorry for his family. His wife . . . she was a real piece of work. They were both young, and I guess she never learned to be faithful. This petty officer figured out what was going on and realized there might be . . . paternity issues with a couple of his kids. He couldn't take it. Hanged himself."

"Wow. That's awful."

"NCIS investigated, of course. I leaned on them to look into everything. Together, we figured out who the father of those kids really was. I made him pay for the funeral, and then I made sure the son of a bitch went on the beach." After a beat, he added, "Means I ran him out of the Navy. Prick. Don't mess with my men."

"Got any less depressing war stories?" Lexi asked.

Her grandfather smiled. "Sorry. You didn't come here to listen to me prattle on about old times."

"It's all good."

"Your dad talk to you about his latest situation?"

"Yeah."

"I haven't seen anything unusual," the old man said. "You?"

Lexi recalled seeing unfamiliar cars a couple times. She lived in a college town, however, and a vehicle sitting in a lot nearby wasn't automatically suspicious. "It's been quiet on my end, too." She paused. "You ever deal with anything like this before? Someone hunting down a bunch of the guys you served with?"

"No. Your dad went up against some rich and powerful people over there. Taliban supporters were no joke."

"Most of them died, though," Lexi said.

"Not all. Even the dead ones have families."

"It's been ten years. Even longer in some cases. Hell, probably twenty or more for some of the early raids they did."

"The clock never runs out on revenge," Zeke said.

Lexi didn't care for the saying, but she didn't comment on it. "What do you think is going to happen?"

"I think someone's going to come for your dad eventually. I doubt it will go well for whoever does."

"I hope this asshole gets capped somewhere along the way," Lexi said.

"It'd be nice." Her grandfather stood. "Want some coffee?"

"Sure." Lexi smiled. Zeke didn't seem too worried about someone gunning for his son. Maybe she should join him in not fretting so much.

MALACHI DIDN'T CARE for providing updates, but it came with the territory when working for someone else. As his career progressed in Mossad and especially Shin Bet, he could pawn off paperwork and keeping the brass in the loop onto lower-ranking colleagues. Here, it was just him. "Sadozai is dead," he told Pazir after the indignity of being left on hold for five minutes. "I found a local to send after Tyler. He didn't do much, but he got me some useful video."

"What happened to this man?" Pazir demanded.

"Tyler injured him. He then wanted more money to maintain his silence. I handled it."

"Excellent. What are your current plans?"

"I'm watching the daughter," Malachi said. "She's far more security conscious than her two roommates."

"Do you think you could get her?"

"Of course."

"Good. If an opportunity presents itself, take it. Nothing would make Tyler suffer more than the abduction of his precious daughter."

"Didn't Durrani try to get her?" Malachi asked.

"Tried and failed," Pazir said. "No doubt, this contributed to his downfall. But you will succeed, my friend."

Malachi bit down the reflexive response of telling Pazir they were not friends. Instead, he said, "What of the other two girls?"

"They do not matter. Killing them may be messy, but I trust you to do it if you need to." Pazir chuckled. "Of course, if you could take them, too, I still know some men who would find a use for them. Feel free to sample the merchandise first, of course."

A shudder crawled down Malachi's back. He would help Pazir get revenge on Tyler for the challenge and the money.

Both were potentially greater than he'd seen in a while. He had no intention of sending any young women into a dreadful life of servitude—or worse—with anyone Pazir knew. Killing them would be far more merciful. "I'll have to see how it all plays out," Malachi said, summoning whatever diplomacy he could before changing the subject. "They have another unit mate nearby. He's making some noise online."

"Any good data? Something we should worry about?"

"Not at all." Malachi brought up the post. "'Three of my friends are dead, and the government we served doesn't seem to give a shit. Whoever's out there doing this should come after me next.' Then, he uses a bunch of made-up hashtags."

"You can safely ignore him," Pazir said.

"I could," Malachi acknowledged, "or I could drive one state north and gut him in his own home."

"Do you think it will make John Tyler suffer more?"

"I think every death adds a little."

"Do it if you think it's best. Otherwise, the daughter would draw him out. His anguish is what matters."

"Understood."

"I'll be arriving soon," Pazir said. "I want to see Tyler beg for death myself. Once I'm secure, I'll let you know."

Malachi hoped Pazir would not travel here. He didn't need the complication of taking Tyler somewhere else. Maybe Malachi would discover a way around this. He could kill Tyler at a place he controlled rather than some lavish home his benefactor rented from an unsuspecting American family. An idea of how to do it formed in his mind. He would work out where later, but it wouldn't be a fancy Airbnb. "Fine," he said and pushed the End button.

Ortiz and Smitty both left in the last fifteen minutes. Tyler needed to put two tires back onto a Trans Am which got its brakes completely redone, and then he could head out for the day, as well. He heard wheels on the asphalt, and a quick look at the monitor in the service bay showed a vehicle pulling into the lot. It was a late-model Hyundai SUV. Tyler knew the logo but didn't keep track of the models enough to know which this one was.

He finished putting one tire back on and re-entered the shop. A pretty woman with a head full of red hair climbed out. Her tight jeans clung to her in all the right places as she retrieved a purse and headed toward the front door. She wore tennis shoes. A casual visit. Tyler preferred letting Smitty work the counter and deal with people who came in, but he would need to handle this one himself. "Good afternoon."

"You're Mister Tyler?"

"I am."

The lady smiled and held out her hand. "Veronica Fitzgerald."

Tyler shook her hand and then scanned the list of jobs on

the computer. "I don't think we have any work waiting for you, Miss Fitzgerald."

"I'm not here for a car," she said. Her green eyes peered at Tyler, and she didn't flinch when he stared back. People told him he had a killer's eyes due to their almost black color and his thousand-yard stare. "I'm here for you. Can we talk somewhere?"

"What's this about?" Tyler wanted to know.

She pointed to something over Tyler's shoulder. "That your office?"

Tyler frowned but headed toward it. Veronica Fitzgerald followed without being invited. Tyler sat behind his desk, and she took one of the other chairs. "We've never met, but we've helped each other already."

"I'm afraid I'll need you to explain."

"Your daughter reached out to me with some information about the Sappony people and Ramseur County," she said.

Tyler bobbed his head. "Now, I know your name. You wrote a bunch of articles. I appreciate you keeping me out of things." Tyler wondered if the North Carolina police's renewed interest in him compelled Veronica to drive here. Or maybe it went the other way. She got pressed for information and gave him up.

"That's kind of why I'm here. You're a story."

Tyler snorted. "No, I'm not."

"You are," Veronica said. She took out her phone and looked at something on the screen. "Decorated Green Beret, a long list of awards and commendations, and eight years in private security."

"I'm quite aware of my own CV," Tyler said.

Veronica grinned. "I hadn't gotten to the interesting parts yet. About two years ago, your former commander gets out of prison. Not long after, he and a bunch of his cronies are dead in a building near the Port of Baltimore. Fast forward a few months, and the shop you used to work at burns to the ground. Around the same time, guys working for a Mexican drug cartel start turning up dead. Then, a whole bunch of them die in a shootout in Bel Air. Harford County police chalk it up to the work of rivals."

"Sounds like a solid investigation."

Veronica continued as if Tyler hadn't spoken. "A couple months after that, you end up on the security detail for Alex Anne. Good singer. Someone abducts her following a concert. In short order, a hangar full of men at the airport die, and someone shoots the pilot of a private plane filled with kidnapped girls."

Tyler remained silent.

"Then, killers take out four people in a house in Cecil County. One sister goes missing, and the other was en route from the airport when all this went down. In your vehicle, as far as I can tell. State police arrested a crooked senator and his wife but only after a major shootout up there. Bunch of guys dead. Then, we get to your work in West Virginia. You took out an entire militia."

"Technically, it was two," Tyler pointed out. Denying everything seemed like a bad play. This woman did her homework and connected dots no one ever bothered lining up before.

"What?"

"Two militias, though I'm not sure either deserved the term. Meal Team Six all the way for the first one."

Veronica smiled. "And then we get to your work in Ramseur County. Chief Heap threw you in jail for some bullshit, you broke out with three felons, exposed a mining operation, and basically turned the county upside down." She put her phone down. "How can you say there's no story here?"

"Because I don't want to be a part of it," Tyler said. "Nothing I've done has been for glory or fame. I don't give a shit about either one. You left my name out of a story once. Clearly, you can do it again."

"The public has a right to know," Veronica said.

"Do they have a right to come after me, too?" She frowned at Tyler's question. "Or come after Lexi? You want to know why Leo Braxton and his band of assholes died? He kidnapped my daughter to get to me. I'll go after anyone who puts her in danger." Tyler paused to glare at Veronica for emphasis. "Reporters included."

"But I—"

"This is also a bad time," Tyler said. "If you're so good at following stories and making connections, you know some people I served with recently died. Someone's coming after our unit. I don't know why yet, but if you're going to insist on making me a story, I can't guarantee you'll get to write it in peace or safety."

"I don't need your protection."

"Neither did the three men this asshole killed. I like their chances a hell of a lot better than yours."

"You're not a big fan of the press, are you?" Veronica demanded.

"Not really, no."

She crossed her arms. "Why not?"

"It's nothing personal," Tyler said. "My experience is embedded journalists get it right, and no one else really bothers trying. We're heroes when things were going well, but if the political winds shift, we become baby killers. Ask soldiers, sailors, airmen, and marines who made it home how they got treated. Puff pieces at first, but then we're all struggling to readjust or mentally ill." Tyler waved a hand. "Maybe you're better than the reporters I've run into. You played it straight with the Sappony mess. If you want to make me a story, however, I'm sure as hell not going to cooperate."

Veronica stood and smoothed her sweater. It was loose

enough to look a little boxy but still showed an attractive figure underneath. She was a pretty woman and epitomized a fiery redhead. Tyler didn't want to see her harmed, but he also knew the only person who could really keep her out of danger was Veronica herself. "I'll be around, Mister Tyler. When I'm done, I'd like some comments from you for the story."

"Piss off," Tyler said. "There's my one and only comment for the record."

"And off the record?"

"You're taking your chances being around right now. They're yours to take, but I'm not riding to your rescue if you get too close."

"I don't need you to rescue me." Veronica scowled and stormed out.

"We'll see," Tyler said to his empty office.

AS THE SUN completed its inevitable descent, Malachi watched his target.

Before leaving Maryland, he hired someone else to go after Tyler and get more film. This time, it was a pair of men willing to crack skulls for the right price. They looked, talked, and acted like brutes, so Malachi didn't like their chances against an operator like Tyler. Still, they might get some useful video out of it, and if they managed to leave him with a lingering injury, so much the better.

Harvey Lee shared three combat deployments with Tyler. He transferred units and did another after his friend retired. Lee left the service seven years ago. Since then, he bounced between jobs and lived in a few places before settling into York, Pennsylvania. Word obviously reached him about the fate which befell his former unit mates, and

Lee invited a challenge from the bastards going after his friends.

He would get his wish.

Lee's townhouse stood among other similar homes in a newer development. Malachi sat atop a nearby hill in a stolen mid-2000s Escalade. His vantage point offered him an excellent view of Lee's street. Signs near where he parked mentioned a builder would divide the area into lots in the near future. More homes. More sprawl. Malachi wondered how so many people tolerated it.

It had been a few days since he enjoyed a nice meal, so he indulged in a steak tonight. The restaurant cooked it exactly how he ordered it. Before they grew cold, the mashed potatoes were excellent. Lee appeared at a rear window of his house. A refrigerator filled the space behind him. The man lived alone. Malachi would watch tomorrow to see if he left for a job. Lee's employment remained spotty, though some of his social media posts mentioned a job he could do from home.

On the street, three men walked dogs who tugged at their leashes as another animal approached. One road away, a park welcomed people and pets. Cars sat in driveways and crowded the street. Neighbors lived on both sides of Lee's interior unit. Depending on the time, people would be milling about. This one needed to be quick, quiet, and precise. Making a clean getaway after firing a gun would be harder. Even at spirited driving speeds, it would be six minutes to the nearest interstate on-ramp. Plenty of time for someone to call the cops and for them to respond.

Malachi took another bite of steak and wiped a bit of juice from his chin. He relished a challenge almost as much as a good meal.

27

At the hotel, Malachi eschewed a room service breakfast and ate in the restaurant. When he expressed a religious aversion to bacon, the chef was happy to make him a steak. The generous tip probably helped. When this job was over, and he could no longer spend Pazir's money, he would need to live within his means again. For now, however, he would enjoy the perks of the budget.

After getting dressed, Malachi made a brief stop in the business center, then at a local print shop before heading back out to observe Harvey Lee. Lights flickered on and off inside the home, eventually settling in one area. Malachi needed several angles to get something approaching a good look through the window, but it appeared Lee worked from a converted bedroom on the second floor of his townhouse.

He continued doing so for a couple of hours. Malachi reviewed Lee's online activity. The statements the man made about himself indicated he didn't leave home often. He took some photos near weights and exercise equipment. Rather than the mirrored wall of a gym in the background, however, drywall formed Lee's backdrop. An overhead pipe appeared in one photo. Malachi surmised Lee converted part of his basement into a fitness center. With a gym downstairs, a home office on the top floor, and no social life, he rarely needed to leave.

Time to beard the lion in his own den.

Malachi slipped the costume wig and glasses on and then drove into the neighborhood. He left the Escalade in front of a house on the opposite side of the street. He carried a small notebook with him and knocked on Lee's door. No answer. He rang the video doorbell. It would record footage. The disguise would deflect suspicion for a while, but good facial rec software could still match his features if American law enforcement obtained a sample for comparison. He had no reason to think they were onto him yet. Pazir's team did a good job setting things up, and Malachi took care to keep himself out of the spotlight as much as possible.

"Yes?" a voice came through the doorbell's speaker.

"Mister Lee?"

"Yes . . . who are you?"

"I'm Michael Gordon," Malachi said, using the main alias provided for him. He risked burning it here but still had another to fall back on should he need it. "I work for an online magazine in Maryland. Your recent posts caught our attention, and I'd like to talk to you about them if you have time."

"You're from Maryland?" Lee wanted to know.

"Yes."

"Why are you up here, then?"

"I live close to the line." Malachi recalled looking at maps as he plotted his movements. "Norrisville. It's not a bad drive."

"I'll be down in a moment." Malachi waited and avoided looking into the video system directly. Lee's footsteps announced his presence. He opened the door with his left hand hidden. Malachi knew the other man held a gun, but Michael Gordon the blogger and would-be journalist probably didn't. "You have some ID?"

"Sure." Malachi took out a fake press ID he'd printed at the hotel business center and laminated in the copy store this morning. It identified him as working for the *Investigative Voice*, a real online news publication in Maryland. If Lee decided to check on this, the jig was up. He scrutinized the ID for a few seconds before nodding and opening the door all the way. "Come on in."

"Thanks." Despite being spartan, the interior was fairly cluttered. Boxes and bins sat against the right-hand wall, and a few lay scattered throughout the living room.

"Sorry for the mess," Lee said. "I'm reorganizing a bit." He slipped the gun back into a small table just inside the entryway. Beige carpet covered the floor in the main area and the attached dining room. The primary level featured an open concept layout Malachi had seen on several American home-buying shows. The little-used dining room led into the kitchen, where the tile hewed close to the carpet's color.

"No worries," Malachi said. "I can't settle on how to lay out my place."

"Where are you from?" Lee eased himself onto a recliner and gestured toward a matching brown sofa. Despite being about fifty years old, worry lines and gray hair made Lee look closer to sixty. Malachi wondered how much the recent developments with his former unit added to the man's anxiety.

"I was born in Israel. Never completely lost the accent." Malachi could moderate it, but this was true. He rarely got picked for undercover work because he couldn't hide where he came from, and getting outed as an Israeli would mean a death sentence.

"What did you want to talk about?"

"We noticed your social media posts about the members

of your old Special Forces unit," Malachi said. He flipped to the first page of the notebook and took a basic pen from his pocket. "I'm sorry about what happened to your friends. Doesn't really seem like anyone is running with the story."

"They're not," Lee said. "We scattered across the country after retirement. Guys get killed a thousand miles apart, and everyone thinks they're totally separate events." He shook his head. "They're not. Someone's coming for us."

"You seem pretty certain. Far more than any law enforcement agency."

Lee waved a hand. "They won't talk to one another unless they really think something's going on. I've called all of them. 'No sign these events are connected,' someone tells me every time. Whoever's doing this is smart. Well-planned. It's the kind of op we might've run if we had the time to set up something so elaborate."

"Everything I've read indicates your unit was very successful."

"How much did you read?" Lee frowned. "I'd think a lot of it is still classified."

"I'm sure it's a pretty high-level account," Malachi said. "There's also the fact someone wouldn't be targeting you today if you weren't so effective a decade ago."

Lee shifted in the seat and stared at Malachi. The Israeli felt Lee size him up. The other man didn't press anything, however. "You followed this story for long?" he asked.

"Not really, no. Your post is what tipped us off. My editor and I did some background work based on the other names you mentioned. Looks like there's something there, but like you said, it must be an advanced operation."

"And well-funded. Whoever's been doing it has crossed the country quickly and without getting caught or flagged anywhere. Ain't easy to pull off."

Malachi jotted a note. He realized he'd been deficient in

this area. At least Lee hadn't called him out for it yet. "What kind of person do you think could do it?"

"Someone skilled, for one," Lee said. "Must have a good bankroll. Also needs to be able to blend in. You can't sneak up on people like me too often, but this guy did it."

You have no idea, Malachi thought. Instead, he posed a question. "A foreign intelligence service you angered over there?"

"I don't know." Lee shrugged. "Maybe. Could just be someone doing it for money and kicks. The kind of guy who likes traveling and doesn't mind killing men who never did him any wrong. Same kind of man might even come into a house as a reporter pretending to ask questions."

"Are you suggesting—?" Malachi's question died in his throat as Lee sprang out of the chair and came at him. Malachi gathered his feet, pushed off, and went over the back of the couch. He returned to vertical by the time Lee stepped around. "How'd you figure it out?"

Lee came in with a flurry of hard punches. Malachi blocked them all and slithered off to the side. His attempt at a side kick met a lowered forearm. "Why do arsonists always like to look at their own work?" Lee asked rhetorically. "Your glasses are fake. Lenses are clear. The way they catch the light is the tell. Your hair is probably a wig. No reason to come here in disguise unless you have bad intentions."

"You must have been the brains of the unit."

Lee shrugged and launched another attack. Malachi turned a couple more punches aside, but one slipped through and caught him hard in the solar plexus. He sucked wind and didn't have time to recover. Lee shoved him in the left side to spin him around and then cinched in a chokehold.

This was the kind of challenge Malachi wanted.

He'd trained for this type of scenario many times. Malachi raised his fist high and drove his elbow backwards into Lee's body. He grunted but didn't release the hold. It took two more hard elbow strikes to loosen his grip. Malachi slipped free, kneed Lee in the groin, and dropped him with a pair of hard punches. Lee tried to kick him while prone, but Malachi caught the leg against his body, braced it, and twisted hard enough to snap the ankle. Lee howled in pain. He wouldn't be able to get back to his feet.

Malachi kicked him hard in the ribs, then twice in the face. Much of the fight went out of Lee, though he remained conscious. "Thank you for at least putting up an effort," Malachi said. He slipped on a pair of thin black gloves, walked into the kitchen, retrieved a knife from a wooden block, and carried it back to the living room. Cooking knives were ill-suited for long combat because of their lack of blood grooves, but they were perfectly fine for delivering a killing blow.

Lee kicked at Malachi's legs, forcing the Israeli to retreat a step. The prone man sat up and tried to fend off the inevitable, but his position put him at a disadvantage. Malachi caught one of his punches and raked the blade along his foe's forearm. Lee grunted and pulled his arm back. Malachi gave him a vicious cut across the chest, then one across the throat which sprayed bright red blood onto the wall. Lee's eyes widened and took on a glassy look. "Soldier to soldier," Malachi said, "you don't need to suffer." He drove the knife through Lee's sternum. More blood bubbled from the man's mouth before he slumped over.

Malachi checked his clothes. Several red spots dotted his shirt and pants. Lee was about an inch taller, but they were of similar build. He stripped his shirt and pants off, started a fire in the gas fireplace, and tossed them in. Upstairs, Lee's closet was full of boring stuff, but Malachi picked a basic black hoodie and a pair of jeans. He made sure to pull the cowl over his head before walking out the door a minute later.

28

Tyler sat in his office while Smitty dealt with a new customer at the counter.

Ortiz had the day off, so Tyler knew he'd get pressed into working in the bays. He enjoyed it. One of his hopes for opening the shop had been to keep his mechanic skills sharp and not just be a project manager in a stained work shirt. So far, so good. He didn't need to start a job right away, however, so he pulled up Flanker's email and read the file on Malachi Golan.

Whoever chose this guy to carry out a campaign of vengeance made a good selection. Malachi served with distinction in the IDF, was extremely proficient in shooting and Krav Maga, and then went on to a career in intelligence. Tracking him would be difficult. Even if he lacked a wealthy benefactor, the Israeli made up for it with years of counter-intel and counter-surveillance experience.

Even the murders of Tyler's old unit mates didn't point to any specific person. The various law enforcement agencies found nothing to indicate the same person carried out all the crimes, but at least they were talking to each other. This meant Malachi found clever ways of getting from place to place—like taking a bus from Louisiana shortly after killing Burns in Texas. He would also need an alias. Tyler flipped through the report Flanker provided. The name Malachi Golan never turned up after the initial flight from Tel Aviv. The closest name on the Greyhound manifest was Michael Gordon, which could have been a *nom de guerre* or simply another passenger with no connection to anything.

The one data point the CIA's papers never came to a conclusion about was who wrote the checks. Someone hired Malachi to do this grisly work. Flanker mentioned Farzaad Durrani, the trafficker Tyler killed at BWI Airport last year. The man would have a network of wealthy undesirables he could contact. Did he get the word out before he died? If so, who bankrolled Malachi now? The report offered no answers and no useful speculation. Maybe those details remained classified.

Footsteps heralded Smitty's approach. Tyler closed the email. "Everything all right?" Smitty asked.

"Yep."

He jutted his chin toward Tyler's monitor. "About what's been happening to your friends."

"Yep."

"You gonna give me anything more than one syllable answers?"

"Nope," Tyler said.

Smitty smirked. "I know you're good at planning these things out. What are you going to do?"

"Not much I can do right now." Tyler blew out a deep breath. "We're up against someone who's very hard to track."

"You trying to find him?" Smitty asked.

"My one friend in intelligence is working on it," Tyler said. "He has a team he can task with finding this asshole." Smitty fidgeted in the doorway. "Don't worry. If he comes here, I'll deal with him. He's not going to be interested in anyone besides me."

"I'm not worried." Smitty walked back to the service bays.

Tyler didn't believe him.

~

LEXI DIDN'T SEE the car from before.

She still didn't know if anyone watched the building at all —or her specifically. It could have been someone sitting in a lot for any of a number of reasons. She parked her coupe, used her right thumb to unlock the front door, and walked into her apartment. Emily and Kim would be back soon. Lexi put earbuds in and listened to a playlist someone recommended while looking at her workload.

Not spending as much time in the shop helped, but even a supposedly easy schedule still stuck her with a fair bit of work. She was in the middle of writing a four-page paper when her roommates got home. Lexi popped out her earbuds and headed to the living room to greet them. The smell of pizza reached her when she was still in the hallway. "Ooh, I didn't know you were bringing lunch," she said.

Emily got three paper plates down from the cabinet. "My boyfriend bought it," Kim said. "I met him for lunch and took this veggie to go." Lexi only met Kim's boyfriend once. She didn't remember his name but definitely recalled how he liked to be seen as a guy with money and connections. The things that mattered to young men her own age often struck Lexi as ridiculous. No wonder she remained unattached.

"Lexi, can I take your car after Econ tomorrow?" Emily asked. "Mine's still in the shop."

"As long as I can catch a ride with Kim." Kim nodded. "And as long as you don't burn up my clutch."

Emily grinned. "I've gotten lots better. I don't even stall the car anymore."

"You can still burn up the clutch," Lexi said, "but sure. It's a short drive. I think my baby will be fine."

"You seem a little better today," Kim said after a delicate bite of pizza.

Lexi picked off a large piece of onion. "I guess."

"The grind not getting to you anymore?" Emily asked.

Again, Lexi struggled with how much to tell her friends. She came up with a very limited version of the truth. "My dad's going through some things right now. I guess that doesn't help."

"Is he all right?"

"He'll be okay," Lexi said. "Just a rough patch."

"What's going on?" Kim said, frowning and pushing her hair to hide the thin scar remaining on her forehead.

Some really dangerous psycho is killing a bunch of his friends, and I'm worried he's going to be in the crosshairs himself pretty soon, she thought. Instead, she took a deep breath and said, "I think it's a few things. Running the shop when it's busy, managing his workers, worrying about me, trying to have some kind of a life . . ."

"He still have a girlfriend?"

"Far as I know."

"You like her?" Emily asked.

Lexi nodded. "I do. I was eighteen when I met her, and maybe that helped. Sara hasn't tried to act like a surrogate mother or anything. I appreciate that."

Emily nodded around a large bite. "I hope your dad's all right," she said after chewing.

"Thanks." Lexi plucked an olive out of the melted cheese. She knew the current situation weighed on her dad. He was used to coming up with plans and solutions. At times, he explained it as part of his duties as a warrant officer. Lexi still didn't really know what a warrant officer did, but in her dad's case, it meant strategizing, kicking in doors, shooting bad guys, and occasionally fixing a Jeep or Hummer. Now, he was a decade older with more things crowding his plate. She worried about him as much as he did her. "Me, too."

29

Tyler again stayed after Smitty left.

He needed about twenty minutes to finish suspension work on a classic Honda S2000. It wasn't the usual kind of car the shop accepted, but Tyler appreciated the little roadster for its high-revving engine and generally fun drive. Once the car was back on the ground, Tyler washed his hands and retreated to his office. He pulled up the file Flanker sent again. Somewhere, it would hold a detail he could use to turn the tables and take action against Malachi Golan rather than simply reacting to someone else dying.

Movement on the monitor caught his eye. Two men walked across the lot. One skirted the weeds just past the northern end of the asphalt. A few cars remained outside, but the duo didn't seem to care about them. They spent their time looking at the building. Tyler used the controls to zoom in. One guy was white, the other black. Both were tall and brawny, and he got the distinct sense neither man came to pick up a vehicle.

He'd passed the first test. Now, Malachi sent two guys. Would a trio descend on the shop after a few more days? And what did the one man do in the overgrowth off the lot? Tyler wouldn't find answers by sitting in his chair. He walked outside via the service bays. If these guys were heavy hitters, Tyler and Ortiz kept guns hidden in the area. Both men sized him up as he approached. "We're closed," Tyler told them.

"You're working late," the blond guy said. His hair was short, and his crooked nose suggested he took part in his share of fights. The guy with long dreadlocks stood maybe an inch taller. He clenched and unclenched his fists while glowering at the smaller Tyler.

"So I am. You taking a survey?"

"We're here to beat your ass," Dreadlocks growled.

Tyler shrugged and assumed a defensive stance. "Get on with it, then."

Blondie hung back while the other man rushed forward. Tyler ducked under a wild swing, grabbed his adversary's twisted braids, and pulled hard. The guy yelped as the force pulled him backwards and toppled him over. He landed awkwardly on the asphalt. Tyler whacked him in the face with an elbow, dropped a hammer fist behind it, and then stood ready for other man as he advanced. "You better than him?"

"Yeah," he said.

"Not exactly clearing a high bar," Tyler said.

Three punches came in quick succession. Tyler turned them all aside. His foe launched a kick. Tyler stepped inside it, deflected the ankle with his forearm, and landed a hard blow to the guy's midsection. He backed off a couple steps, but Tyler pressed the advantage when he noticed the other one stirring. A side kick bent the man in half. Tyler elbowed him above the ear and put him down with a knee to the face which snapped his head back and sprayed blood on the ground. Despite bleeding and landing flat, the guy tried to push himself back up. Tyler punted his forehead.

He got clubbed across the back and nearly tripped over the prone man in front of him. Before he could turn around, the black guy wrapped Tyler up from behind. Powerful arms squeezed the air out of his lungs and lifted his feet from the ground. Taking away leverage was a smart play. Basic—but smart. Some combatants wouldn't know how to respond.

Tyler was not among this number.

He reached back, grabbed a handful of twisted hair, and drove his head straight back. It hit something solid but didn't loosen his enemy's grip. Tyler did it again. The hold weakened a little, and Tyler drove his elbow down, knocking the guy's arm loose. Tyler dropped to a crouch and struck to the rear with another elbow, catching his taller foe right in the family jewels. It wasn't hard enough to put him down, but it kept him stunned long enough for a punch and two kicks to send him spiraling to the asphalt.

The white one managed to get back to all fours. Tyler dashed forward and kicked him hard under the chin. His head snapped up, and he flopped onto his back unconscious. The other remained awake but lay on the asphalt coughing and sputtering. Tyler jogged to the service bay, retrieved a 9MM pistol, and stalked back to the fallen man. "I'm going to leave," he said. "If you two are still in the lot when I bring my car around, I'm running you over. If the Olds doesn't finish you . . ." He shook the gun. ". . . this will."

"He's knocked out," the man said, sitting up and pointing toward the unconscious blond.

"And you're a big, strong guy. You can either carry him alive or carry him dead. I don't really give a shit which one." Tyler walked backward to the 442, climbed in, and fired up the engine. The black man rose to unsteady feet. He trotted to the other fellow and shook him. It must have jostled him awake. The white guy needed a fair bit of help to get back to vertical, but the two of them left the property and headed up the sidewalk of Northern Parkway as Tyler backed out of the spot and started forward.

Once he confirmed they were gone, he locked up the shop and set the alarm. He left the 442 pointing to the north, its headlights illuminating the area where one of the guys did something before their ill-fated attack. Tyler rummaged through the growth and found a small digital camera sitting atop a tripod mount. Two small lights—one red and the other blue—were lit on the top of the device. From what Lexi had told him, this meant the device was powered up and transmitting. Tyler centered his face in the lens, held up his middle finger, and swung the tripod in a hard downward arc. The camera smashed against the blacktop, scattering bits of plastic everywhere. Tyler stomped on the remains a few times for good measure before walking back toward his car.

Malachi Golan wanted to collect footage on him. Tyler wondered if he did something similar for the other victims. What if someone like Durrani reached another sicko who could bankroll the operation? Tyler might be the real target, and everyone else was just collateral damage. He hoped this wasn't the case. There were much worse ways to hurt him than going after men he hadn't talked to in years.

MALACHI AGAIN WATCHED Plato's Parlor.

He'd gotten used to the buzz of the college town. Lots of cars left early in the morning. A few returned before twelve, but most made their way back mid-afternoon. In the evening, many of them left again, especially on weekends. Without even realizing it, these college kids were aping their parents. Go to work—or school—and venture out at night, but spend the rest of the day bored at home. In all his visits to the States, Malachi never really understood the American lifestyle.

He killed some time watching camera footage of John Tyler taking on the two men at the shop. Neither was very good. Their reputations indicated they could present a challenge working together. Short from a minor strike and grapple toward the end, they didn't get much offense against Tyler. Despite being twelve years older than Malachi, Tyler still moved well. He anticipated. He struck hard and decisively. At the end, he found the camera and gave it the middle finger before the feed cut out.

No matter. The device did its job before meeting its end.

Around eleven-forty-five, the blue Accord coupe made an early return. Malachi didn't expect Alexis to make it back so early. Maybe a professor canceled class, or she simply decided to skip. Americans didn't dedicate themselves to things like learning and careers the way his people did. The brake lights went out, the door opened, and Tyler's daughter emerged. She wore her dark auburn hair in its usual ponytail, but the denim jacket was a new look. It was a good one, too. For a man of middling mien, Tyler certainly had an attractive daughter. Malachi remembered Pazir telling him to do what he wanted with her.

Tight jeans hugged her hips and butt as she walked. Maybe he would. There were things besides good food to indulge in, after all.

Malachi stepped out of the stolen delivery van. He wore a long-sleeved shirt and jeans close enough in color to count as a uniform, and he carried a large envelope under his arm. The ruse should get him into most buildings, but this one took security seriously. Alexis crossed the parking lot in front of him. Malachi got treated to another view of her sauntering toward the steps. He remained about five paces behind her.

As she reached the door, she turned to her left, and her eyes took him in. He offered a small, quick smile as he started up the stairs behind her. "You mind letting me in?" he asked.

"Who are you delivering for?" she wanted to know.

Malachi anticipated getting challenged. When a legitimate driver left a package near the main entrance two days ago, he got a look at it before someone carried it in. He made a show of looking at the envelope. "This is for a Mister Mullens."

"All right." Alexis used her right thumb to open the electronic lock. She stepped inside, and Malachi followed on her heels. He checked out the area and found no one watching them as Alexis moved to the mailboxes on the right side of the small lobby. Malachi pressed a pistol into her back. "Upstairs now. Do as I say and be quiet, and you won't get hurt."

30

ALEXIS LED MALACHI TO THE APARTMENT. HER HANDS SHOOK as she fumbled the keys out of her purse. Curiously, she kept her car keys on a separate ring. It took her a few seconds, but she found the one for the door and unlocked it. He pressed the gun into the small of her back and followed her inside. A soft beep came from a box on the wall. The unit had its own alarm. He didn't know this but wasn't surprised considering the place's focus on security. "I'll need to turn it off," she said.

Malachi shook his head as he pushed the door shut and engaged both locks. "Tell me your code. I don't trust you not to trick me and summon the cops."

She rolled her eyes. "Fine. Three six four seven nine."

Malachi believed her. She offered it quickly with no attempt to make up the digits. He keyed in the numbers, pressed the main button, and the small screen showed *DISARMED* as its status. "In the living room." Malachi waved the pistol in the proper direction. Alexis raised her hands and walked toward it.

"Don't hurt me," she said in a small voice. A tear slid from her left eye.

"You're not as tough as I expected," Malachi said. "I guess all American girls are soft in the end."

"Expected?" Alexis frowned. "What the hell are you talking about? I don't know you. I've never even seen you before."

"Ask your father." Confusion pulled her brows into a deep frown. "I guess it doesn't matter."

"What are you doing here?" The girl wiped her eyes, which continued leaking occasional tears. "If you came here to rape me, I'll fight back. Gun or not. You might be bigger and stronger, but I won't make it easy for you."

"I didn't come here to violate you," Malachi said. He remained tempted by the idea, however. The young woman's sweater was not provocative, but it was inadequate at hiding the size and shape of her breasts. Malachi didn't remember Alexis being quite so chesty in the photos Pazir's team gave him. "You're a pawn in a bigger game."

"I have literally no idea what you're talking about," she said. Despite being near a sofa, Alexis remained standing. Malachi thought the three women did a good job with the place given their limited funds. Nothing in the living room really matched, meaning the girls brought odds and ends from their respective homes.

"Like I told you before," Malachi said, "ask your father."

Alexis frowned. "My dad's a plumber."

Malachi snorted. "Do you really think he's done nothing else with his life?" John Tyler didn't work as a plumber, though car mechanic seemed equivalent. What was this girl talking about? She probably tried lying to throw him off the scent. "Men like him make enemies, and sometimes, those enemies pay someone like me to make things right."

"He's been a plumber my whole life," she said, raising her voice. "What the hell are you talking about?"

"Don't try to deceive me, Alexis. It will only—"

"You think I'm Lexi?" She chuckled and lowered her hands. "What do you want with her and her dad?"

"Who are you?" Malachi demanded, his grip tightening on the pistol. He knew he'd scouted the right building. This girl even got out of the blue Accord coupe.

"I'm her roommate."

"I don't believe you."

"Screw you."

"Show me your ID," Malachi said.

The young woman scowled at him but complied. Both her driver's license and University of Maryland student card identified her as Emily Utter. "Satisfied?"

"You look quite a bit like her."

"She's two inches taller than me." Emily crossed her arms. "What do you want with Lexi and her dad?"

"My business," Malachi said. "I wasn't planning to hurt your friend, but you might be a different story."

"Before you pull your pants down, you might want to know the cops will be coming soon."

Malachi scoffed. "I don't think so. You haven't called them."

"The code I gave you? There are two." She plastered a fake smile onto her otherwise pretty face. "One deactivates the alarm normally. The other turns it off but also calls the police."

"You're bluffing."

A distant siren drew closer. The artificial smile remained. "Am I?"

Malachi leveled the pistol at her chest. "I could kill you and be a quarter-mile down the road before they get here."

Emily swallowed hard. Her face lost its color, and her eyes welled again. The mirth she faked was gone. "Please . . . just go."

Malachi stepped toward her. The girl winced like she

expected him to fire or hit her. Both were tempting options. She'd deceived him twice. Still, he had to admit the alarm trick was smart. His fight was with John Tyler, and Alexis served as a means to an end. Killing one of her friends wouldn't have the right effect. Demoralizing the daughter didn't matter. Malachi prided himself on not killing innocent people. He pocketed the gun and dashed out of the apartment.

The siren was closer now. Malachi took the stairs two at a time on the way down, leaped to cover the last three, and opened the door. He ran to the van, fired it up, and pulled out of the spot. Even if the cops arrived before he left, he drove a vehicle which could plausibly visit the apartments, and officers knew nothing of what he looked like. They were simply responding to an alarm. Considering the settings Emily described, a certain number of false positives had to be baked into the system. Still, he didn't want to stick around any longer than he needed to.

Malachi made a right turn onto Route One. Two police cars zoomed past him in rapid succession and slowed to make the left into the complex's parking lot. Malachi ran a light which recently changed to red. He made a right with screeching tires onto a side road. Plenty of chances to ditch and torch the van down here once he got a mile or so away from the main drag. Malachi ran a hand through his hair. He got careless assuming Emily was Alexis, and it almost cost him.

It was imperative for him to be better and sharper for the sake of the mission. Pazir didn't need to know about this minor setback. Everything would proceed.

31

LEXI WONDERED WHY POLICE CARS SAT IN THE LOT NEAR THE building. She checked her phone but didn't have any messages from Emily. "What do you think happened?" Kim said as she stopped her Toyota Avalon and put it in park.

"No idea," Lexi said. "We don't usually see a lot of cop cars."

Kim chuckled. "If we do, they're usually for weekend keggers. Those frat boys in the next building never learn."

"They'll be living somewhere else next semester." Lexi got out of the car. As they walked by the trio of police cruisers, Lexi noticed two officers sat in each. Kim unlocked the front door with her thumb, and Lexi handled the entry to the apartment. Emily paced in the living room. Her hands were clenched into fists, and her cheeks were wet. "What hap—"

"What the hell, Lexi?" she barked.

"What?"

"Why was some asshole with a gun just here thinking I was you?"

Lexi's heart thudded in her ears. "Are you all right?"

"I'm fine." Kim walked to their friend, but Emily shook her head. "Answer my question. Why was he here?"

"I don't know."

"What the hell is your dad mixed up in?"

"My dad?" Lexi said.

"Yes! Your dad." Emily jutted a finger toward Lexi. Fear and anger twisted her features. "When I wondered what the hell all this was about, he told me to ask my father."

Lexi knew three of her dad's old unit mates recently died under suspicious circumstances, and Musa almost made it four. From what she'd been told, they were straight-up killings. Whoever took the men out didn't involve family. Why was it different this time? Was her father the target all along?

"Well?" Emily demanded.

"We need to know what's going on," Kim added, crossing her arms.

"This feels a little like an interrogation," Lexi said.

Emily shrugged. "You'd know. You shot two men on campus last year."

Lexi took a slow, deep breath and didn't respond to the barb. She understood Emily was upset, and provoking her wouldn't accomplish anything. "You're aware my dad was in the Army. Green Berets. He's been retired for about ten years now. Recently, someone killed three of the guys he served with, and a fourth man barely got away."

"That's awful," Kim said.

"Is this what you meant when you told us he was going through some things?" Emily asked.

"Yeah." Lexi nodded.

"And you didn't think to let us know?"

"Whoever's been doing this never went after family. He just straight up killed three guys. I never thought I was in danger."

"Well, guess what?" Emily said. "You are . . . and now, we are, too."

"I had no idea," Lexi said. "I would never put you at risk. I love you guys."

Emily shook her head hard enough to unscrew it from her neck. "I'm not sure this roommate thing is going to work for me."

"Emily, I—"

"Lexi," Kim broke in, "I think we need to hear what Emily is saying. She's the one who got traumatized even if the man who came here was after you."

Lexi closed her eyes and nodded. Emily and Kim had to realize she'd never put them in danger. Still, danger came right to their doorstep and into the apartment. Emily was probably lucky to survive unharmed considering the violent actions the killer had taken so far. "If you want me to go, I will," she said in a quiet voice.

"I think it's best," Kim said. Emily bobbed her head in confirmation. "Just for a few days." No confirmation came this time.

"All right." Lexi knew she needed to fix this but didn't have any idea how to even start. Emily and Kim were her best friends, and she couldn't lose them over some asshole who came gunning for her dad. She walked down the hallway, grabbed a duffel bag, and threw some clothes into it. She was overdue for laundry, so she packed some dirty clothes into a trash bag and stuffed that into the duffel.

"You going to your dad's?" Kim asked from the doorway, causing Lexi to jump. "Sorry. Didn't mean to startle you."

"Yeah," Lexi said. "He's kept my room ready. I didn't think I would need it so soon."

Kim took a few steps in. "Look . . . you have to understand Emily is freaked out."

"I get it."

"Just give her some time and space to process everything. She'll realize this wasn't your fault."

"Does it matter?" Lexi set the bag on her bed. "Some jerk came into the apartment. She doesn't feel safe. No matter whose fault it is, that's hard to get over."

"I'll keep you posted."

"Thanks," Lexi said. Kim offered a smile, and the two embraced.

"Let me finish packing, and I'll be out of your hair." Lexi grabbed some supplies from the bathroom, put them in a smaller bag, and added it to the duffel. Only Kim sat in the living room as she headed toward the front door.

MALACHI PICKED a secluded spot to ditch the van.

He pulled it off the road when he reached what looked like an unused industrial park. A circuit of the perimeter showed no security cameras. No other businesses or homes were nearby. Malachi left the van behind the building and used the contents of the gas can to set it on fire. Once the flames crackled, he walked away. People could see the smoke, but someone would actually need to visit the site to find the source. This would give him time to get away.

After about a mile of walking, his phone vibrated. Pazir called. If Malachi ignored it, his benefactor would keep dialing him. Might as well get it over with. "Yes?"

"Did you get the daughter?" Pazir demanded. "I want to know if you treated her like a whore."

The older man was obsessed with whores and trafficking. It made sense in his line of work, but Malachi found some of their conversations distasteful. He felt a little ashamed he'd objectified Emily when he saw her jeans and the hang of her sweater. "No. I decided it wasn't a good move."

"*You* decided?"

"Are you in the field with me?" Malachi asked. Pazir didn't answer, so Malachi kept taking. "No. I'm out here. I wanted to get her, but operationally, it wasn't a good call at the time."

"Will you try again?"

"No."

Pazir sighed. "I am disappointed. This is a guaranteed way to make John Tyler suffer. He must pay for what he did to my friends."

"The girl is in a secure building," Malachi said. "Yes, I could get in, but it's very easy for someone to trigger an alarm secretly. Police response is fast."

"How do you know these things?"

"Research and testing."

"You ran a test?" Pazir asked.

"Yes."

"And you concluded it wasn't worth it?"

"I recognize you think the reward is great," Malachi said, "but so is the risk, and I'm the one who bears all of it."

"Fine," Pazir said. "It sounds like you made the right call." Disappointment still bled into his tone, but he would get over it. "You've already done quite a bit. I think you should make contact with Tyler soon."

"Very well."

"I will be settling in tomorrow. Let's stay radio silent until then unless there's an emergency."

"Understood," Malachi said, and he ended the call. He wanted this job to be over. The money was good, and he didn't mind killing old soldiers, but working for a man like Pazir was too much. Malachi never should have accepted the job. The size of the paycheck compelled him to say yes. He would finish the mission and collect his money.

Then, he would finish Pazir.

32

———

Ortiz had just left to pick up lunch when Tyler's phone vibrated in his pocket.

Musa's name showed on the caller ID. He hadn't been the bearer of any good news for a while. Tyler answered the call. "Hello?"

"You all right, Tippy?"

"I feel like I should ask you. You're the one who's been shot more recently."

"I'm fine," Musa said. "Oswald's dead."

"Christ," Tyler said. "I called him a few days ago to warn him." Tyler balled his left hand into a fist and rested his forehead against it. "I'm tired of this asshole killing good men."

"Me, too."

"How'd it happen?"

"In Oswald's house. Cops are calling it—"

"Lemme guess . . . a home invasion."

"You got it."

Tyler sighed. "Are they even going to talk to the other departments?"

"No idea," Musa said. "Look, we both understand this was a killing. The cops need evidence. They're trying to close cases, and they're going to start with the easiest theories. They're not trying to do a bad job."

"I get it," Tyler said, "but it ends up being one."

"A fair number of cops come from the military. They wouldn't want to let the services down and not solve this one. Speaking of which . . . you talk to Flanker more?"

"Yeah. We have a name. I'll forward you an email." Tyler opened the app on his laptop, found Flanker's message with Malachi's dossier attached, and sent it to Musa. "You should have it."

"Let me take a look." The line went silent for a few seconds. "Heavy hitter," Musa said when he came back on.

"Smart, too," Tyler said. "He's really picking good times and places to strike."

"Flanker have more?"

"Some. He gave us the public version. There's not much more to help us find this prick right now, though. He moves without being detected. We found the one alias, but it's hard to track."

"I'll see if my people can help," Musa said. "We know more now, so there's a chance."

"I had a thought," Tyler said.

"Can people around you smell smoke?"

"Probably. Two guys came to the shop last night. They were trying to rough me up, but they didn't get very far. When they limped away, I found a camera nearby. Online and transmitting." Tyler caught himself almost using Malachi's name on an open line. "Our man must have been trying to gather some info on me."

"Sounds like it," Musa said. "What's the thought you had?"

"He didn't do this for anyone else as far as we know."

"You think he's after you specifically?"

"Maybe," Tyler said. "I busted up a trafficking ring last year."

"I remember."

"One email before the end is all it would take. Now, some other asshole wants revenge, and he hires a very qualified person to make it happen."

"I'm not sure it explains why four other men are dead, Tippy."

"I've been thinking. Maybe he's trying to make me feel isolated . . . suffer. Psychological warfare."

"Is it working?"

"I feel bad for our friends and their families," Tyler said. "None of them deserved this. I'm not going to go cry in the corner, though. If this prick comes, I'll be ready for him."

"Remember, I'll help. I might be on light duty, but I can help you scout and be an extra gun. I'm still a good shot."

"I would expect nothing less. I'll let you know if anything changes. Thanks for calling, Musa."

"You got it," he said.

Tyler set his phone down. Four dead plus Musa, who nearly made it five. This needed to end. Tyler called Flanker. "They got Oswald," he said when the CIA man picked up.

"Shit."

"We got any more intel?"

"Not really," Flanker said. "I have people working on it, but our guy has proven himself to be good at not popping up on the radar too often."

Tyler relayed the story of the two alleged tough guys who came to the shop, the camera, and his theory about being the real target. "I want to do something. Four of my friends are dead, and a fifth one almost joined them."

"I understand."

"I'm the guy who comes up with a plan, helps kick the door in, and shoots people. The problem is I need intel to make it happen."

"We're working on it," Flanker said.

"Work faster," Tyler told him, and he pushed the button to end the call.

He set his phone down again—much harder this time—and stared out the open office door.

WHEN SHE LEFT COLLEGE PARK, Lexi grabbed food from a nearby McDonald's. She wasn't hungry after the events of the morning, but she needed to eat. It took her a while, and she ended up parked outside the restaurant way longer than expected to down a simple chicken sandwich and fries. When she finally finished, she went back inside, ordered a chocolate shake, and then headed north. She pulled into the lot at her dad's shop just after one-thirty.

As she walked in the front door, Smitty and Ortiz toiled away in separate service bays. Her dad sat in his office looking at something on his monitor. He smiled when she walked in. "Didn't expect to see you today." Lexi dropped onto a guest chair, and her dad's happy expression faded. "It's not like you to sink into a seat so heavily."

"I just had a shake on the drive up. Might've gained a pound."

"You get what I mean."

"Yeah," Lexi admitted.

"What's wrong, kiddo?"

Lexi sighed and stretched her legs. It put her feet under the large metal desk. "Emily and Kim gave me the boot." She put up a hand when her dad's mouth opened. "Before you object, I think they were right to do it."

"What the hell happened?" he wanted to know.

"Your boy showed up."

"My boy?"

"The crazy asshole who's been hunting your friends. He came to the apartment." Her father scowled and gripped the edge of the desk hard enough to turn his knuckles white. If it were wood, he might have snapped a piece off. "I wasn't there. He thought Emily was me and held her hostage briefly. She was smart enough to use the alarm code when he made her open the door."

"Where is he now?"

"No idea. Cops would have come in a few minutes, so he probably bolted."

"Is Emily all right?"

"Yeah," Lexi said. "Physically, at least. Mentally and emotionally, she's shaken up. Told me she didn't feel safe with me around right now."

"You think they'll let you back once all this blows over?"

Lexi shrugged. "I hope so. They're my friends. The whole plan was to have an apartment together for three years. Things weren't supposed to blow up so soon."

"I'm sorry this happened," her dad said.

"Me, too. I'm a little bitter about it, but I feel bad for Emily. Subtract two inches, and there's definitely a resemblance."

"You're prettier than she is."

"Dad, you would say that no matter what."

"I would . . . but it's still true."

"Thanks." Lexi smiled. "I take it my room is still ready?"

"You might want to wash the sheets and blanket, but yeah. Good to go."

"All right." She stood. "I guess I'll see you at the house."

"Be careful, Lexi," he said. "This prick has your address, so he has mine, too. There aren't a lot of places you'd logically go, so if he's looking for you, he knows where to find you. If you want to wait here, I can follow you home."

"I'll be all right," Lexi said. "I'm packing."

"There's my girl."

33

Tyler sat at the easel in his home studio.

Malachi went to Lexi's apartment. This represented a serious escalation. It also solidified Tyler's dark thought about him being the target all along. The other killings must have been to throw off suspicion or demoralize him over the deaths of his friends. It was almost enough to work. Tyler felt awful for Bendix, Burns, Orlando, Harvey, and their families. Whoever hated him enough to hire a sicko like Malachi Golan would have a lot to answer for.

An M4 carbine sat propped up against the wall near the door to this spare bedroom. Tyler kept a gun in every room in case he needed to get one quickly, but for now, he carried the reliable rifle with him as he moved throughout the house. Malachi would not catch him by surprise. Memories of his fallen friends rushed into his mind. Bagging on the lousy food in the mess hall. Riding in Hummers over whatever passed for roads in parts of war-torn Afghanistan. Gunfights with the Taliban. The adrenaline rush of kicking in a door and sweeping a shotgun across a room. Hours spent rating women in skimpy clothes on long-defunct websites. The unit laughed, cried, fought, swore, and bled together, and now they were diminished by four men.

Malachi and the coward writing his checks would answer for the deaths.

A few minutes into his painting, a vibrating phone interrupted Tyler. *UNKNOWN CALLER* showed on the display. He usually ignored calls like these, but after recent events, Tyler pushed the green button to answer. "Hello?"

"Is this John Tyler?" A male voice. Strong. A baritone but with an accent. It sounded Israeli.

"It is."

"I'm glad we're finally getting to talk, John."

"It's Tyler." Despite knowing who was on the other end, Tyler didn't want to give any info away. "Who's this?"

"I think you have a good idea," Malachi said. "You may not know my name, but my actions over the last several days will speak for me. I've killed five of your friends."

He still thought Musa was dead. Good. Let him remain in the dark. "Enough playing around, then," Tyler said. "Stop sending chumps to try and soften me up. Come after me yourself."

"All in good time. You have made some enemies, John. Many people would pay good money to see you dead."

"And hire an asshole like you, apparently."

"There's no need for name calling," Malachi said in a tone reminiscent of a teacher scolding a disruptive student. "This was inevitable. You have made your choices. Now, the events and decisions of your life are backfiring like the old cars you love to work on."

"Maybe I shouldn't take you seriously," Tyler said. "You can't even menace the right college girl."

"You would underestimate me at your peril. Ask your friends how good I am. Oh . . . you can't, can you?"

"Name your time and place. Wherever you are, I'm going

to paint the walls with your blood before you tell me who's bankrolling you." Tyler realized trying to get location data from the call would be pointless. Malachi would use a burner, and he was smart enough to ditch it and head somewhere else in the next few minutes.

"I might have found the wrong girl in College Park," the Israeli said. "How many places could your precious Alexis go? It's only a matter of time until I find her . . . if I'm looking for her." Tyler didn't take the bait. Instead, he seethed but remained silent. Malachi couldn't help himself. "Or maybe I'll just come after you. What has your American military concluded about fighting a two-pronged war?"

"I don't know. The report must have gotten lost in the billions of dollars we've sent your country over the years."

A light chuckle fluttered in Tyler's ears. "We will see each other soon, John." The line went dead. Tyler set his phone down. He looked at the watercolor page he'd barely started. Talking to Malachi left him too agitated to continue. If it weren't so late, Tyler would head to a gun range and work off some steam by shredding paper targets.

Instead, he stared at the corner of the room and imagined gutting Malachi Golan.

MALACHI WATCHED THE VIDEOS AGAIN.

While he did, he smashed his old burner phone and set up a new one. Clarence and the other two men both failed to get much offense in against Tyler, but it wasn't the point. If chumps like them had made him sweat, Pazir wouldn't need someone with Malachi's skill set and experience. He watched both clips in succession. Tyler still defended well. He moved with purpose. He understood what his opponents were trying to do—to the extent any of the three had a plan. The experience showed. Tyler was an efficient and deadly combatant.

He'd lost a step or two from his peak, however.

While he managed to block a bunch of punches and kicks, slow motion revealed several came close to hitting him. Getting grabbed from behind in the second encounter shouldn't have happened. The John Tyler of twelve years ago would represent an even match for Malachi. Today, however, the Israeli knew he could take the American. He would make sure the fight went long to tire out the older man. Small injuries and even a few cuts here and there would compound Tyler's suffering.

There was no way he would beg for death like Pazir wanted. Men like Tyler were too proud for such wimpy civilian moves. Still, Malachi would make sure he was in agony before he died. The second encounter ended. Tyler spotted the camera, moved it closer to his face, and held up his middle finger. A quintessential American gesture. It made Malachi chuckle. In a different reality, he might have liked Tyler.

In this one, he needed to kill the man.

Once his new phone carried some charge, he called Pazir. "I made contact with Tyler," he said when the Arab answered.

Silence filled the line for a few seconds until Pazir finally spoke. "Do your people have a saying about poking the bear?"

"No."

"Maybe they should."

"Did you not think this was a good idea recently?" Malachi said. "I am not worried."

Pazir snorted. "I like your confidence, but I also know Tyler is a big test. You'll be confronting him in a way you skipped with the others in his unit. I'm sure you think you're going to win, but don't tell me there's not some small part of you wondering if things will go the other way."

"There is always the possibility of losing a fight." This wasn't a productive conversation, so Malachi changed gears. "You are settled?"

"Just recently, yes," Pazir said. "I will text you the address."

Malachi looked at the map his phone automatically opened when he tapped the info. It was farther away than he expected. "I may not be able to bring Tyler to you easily," he said.

"This is our arrangement."

"If I can, I will. If not, I will make sure to get it on video and send it to you. You can enjoy watching it every day if you want."

Pazir grunted. "If we must. The key is his suffering. If I have to watch you from afar, I want to see the blood. I want to hear his cries and screams."

"You will," Malachi said before hanging up.

34

Malachi understood a little of where Tyler came from.

He sat on a side road across from the estate comprising Evergreen Acres. Tyler's father Ezekiel—a good Hebrew name thanks to the old man's Jewish mother—lived in one of the buildings. He'd chosen one with poor visibility when contemplating an attack from basically any angle. If the state's gun registry were accurate, the elder Tyler owned a cache of weapons large enough to hold off a Russian battalion.

It made a frontal assault a poor choice. Tyler would talk to his father. Ezekiel would expect the man tormenting his son to find him. Good attackers logically went after weak spots, and family represented the biggest vulnerability of all. Malachi's dinner grew tepid on the passenger's seat of the stolen Dodge Durango as he moved the car a foot at a time to try and find the best vantage point.

In the spring or summer, he probably couldn't see Ezekiel Tyler's building from here . . . and definitely not his balcony. Now, however, with more leaves on the ground than in the trees, he had a small window through which to spot it. His vantage point was across a field, a fence, and another large wooded area. Probably half a mile away. It would be a hell of a shot. Malachi was a good sniper, not a great one, so he didn't know if he could make it.

He needed to try, at least. What better way to make sure John Tyler suffered than kill his beloved father? Going after Alexis again so soon represented a tactical error. She and her dad would both be on high alert. The eldest of them, an hour removed from his family, may not be. Malachi grabbed the container and opened it. The grilled shrimp smelled great, though they'd started to get a little rubbery as they cooled.

He ate them anyway. The vegetables were similarly cool and a little soggy. It wasn't the restaurant's fault. Malachi took his time. He could have done the work faster but not as well. If a nice meal turned mediocre got him a better chance to kill Ezekiel Tyler, he'd make the trade a hundred times. Tomorrow, Malachi would come back. This area of the side road saw no traffic, and the nearest house stood around a bend. If he moved a few feet into the trees, he could retain line of sight, and be invisible to prying eyes.

The curtain behind the old man's window moved back a couple times. Malachi was far enough away to remain unseen. Distance plus dusk would render his hiding place invisible to someone as far away as Ezekiel. "Enjoy your evening, Mister Tyler," he said around a bite of shrimp. "It's going to be your last."

TYLER HELD UP A GLOVED FIST, and the men behind him stopped.

A few seconds later, he got the confirmation. "Bravo team in position," Giovanni Orlando said in his earpiece.

Tyler took a step to the side. He and his unit poised ready

before the main door of a small compound. It stood just outside a small village in Afghanistan. The warlord who lived here supported the Taliban and terrorized the people who lived nearby. In a just world, he would have protected them, but Tyler realized a just world was a pipe dream years ago. He held up three fingers, then two, then one.

When the final digit fell away, Carl Burns swung a small battering ram, and the front door exploded into the house. Despite outranking the other man as a warrant officer, Tyler went in first. He moved to the left right away. A hostile stepped out of a room on the side. Tyler leveled the shotgun at him, pulled the trigger, and watched him slump to the tiled floor.

Four more tangos came out, and they all went down right away. The warlord didn't possess overwhelming forces, but even a half-dozen armed men could easily overpower a bunch of villagers. Two women—captives from nearby who'd probably been mistreated in the worst ways—pled for mercy. Tyler cut one free, Burns took the other, and another soldier escorted them back outside.

Gunfire erupted near the rear of the house. Alan Bendix stumbled into the main area, blood spurting from a wound in his neck. His head lolled, and he crashed to the floor before anyone could stop him. Burns moved up to pull his fallen comrade to safety, but more bullets shredded the air. Three embedded themselves in Burns's chest and head, and he fell beside Bendix.

Even though asleep, Tyler recognized he was dreaming. He remembered raiding this estate. Bendix hadn't even been there, and his unit suffered no casualties while clearing out the place, freeing two female prisoners who'd been badly treated in predictable ways by their captors, and pumping about a hundred rounds into the warlord. He was a tall, thin man with a hooked nose and a nasty face. When he raised his

AK-47, he got it about six inches up before the torrent of bullets took him down.

Tyler knew it was a dream, but he couldn't wake himself. His brain forced him to watch this twisted memory play out. Another burst of automatic weapon fire, and Giovanni Orlando staggered forward from the rear. He bled from numerous bullet wounds and locked eyes with Tyler before collapsing. Tyler and the rest of alpha team remained along the walls in the main room. After still another exchange of gunfire, Harvey Lee walked in. His pistol smoked from the end, and he smiled.

Before he could say anything, a shot from the rear blew his head apart.

Tyler sat up with a gasp. Sweat covered his face and soaked into his sheets. He gulped in a few deep breaths. One perk of his painting program was a reduction in nightmares like this, specifically ones in which real events ended up distorted in a terrible way. Tyler lay back down and stared at the ceiling.

He got the feeling it would be a long night.

35

LEXI IGNORED HER RINGING PHONE AS SHE DROVE TO COLLEGE Park.

So far this semester, her commute to classes had been easy. Go about a mile down Route One, hang a right onto Campus Drive, and find parking. Now, however, with Emily and Kim giving her the boot, Lexi drove from her dad's house in Baltimore. There was no way to get to school that didn't involve a highway and traffic. She'd chosen what looked like the least congested option, but I-95 South slowed to a 15-mph crawl as she headed south of Laurel toward the 495 split.

The same number called again. She answered this time. "What?"

"Lexi? This is Veronica Fitzgerald."

It took a second to recall the name. "Hi. How are you?"

"Good, thanks. Listen . . . I want to do a story on your father, and—"

"I'm hanging up now."

"Wait. Please."

Lexi sighed. Her Accord coupe didn't have built-in Bluetooth, so she controlled her phone through a speaker clipped to the sun visor. Her thumb hovered above the button that would disconnect the call. "My dad isn't a story."

"I think he is."

"Have you talked to him about this?" Lexi asked.

"I have."

"And."

"His only on-the-record comment was telling me to piss off," Veronica said.

"Sounds like my dad."

"I don't need to tell you the things he's done. You were there for some of them. My guess is you helped with more than just the mess in North Carolina."

"I'm not going to give you a sound bite," Lexi said. "I was happy to help you with the Sappony because they were getting a raw deal, and you could shine a light on it. I don't want you shining a light on my family."

"Honestly, I was hoping you could tell me at least a few things," Veronica said. "We could even talk about when you were growing up. I don't—"

"Did he tell you this wasn't a good time to be around?"

"Yes, though I feel he'd tell me that regardless."

Lexi chuckled. It would be exactly like her dad to do precisely that. "Maybe, but he has his reasons this time."

"I told him I wasn't worried."

"And?"

"He said neither were the three dead men," Veronica replied.

"You might want to listen. You being around isn't doing him any favors, but he's only telling you this stuff to try and keep you alive."

"Lexi, I'm going to write my story. Your father is an interesting man, and I think people will want to know what he's doing."

"And when someone comes after him?" Lexi said. "Or me?"

"I can't control how people react to something I write."

"Sure you can. Don't write it in the first place . . . or at least don't mention him by name."

"I'm moving ahead with this."

"I could tell you good luck," Lexi said, "but I wouldn't mean it." This time, her thumb hit the button, and Veronica's next question ended in mid-sentence. She glanced at the clock in the dash. Her first class started in twenty minutes. Once she could get to 495, the journey was pretty direct. Heavy traffic was the one time Lexi didn't enjoy driving a clutch. At least it was light and predictable. The congestion didn't ease, and she pulled into the closest spot she could get three minutes after the class started.

This arrangement was bullshit. She needed to be back in the apartment with her friends. Hopefully, they would come around. For now, she would give them time . . . and try not to get further embroiled in the mess surrounding her dad at the moment.

ZEKE CARRIED his steaming mug of black coffee into the living room. He'd already opened the blinds on his lone kitchen window, and now he did the same for both in here. Last night, an SUV sat across the way, past the Evergreen Acres property line and into the neighborhood beyond. Zeke spotted it twice. It was out of place. The particular stretch of road sat between two different subdivisions, and while ample acreage was available, no one broke ground on any construction yet.

Whoever parked his vehicle there didn't know these details.

An outsider. In the end, deducing who sat in the car didn't require any logical leaps. Someone stalked Zeke's son and his old Green Beret unit. Thus far, the assailant had been successful. Now, he targeted family members. A quick look as he walked back into the kitchen showed no one in the spot again. Still, Zeke set his mug down, unpacked his favorite bolt-action rifle, and checked the load. He'd fired it at the range a couple weeks ago. If some son of a bitch wanted to case his condo, he'd get a high-velocity encouragement to move along.

After a few minutes of quiet, Zeke returned to the kitchen to make breakfast. His wife died over twenty-five years ago, and it forced a man who ate on ships his whole life to learn to cook. Nothing he made could touch what she was able to whip together, but he did all right. This morning, he fried bacon, removed it and cracked a couple eggs into the grease, and reheated two biscuits he'd baked the prior evening. Zeke ate at his dining room table. There was no direct line of sight from the windows, but he still kept a pistol beside his plate.

By the time Zeke polished off his second cup of coffee, the situation changed.

The same SUV was back and parked in basically the identical place as last night. It proved easy enough to spot without Zeke making it obvious he looked out the window. With the trees shedding most of their leaves, line of sight to the other neighborhood ended up being good. The same would be true from the other person's end as well, but one of the virtues of living near the top of a building was enjoying the higher ground.

Zeke grabbed a small rug, opened the window, and shook it out. While some dirt and dust came free, the whole thing was mostly for show. He wanted to take the time to get a better look at his potential adversary. One figure occupied the cab of the vehicle. This would be his second observation of the place, and he'd just gotten confirmation his target was awake and in the unit. Zeke moved away from the open window, didn't close it, and retrieved a screw-on suppressor for the rifle. It wouldn't mute the report, but it turned the volume down some.

The other guy needed a little time to get things set up. He would have a good rifle with him. It wasn't an easy shot—especially coming from below the target—so a bipod made sense. Probably a good spot to lie in the grass and brace his body against a tree. Being in line with the SUV would reduce the odds of getting spotted from the road. About forty minutes after shaking out the rug, Zeke walked by again. This time, he spotted a small figure near the vehicle.

The game was afoot.

Zeke picked up the rifle. He fed the barrel through the open window and braced the weapon against the left side. His only problem would be the wind. He didn't measure it. Trees in the distance rustled, and their leaves indicated the breeze blew from left to right. Zeke would need to make his best guess. He'd been shooting a rifle for sixty-odd years. Even if he didn't plug the bastard, he could chase him away.

Looking through the scope, Zeke found his enemy setting up shop. As predicted, he used a bipod and screwed a suppressor of his own onto the rifle. It was a newer weapon. Semiautomatic of some kind. Definitely a higher rate of fire than the bolt-action model Zeke still preferred. He would need to make his shot count. The man below looked to be about forty. He had a Middle Eastern complexion, and Zeke judged him to be in good shape despite a small paunch visible beneath his jacket.

After adjustments for windage and angle, Zeke placed his adversary's center mass in the crosshairs, exhaled, and squeezed the trigger.

The bullet tore through the air. It went wide about two

feet to the right but tore a chunk out of the tree. The man below nearly leaped out of his skin. He grabbed everything as Zeke fed a new cartridge. He adjusted for his prior underestimate. The wind must have been stronger than he thought. The second shot narrowly missed, burying itself in the door of the SUV.

The guy made it back inside. Headlights came to life. Zeke took a third shot, blasting the passenger's side window, but his foe made an escape with screeching tires. "Get gone, you son of a bitch," Zeke said to the fleeing vehicle in the distance, which soon disappeared behind a cluster of townhouses. He brought the rifle back inside and got his cleaning supplies out. People would have heard the reports even with a suppressor, and most of his neighbors had been awake for hours.

Zeke chided himself for missing three shots even under the current conditions. He needed more time at the range.

36

Malachi relaxed in the hotel's jacuzzi tub.

He'd ditched the SUV nearby. Keeping it would have been nice, but he couldn't drive it with a bullet hole in the side and a window shot out. Maybe it was time to stop stealing older cars. He could use some money from Pazir to buy himself something. The mission was in the final stages. The risks of getting seen entering or leaving an area had declined since his initial attacks against Bendix and Burns. Now, he could focus on surgical strikes against his ultimate target.

John Tyler.

Malachi sipped wine from a plastic hotel cup. He hadn't expected Tyler's father to spot him. It was a good place to set up and take a shot. The old man remained observant, however, and if he'd been better with the rifle—or if there had been no wind to push the large bullets wide of their marks—Malachi would be dead right now.

Tyler and his father would talk. Same for the daughter. If recent events combined with Malachi's phone call didn't hammer home the idea Tyler was the target, nothing would. For a man without a college degree, Tyler seemed smart and intuitive. He knew what went on. What he couldn't predict was where his unknown enemy would strike.

There were two places Tyler frequented—his house and the classic car shop he owned. The former stood among a bunch of similar homes. They were close enough together for people to notice what went on. Kicking in the door and firing a bunch of bullets wasn't a good idea. The shop was at a major intersection. Well lit. Plenty of cars going by and pedestrians on the sidewalks. Making a getaway would be easier from there with an interstate nearby, but Malachi knew he had very little chance of killing Tyler there without someone seeing or hearing something.

One option remained, and it was the best one of all. He could make Tyler come to him. Considering how going after Ezekiel went, Malachi concluded he would need to grab Alexis. Not her roommate this time. The prior mistake set him back two days. He could be on a flight back to Tel Aviv now. Instead, he still toiled for Pazir. Alexis was a pretty girl. Taking out his frustrations on her could be quite enjoyable.

He wondered if her friends let her stay in the apartment. A mistaken kidnapping could sink their relationship. Later, he would drive by Tyler's house. If the girl were there, he would abduct her. Then, he would get his showdown with Tyler and be able to put Pazir in his rearview.

MALACHI DROVE to Baltimore in his new BMW.

He paid cash for a 2005 5-Series sedan. It was black, came with an inline-six engine, and the auto repair shop owner specialized in not asking too many questions. The fellow registered the vehicle in an alias Pazir's team prepared. Despite being nearly twenty years old, it only had 133,000 miles on it, and the engine purred when he pushed his right foot down. Malachi never considered himself much of a car guy, but he would enjoy driving this one.

He slowed when he reached Tyler's street. Two vehicles sat in the man's driveway: a white Tesla SUV, and Alexis' Accord coupe. The daughter was home. Malachi smiled as he left the BMW at the curb across the street. Alexis was a co-ed. Despite who her father was, she wouldn't be much trouble for a trained operative. Malachi ditched the disguise he wore to get into the College Park apartment. Let her see him for who he was.

Dusk settled over the neighborhood. No one walked along the sidewalks. Street lights lifted the growing gloom, and a chill settled in with the sun in retreat. Malachi approached the house. Curtains covered the windows, so he couldn't see inside. Anyone raised by John Tyler would keep the doors locked. Malachi opted for the direct route and knocked. When no response came after a moment, he did it again.

Footsteps approached from the interior. Two locks clicked back, and Alexis pulled the door inward. She wore yoga pants and a sweatshirt from her school, and Malachi realized she was both taller and prettier than her friend. Not quite as busty, but she would still provide him with hours of entertainment. If Pazir weren't such a scumbag, he would hand the girl over to him once he'd completed the mission. Alexis frowned and started to ask something when Malachi pulled on her right wrist, yanking her onto the porch.

Her left arm had been hidden behind the door jamb. Now, he saw why—she carried a Glock 19. As she raised it, he kicked at her hand and knocked the gun loose. It landed with a dull thud in the grass. She was smart enough not to waste time and leave herself exposed by trying to pick it up. Malachi never enjoyed fighting women, but the ends justified the means in this case. He threw a hard right cross, expecting to knock the girl out with a single blow. Her upraised forearm deflected his strike high and wide.

She countered with a jab at his midsection, which he blocked. Before he could pull his right arm back, however, Alexis caught him with a kick to the side. The girl had some training. Maybe her father taught her a few things. Before he had time to ponder her experience, she came at him with a flurry of blows. Despite his combat experience, the young woman's ferocity and speed caught him by surprise. A hard kick to the gut staggered him backward. He tried to spin away, but her left foot took him square in the balls. Malachi caught a break when he slumped to the ground within reach of the Glock.

Alexis turned and sprinted past her house as he grabbed the pistol and brought it to bear. She was already out of sight. "Dammit," Malachi muttered as he rose to his knees. He took a deep breath and made it back to shaky feet. A quick look around told him no one took an interest in what happened. Yet. There were enough houses around for people to discover what went on. A man out to walk his dog would be an unwelcome complication.

Malachi ran after Alexis. He hopped the fence into the Tylers' backyard, then did the same to leave it at the other end a moment later. No sign of the girl. She'd bolted away, and she knew the area, so Alexis could be anywhere by now. Malachi couldn't stand around holding a gun for long. He tucked it into his rear waistband, walked around the property until he came back to the road, and looked around again.

Still no sign of her.

Clearly, Malachi underestimated Alexis Tyler. It made him want another shot at her. He'd always liked it when women fought back. Something told him she would be particularly difficult to tame. While he'd normally relish the challenge, she could also be calling her father right now. Malachi preferred the meeting to be on his own terms, so he hustled a return to the BMW, fired it up, and drove away.

37

When Lexi made her break, she sprinted away and to the right behind their neighbor's house. She'd run track in high school, and even though kickboxing was her preferred method of exercise these days, she could still make a mad dash when she needed to. Three homes away, she peeked out from the side of the building. Malachi tucked her pistol into his pants, got into some German car, and drove away.

Lexi remained in place. She waited five minutes, but he didn't come back. Once the coast was clear, she returned to her dad's from the rear and went in through the kitchen door. She called him once she was safe inside and her pulse and breathing returned to normal. "Malachi came to the house."

"Are you all right?" he asked right away.

"Yeah. He tried to grab me, but I got away."

"You at the house now?"

"Yeah, I'm back inside."

"Lock the doors and stay there. I'm coming."

"It's fine, Dad," she said even though it felt far less than fine a few minutes before. "He left. Got into some German sedan and drove off. I waited a few minutes. He's not lurking somewhere close."

"If he does, get yourself a shotgun."

"Speaking of weapons, the son of a bitch ended up with my Glock."

"I'll be sure to get it for you when I kill him."

"Please do," Lexi said. "I think I'm going to go to Grandpa's until all this blows over."

"Wow. Willingly."

Lexi chuckled in spite of the gravity of the situation. The last time she stayed with her grandfather, her dad insisted and practically shoved her out the door. "His place is harder to get to and easier to defend."

"True," her father said. "Be careful. If this prick follows you, let me know. I'll come and take care of him."

"I think you're the one who needs to be careful, Dad. This guy is gunning for you, and he's obviously willing to use me to make it happen."

"I know. I'm working on finding him. My one friend in intelligence is on it, too. Our guy is a slippery bastard, but we'll find him."

"I hope so." She sighed. "I'm going to get my bag. I'll let you know when I make it to Grandpa's."

"Please do."

Lexi promised she would and ended the call. She headed upstairs and got her duffel. Having only taken a few things out, packing it again was quick and easy. With her main pistol in Malachi's hands, Lexi fetched another from her closet. It was a .38 revolver with a five-inch barrel. Her first gun, and a gift from her grandfather when she turned twelve. By fourteen, she was already a good shot with it—much to her mother's chagrin.

The coast remained clear as Lexi got into her car and backed out of the driveway. She kept an eye out for Malachi, but no one followed her. The prick came for her in College Park and now chased her out of her father's house. She wondered what Emily and Kim would think of the recent developments. They probably wouldn't have a lot of sympathy. She didn't blame them. Feeling safe in your place was important. This mess her dad landed in threw everything into upheaval.

She knew it wasn't his fault, but a small part of her still felt angry about it.

MALACHI RETURNED to John Tyler's street a couple hours later.

It was fully dark by now, and only the street lamps and ambient light from the city offered illumination. The Tesla sat as the lone car in the driveway. Alexis's Accord remained gone, and Tyler's muscle car was conspicuous by its absence. Malachi wondered if Tyler came home. His daughter would have told him what happened. Maybe he stashed the car somewhere else and hoped for a break-in. No lights were on inside. If the man waited for him, he did so in total darkness.

It seemed unlikely.

Another car came to life. Its quiet engine turned over, and the headlights flashed on for a moment before the driver killed them. Malachi remained in place. His BMW sat on the opposite side of the street two houses to the rear of the small Hyundai SUV. Illumination from within the cabin showed a woman's red hair sticking up over the headrest. Who was this? The mystery lady alternated between angling her head toward Tyler's house and something in the car. A notebook maybe . . . or a computer? She could have been a cop. Even a reporter.

Malachi doubted anyone watched Tyler's house without the man being aware of it. His paranoia and PTSD wouldn't allow it. Since Alexis resisted attempts to become a useful hostage, maybe this woman was the answer. When Tyler rode to her rescue, Malachi would get to confront him on his own terms—a factor far more important than picking a spot convenient for Pazir.

The Israeli opened his car door, exited, and closed it as quietly as he could. He checked for people moving around or looking out their windows and saw no one. Malachi kept low and padded up the street. He stayed wide of the SUV's side mirror to avoid tipping off the driver. Pulling even with the vehicle, he watched her look at Tyler's house and then back to something on her lap. The seat was pretty far back for a woman. She must have used a computer or tablet.

Malachi drew the Glock 19 Alexis dropped. He considered killing the woman in the Hyundai. The pistol would be on file, and making a mess of things for Alexis would be a nice way to get revenge for her kicking him and running away. He decided against it. Complicating her life—however satisfying it may be in the moment—was not his mission, and Malachi didn't kill innocent people if he could avoid it. Especially non-combatants.

Instead, he approached the Hyundai, stood, and tapped on the glass. The woman inside was a pretty redhead dressed for the cold in a sweater and a coat. Her eyes widened when she saw the pistol. Malachi smiled at her.

38

———

Tyler worked late with Ortiz.

It kept his mind off everything. Lexi texted earlier to let him know she'd made it to Zeke's. There were enough guns there to hold off an entire team of Mossad agents, let alone a single asshole. Ortiz insisted on staying in case something happened. Tyler stopped asking him to go home about two hours ago. Even though the circumstances were less than ideal, this late-night session gave them a chance to catch up on service orders from the last few days. The shop's business hummed like a well-tuned engine, and Tyler stepping away to deal with outside matters slowed things down.

The phone in Tyler's office rang. Not many people knew he would be here, so he stopped working to answer it. Ortiz followed. "Hello?"

"Good evening, John." Of course, it was Malachi. Tyler's stomach clenched. Did the Israeli overcome the odds and abduct Lexi or Zeke? "I have someone here who's interested in you."

Tyler pressed the button to put the call on speaker. "Who?"

"Her name is Veronica. She says she's a reporter." Tyler let out a sigh of relief. "Did you hear me, John?"

"Yeah." Tyler tried, but he couldn't suppress a fit of laughter.

"I don't think this is funny. The lovely Veronica here probably agrees."

"You sure you got the right woman this time?" Tyler said, knowing he was egging Malachi on. "Your recent history there isn't exactly strong." Malachi's sigh hissed in Tyler's ear. "Terrorizing college girls . . . kidnapping reporters . . . I'm glad you finally found your real skill level. I don't know what kind of money you're getting, but I think your benefactor overpaid."

"Don't trifle with me," Malachi said, and the annoyance in his tone came through loud and clear.

"What do you want?"

"You'll meet me at a time and place of my choosing. We'll end this once and for all."

"And if I decline?" Tyler asked.

"I kill the reporter."

"Go ahead."

Malachi didn't answer right away. After a few seconds, he came back with, "What?"

"She's a nosy journalist threatening to write a story about me. Why would I give a shit if she lives or dies?" Ortiz frowned, but Tyler held up a hand to let him know it would be fine. "If you kill her, you're doing me a favor. I won't thank you because I'd rather cut your throat and watch you bleed out, but I'm pretty sure whoever's bankrolling you doesn't want you helping me."

"I'll murder her," Malachi threatened again.

"Fine. Go ahead. Be a peach and let me know when it's done." Tyler hung up.

"You're taking a risk," Ortiz said, his arms crossed.

"No, I'm not. He won't kill her."

"What makes you so sure?"

"He had a chance to kill Lexi's roommate and didn't take it. Whoever this asshole is, he was a soldier, and I don't think he wants to snuff out someone who's not involved in his mission."

"Some reporter really wants to do a story on you?"

"Yeah," Tyler said. "I tried to tell her I'm far too boring. She won't hear it."

"What does she know?"

"A lot. She's good. Don't worry . . . I'll keep you out of it. So far, she seems to think I acted alone in West Virginia."

"I'm more worried for her," Ortiz said. "You told me about the guys this prick killed. None of them were lightweights."

"She'll be all right. Malachi is stewing right now because I threw a wrench in how he wanted to do things, but he'll call back."

"You sure?"

"I am," Tyler said.

~

"GODDAMMIT!" Malachi squeezed the phone hard enough to turn his knuckles white. "Son of a bitch. Who does he think he's dealing with?"

They sat in his BMW in the main lot of a state park in Harford County. Malachi had done some location scouting trying to find a great spot to get rid of Tyler once and for all. This area, closed for trail renovations which the local papers said were on pause over budget issues, offered exactly such a venue. He'd even picked out the place and knew he could set up several cameras to film it all for Pazir. This reporter made the perfect bait . . . until Tyler laughed and issued his silly American taunts.

"He'll call back," Veronica said quietly in the passenger's seat.

"You just want to stay alive."

"Doesn't everyone?"

Malachi's head bobbed automatically. He'd been impressed with Veronica. She never screamed, never tried to claw at him to get away, or any other ridiculous thing many captives did. It made him wonder if she'd worked an assignment which went wrong and saw her get kidnapped before. "I didn't think he would laugh and hang up."

Veronica let out a dry chuckle. "I'm not surprised."

"Really?"

"What he told you is true. I'm investigating him for a story. I don't know what your beef is with Tyler, but he's taken out some very bad people and managed to keep himself out of the headlines and mostly off anyone's radar. I only landed on him by good fortune."

"You think he would prefer to stay off the radar," Malachi said, nodding. "I understand. I wanted the same thing for a while."

"And now?"

"This job forces me to work in the shadows. When it's over . . ." He shrugged.

"You'll go back to Israel?" Veronica asked. Malachi shot her a sidelong glance. "Your accent. I've interviewed Israelis before."

"Ever the journalist." He smirked. She was getting material for a story. "I'm not someone to write about." Malachi looked at the phone. Nothing. "I wonder if he'll call back. John Tyler seems like the kind of man who tries to keep people safe."

"Generally, I agree. He sees my story as putting him out there. If the wrong people read it, he and his daughter could be in danger. His concern for her definitely trumps any he might have for me . . . or pretty much anyone else in the world as far as I can tell."

Malachi let out a long, slow breath and stared at his phone. No activity. Tyler wasn't calling back. The man pegged him right: he didn't want to hurt Veronica. He figured Tyler would come riding to the rescue like some white-hatted cowboy in a silly American film. Clearly, this wouldn't happen. Malachi could still get him to turn up, however. As much as he didn't want to, he called back.

"Sure you have the right woman?" Tyler asked. "Maybe you should check her ID."

"Enough of your taunts. Maybe you don't care about this woman, but I'll find your daughter next."

"Good luck."

"And what if I had some good luck?" Malachi said. "I almost had her before. If her friend hadn't been driving your precious Alexis's car, I would have." Tyler offered no response. "Her apartment sells security . . . probably so parents like you can feel good about paying to let their kids live there. Wherever she is, I can get to her."

"Fine. What do you want?"

"You're going to meet me somewhere, and we'll settle this."

"Where?"

"Do you know Susquehanna State Park?"

"Not offhand, but I'll find it."

"Come to the main lot. Two hours. I won't bother threatening you with the reporter again, but if you don't show up, I'll make it my mission to find your daughter."

"I'll be there," Tyler said, and he broke the connection.

"Why two hours?" Veronica wanted to know. "He doesn't live more than an hour from here."

"A man like Tyler will want to arrive early to scout the

area. No matter. I've already done it, and I know how this is going to go."

Veronica frowned. "I'm going to be bait, aren't I?"

"I'm not sure he cares enough about you, my dear . . . but you're not wrong."

39

"Let me help, boss."

Ortiz sat in one of the chairs in front of Tyler's desk. The monitor—angled so Ortiz couldn't see it—showed the location of Susquehanna State Park, nestled deep in the woodland portions of Harford County. Tyler couldn't imagine anyone finding it unless they already knew where it was. A recent article in a local paper mentioned trail and other construction work getting delayed by the usual budget overruns which seemed endemic to government contracts at any level.

Tyler shook his head. "Go home. Thanks for your offer, but I'll deal with this prick myself."

"What if he has someone else?"

"He's operated alone so far."

"You sure he's going to continue to?"

"I'll take my chances," Tyler said. "He wants me, and he'll get me. If he sees someone else, he might kill the reporter."

Ortiz smirked. "Don't tell me you care what happens to her."

"I don't want her writing a story about me, but I also wouldn't want her getting killed in my place."

"Careful, boss. You're almost getting sentimental."

Tyler jerked his thumb toward the door and grinned. "Thanks for your help this evening . . . and your offer to do more. You're a good man, Ortiz."

"Thanks. I'd better see you here in a couple days."

"You will."

Ortiz frowned, but he got up, straightened his work area in the service bay, and climbed back into his pickup. Tyler looked at the map on his monitor. The main lot led to a large grassy area covered with trees. Hiking trails began about a quarter-mile later, and there was some kind of ranger house nearby, as well. The park stayed closed while the renovations remained incomplete.

Malachi picked a good location.

Tyler unlocked the supply closet in his office. He slipped a bullet-resistant vest on over his shirt, grabbed an extra magazine for his trusty Sig Sauer pistol, and secured the shop. In the car, he keyed the park into his phone's GPS and headed north up Harford Road toward the Baltimore Beltway. From there, he took I-95 into Harford County. Despite larger cities like Bel Air and Aberdeen, much of the county's acreage was rural.

Susquehanna State Park encompassed a large area near Havre de Grace. Signs and jersey walls marked the campground avenue as closed. Tyler turned into the main lot off Wilkinson Road. No other vehicles occupied it. This meant Malachi wasn't here yet, though he must have picked the location because he'd scouted it already. More signs made sure to alert everyone the trails remained shut down for renovations. The entrances were taped off, though any enterprising person could simply walk into the woods and get onto the pavement soon after.

Malachi could have set some kind of trap on one of the trails. To the east, the park bordered on the river for which it was named. Too far from the entrance, and the water was open, so anyone in a boat could potentially see whatever happened nearby. Hundreds of acres of grass and trees offered plenty of places to lie in wait. Tyler took in the surroundings and headed up a short hill. He didn't want to use a light and give away his position. From his vantage point in the late evening gloom, he didn't see anyone or anything.

Trails wove their way through the forest. Tyler found a spot near where three converged. He stepped into the trees at the mouth of the Y intersection and moved into the moonlit shadow of a large tree. The night was never as quiet as people thought, especially in the county. Crickets chirped. A vixen howled like an old woman being stabbed to death. Tyler kept his breathing quiet, held his Sig against his thigh, and listened.

FROM HIS VANTAGE point in the woods, Malachi watched Tyler pull in.

The man moved with the mix of easy confidence and caution which came from years in special operations. Malachi could always spot it. It was something about the gait. Despite most of the light coming from the moon, Tyler picked his way up a hill and took up a spot in the trees. It made sense. He thought he'd gotten here first. "He might save you yet," the Israeli said to Veronica.

"Or he might kill you."

Malachi smiled. "I think not."

"Are you going to kill him?" Veronica asked.

"Eventually."

"You're going to torture him first?"

"You don't need to know my goals," Malachi said. "This isn't some story you're writing."

"How do I know you're going to let me go?"

Malachi shrugged. "I guess you don't. I could shoot you in the back as you ran away." She swallowed hard. "Relax. I'm not interested in killing you. Unlike your American military, I actually try to avoid civilian casualties." He stared at her. "Do I need to put a gag in your mouth?"

"No," Veronica said in a small voice. It didn't matter. He knew she would try to warn Tyler regardless. In the end, she served as a distraction. Try as he might, Tyler wouldn't be able to tune out her running and yelling, and it would give Malachi the opportunity he needed. He'd made plans and bought equipment for the morning, and all of it hinged on the next few minutes going off without a hitch.

"Good. Stay there. I'll do the doors." Malachi climbed out of the sedan and shut the door as quietly as he could. He'd taken the car into a clearing, driven up a trail, and parked past the ranger station. Even if John Tyler heard anything, he wouldn't be able to pinpoint a location. A cautious man like him would stay put and let the action come his way. Malachi would indulge him. He padded around the car, let Veronica out, and shut the passenger's side with barely a sound. "Follow me."

"It's dark."

"Of course it's dark," he snapped. "Stay behind me. There's enough light to see a few feet ahead. If you veer off and run, I might forget my principles and shoot you."

"I won't run," Veronica said.

Malachi made no reply. He walked along the trail, taking his time to make sure he kept the pavement under his shoes at all times. Based on where Tyler walked into the trees, the man stood about three hundred yards to the west and a touch south. The trail went west but a little north. They would need to move through the forest to reach Tyler's position. This suited Malachi. More places to hide.

When they'd gone far enough, Malachi held up his fist and stopped behind a tall oak. Veronica brushed into him from the rear. "We're heading through the trees now," he whispered, pointing to the south. "You'll go first. I don't care if you walk or run, but too much speed might cause you to take a nasty fall. You should see John Tyler in a minute or two."

"What do I do then?" she wanted to know.

"It doesn't matter."

"How do I get back to my car?" They'd come in Malachi's BMW, so Veronica's rental remained parked on Tyler's street in Baltimore.

"Take an Uber."

"It'll be expensive." He raised a pistol. She frowned, turned around, and started walking. Malachi followed her direction if not her path. Veronica possessed no training. She blundered down the middle. If Tyler didn't get a good look at her, he could mistake her for a hostile and open fire. Malachi moved along the tree line. If everything worked right, Veronica would create an unwitting distraction.

She neared the other man's position. Tyler held his pistol up and lowered it. He must have recognized her. Veronica picked up the pace, closing to within about a hundred feet of the target. "Turn around," she called. "He's trying to trap you."

"Are you all right?" Tyler said.

"I am." She waved her arms as she ran past him. "You need to go."

For a second, Tyler turned his head to follow her movements. It gave Malachi the opening he needed, and the woman's noisy progress covered his advance. He closed the distance to Tyler, took a syringe from his pocket, and jabbed it into the American's neck. The plunger delivered the dosage before Tyler swatted Malachi's hand. He brought the pistol around, but Malachi kicked it from his grip. "You coward," Tyler said. He took a fighting stance but already blinked his eyes rapidly.

"You won't die, John. Not yet at least." Tyler threw a punch, but the drugs were already doing their work. His attack was weak and left him off balance. Malachi hit him in the face with a solid left. Tyler lay sprawled on the ground. His eyes closed, and he made no effort to get up.

Malachi looked up. Veronica was gone.

40

WHILE DRIVING BACK TO HIS HOTEL FOR SUPPLIES, MALACHI called Alexis Tyler. "Hello?"

"I'm going to kill your father," he told her.

She snorted. "Like hell you are. You couldn't even tell me apart from my roommate. My dad doesn't need to worry."

Amusement and mockery came across in her tone, like she shared an inside joke with a friend. "Your father is unconscious right now. Soon, I will torture and kill him for an audience of one." Silence served as the only reply. "Where are your jokes now, girl?"

"Bullshit," she said.

Malachi figured she would doubt him. He brought up the picture he snapped of Tyler collapsed on the ground and forwarded it to her. "Still think I'm bullshitting you?" he asked. "Maybe you'd like to remind me how I found your roommate instead of you. Well, I'm pretty sure I've found your father here."

"You'll never get the better of him." The humor in her voice was gone. Instead, a small tremor replaced it, and the pitch went up about a quarter octave.

"Nervous? You should be. Your father will be dead soon. If you're nice, I'll let you watch."

"Piss off. If anything happens to him, I'll find you."

Now, it was Malachi's turn to snort and laugh. "You overestimate yourself, girl. Just because you got away from me at your dad's house doesn't mean you can hunt me down. I'll be a rich man and in the breeze before your tears are dry."

"I'm gonna—" Malachi broke the connection. He didn't know what the girl would do. Did she have some way to try and trace the call? He'd waited until he was about twenty minutes from the park before dialing her. John Tyler was secured. He wouldn't be going anywhere until Malachi went back for him, and then, the man's life would be measured in minutes. Maybe even hours if Pazir really wanted to drag out the torture. Malachi knew how long it took a man to bleed out from a variety of small cuts. He knew how much skin he could flay from a screaming victim before the poor soul passed out. He gave John Tyler thirty minutes.

Malachi stopped his BMW at a light. He was the only car at the intersection. He rolled the window down and tossed his phone out. It clattered to the asphalt, slid to the curb, and disappeared down a sewer grate. He had another at the hotel to replace it. This would be the last phone he needed. Tomorrow morning, he would take care of John Tyler, become a rich man, and then deal with Pazir.

"YOU PRICK," Lexi hollered as Malachi hung up on her.

She needed to take the man at his word and presume he held her father captive. While her dad was capable of getting himself out of challenging situations, Malachi had already killed four men of similar skill level. He'd never abducted any of them before. What did the change in tactics mean? Was her dad the target this whole time? He'd kicked the idea around. It relegated four dead men, an injured fifth, and a traumatized Emily to the status of collateral damage in some sick, private war.

Lexi grabbed her dad's laptop out of her travel bag. After retiring from the Army, he spent eight years working for a company called Patriot Security. Toward the end of his tenure, they gave him a laptop with tools designed and approved by former military red teamers. Her dad didn't understand how to use most of the machine's more interesting—and often illicit—capabilities, but Lexi did, and she brought it just in case shit hit the fan. She fired the heavy machine up and logged in.

A quick search for the phone number Malachi called her from showed the device in an offline status. Probably a burner, and he might have chucked it out the window. The background noise on the call made it sound like he was driving. He could have been heading to or away from wherever the sick bastard stashed her father. Malachi's cell pinged a few towers starting just north of Aberdeen and continuing southwest toward Belcamp.

Harford County was a huge expanse of territory, much of it rural. Lexi couldn't even eliminate Aberdeen Proving Ground. Malachi could have flashed a fake ID to gain access to the base. It would certainly complicate search and rescue efforts. If he headed away from wherever her dad remained, it still left a lot of territory even without considering APG. By square footage, the largest area was Susquehanna State Park. An asshole like Malachi could have left her father tied to any of a million trees. He'd be impossible to find even if he were actually there.

Lexi's phone buzzed. She hoped for something from her dad, but it was a text from Kim. She set her phone down without reading it. While she wanted to go back to the apartment, this was not the time for roommate drama. Lexi pondered other ways to find Malachi. She could use the laptop to search traffic cameras and EZPass usage, but she'd be guessing. The tower data didn't provide precise enough location data to say Malachi drove along a certain stretch of road at some exact time. Her dad's phone was off, and its last communication was with a tower north of Aberdeen.

This still left way too much ground to cover. The state park. Any industrial complex. An abandoned farm. A run-down house rented for just such an occasion. Malachi could have left her father anywhere. Lexi considered calling the county cops, but what would she tell them? "Hi, I think my dad has been kidnapped, but I don't know where. Maybe Someplace in the northern half of your county." Saying it out loud made it sound even more ridiculous.

Lacking a better idea, Lexi knocked on her grandfather's bedroom door. He answered a moment later, and she apprised him of the situation. "Should I call the sheriff's office?"

The old man shook his head. "And tell them what? The son of a bitch could have come from Cecil County and called you when he did just to lead us on a wild goose chase."

She hadn't considered this angle. Considering what she knew of Malachi, it was possible. "What do we do, Grandpa?"

"Not much we can."

"I don't want to sit here and do nothing."

"You're young," he said. "When I was your age, I always wanted to rush into something, beat somebody's ass, and call it a day. It's not always possible. Sometimes, as much as it sucks, you gotta wait for more intel and a better opportunity."

Lexi sighed and pounded her fist into her open palm. "I hate this."

"Me, too."

"Dad could really use our help."

Her grandfather nodded. "Once we know more, we'll do what we can. When we drove off after him to the county estate up north, we knew where he was going. Here, we're clueless."

"But he—"

"He can take care of himself. If he was the target of this whole shitshow, he's going to be kept alive for something. Your dad will find a way out."

Lexi fought the urge to sprint to her car and drive into Harford County. Her grandfather was right. There were a ton of unknowns, too much ground to cover, and her dad remained a capable operator who would seize the opportunity to get away—or kill Malachi—should a chance present itself. "I hope you're right," she whispered.

41

MALACHI ARRIVED BACK AT THE STATE PARK.

Sure enough, John Tyler remained where the Israeli left him. The man lay flat on his back in the grass, one arm at his side and the other above his head. His eyes remained closed. Malachi nudged him with his boot, but Tyler didn't stir. If this were a normal job, Malachi would have executed him already. Pazir wanted to watch him suffer, however, and for the money the man was paying, he could get what he wanted.

Malachi frowned at the unconscious man and gave him a harder kick. A vest. Smart but ultimately pointless. Malachi removed Tyler's jacket, undid the vest, and tossed it aside. He put the man's coat back on. Temperatures would drop overnight, and he didn't want to come back in the morning to find his adversary dead from exposure. To be sure Tyler survived the elements, Malachi retrieved a blanket from the trunk and tossed it atop his supine foe. "I'll kill you soldier to soldier," he whispered, "man to man."

He returned to his car and retrieved two large boxes of gear. Pazir wanted to watch the events, and Malachi made sure he would be able to. He affixed spikes to five posts and shoved them into the ground. They were spaced about evenly apart in a wide circle covering the clearing where Tyler lay. A few small trees would obstruct some of the view depending on where the combatants moved, but Malachi could only control so much.

Once he was confident the posts wouldn't move, Malachi screwed a digital video camera in place atop each one. He connected them all to a mobile hotspot and made sure they could transmit by sending still photos to his phone. Everything worked as expected. Malachi set the timers for the morning. One critical piece remained—securing John Tyler.

Malachi fetched a second syringe from the car. His brief trip to Sinai Hospital had been fruitful. Not only did he eliminate Clarence, but he'd been able to pocket a few vials of useful drugs. He didn't know the interval before Tyler would need a second dose. Giving him too much might kill him. Malachi injected the unconscious man again, this time with two-thirds of the needle's contents. Next, he used a length of rope to secure Tyler's ankle to a tree. Even if he came to before the festivities got underway, he wouldn't be able to escape. Malachi knew how to tie a good knot.

"I'll be back for you in the morning," he leaned down and whispered to Tyler. The park remained closed, and they were about five hundred yards from the closest parking lot. The odds of discovery were so close to zero as to be nonexistent. Tomorrow morning, Malachi would indulge in a final decadent American breakfast, prepare himself for combat, return to the park, and kill John Tyler slowly for an audience of one.

Pazir would be pleased . . . for a little while at least. Then, Malachi would come for him, too, and the money he got for murdering a few retired soldiers would be a pittance to the funds he could access following the trafficker's demise. Malachi whistled a happy tune as he headed back to his BMW.

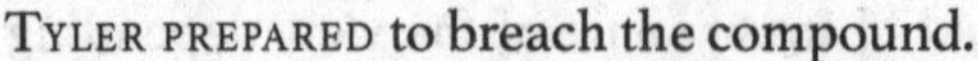

TYLER PREPARED to breach the compound.

The team spent hours going over schematics, aerial photos from drones, and the intel they'd cobbled together from people who spent time there. Fred Flanker vouched for his source, but he always did. Human intelligence was a risky game, yet the CIA man never handed over any incorrect information. Just ask him. They'd rolled up in three Hummers, shot the pair of guards at the gate, prevented the dying men from raising an alarm, and now stood ready to take out another trafficker and Taliban supporter.

A battering ram knocked the ornate doors open. The harsh sun glinted off marble floors as Tyler padded into the room. He went left and carried an automatic shotgun. A mercenary popped out of the kitchen, and Tyler blasted him in the chest. Gunfire erupted in the large foyer as enemy combatants flooded the area.

On some level, Tyler knew he was dreaming. His unit raided a compound much like this one—several, in fact—but events never unfolded quite like this. A bullet slammed into Tyler's midsection. His vest soaked it up, but the impact still knocked him flat. Giovanni Orlando stepped in front of him and took out the shooter only to get dropped by a burst of automatic gunfire. He collapsed beside Tyler, and his dead eyes stared straight ahead.

He proved to be the only casualty, however. Tyler and his unit mates cleared the rest of the area. The trafficker himself sat in a large, lavish bedroom. A door hung open nearby, revealing a golden toilet. Two young women whose bodies showed clear signs of mistreatment and abuse were chained to the bed. A closed door led to somewhere else in the house. Despite being hopelessly outnumbered and outgunned, the Afghan criminal raised a pistol and caught about sixty rounds for his troubles. His lifeless body crumpled to the soft carpet beside his luxurious chair.

While a few people worked to free the captives, Tyler moved on to the other door. He got it open and walked inside. The area remained gloomy, so he used his flashlight to see better. It could have been a large closet or small bedroom. The walls were bare of shelves, racks, or adornments. A few steel posts held two sets of chains. Lexi and Sara Morrison were bound to the wall, bruises all over them, gags in their mouths, and their eyes pleading for help.

"You couldn't save us," the body of Disney said. The wounds to his neck and upper legs still leaked blood.

"You couldn't even keep a maniac away from me," Lexi said. The gag was gone from her mouth, and her eyes bored into Tyler's.

"Some knight-errant," Sara scoffed. "You can't even protect the people you love. What kind of man are you?"

The corpse of Orlando jabbed a finger at Tyler's chest. "She has a point, Tippy. Answer her question! What kind of man are you?"

Tyler gasped as he woke up. Sleep paralysis held him fast. He wanted to sit up, but his body wouldn't cooperate. After a moment, his breathing slowed, and he convinced himself he was awake. The dead talking and the women in his life accusing him never happened. This marked the second dream where he knew he was asleep but still had to watch events unfold in a way they never had in reality. When Malachi and his benefactor were dead, Tyler would sit down for a couple sessions at the easel. Maybe he'd even check in with the doctor who first turned him on to the program.

In the meantime, he realized two things about his predicament. First, he lay on the ground outside, and it was chilly. A blanket half covered him, and he pulled it over his torso. Second, a rope bound him to a tree via his right ankle.

Malachi. Tyler remembered coming to Susquehanna State Park. He staked out a good position. At some point, he heard two other people arrive in a car. Veronica Fitzgerald ran past him a few minutes later. Then, something bit into his neck, and he remembered nothing else.

Malachi wouldn't leave him here to die. The man would be coming back. And Tyler resolved to be ready for him.

42

———

Tyler took a few deep breaths to clear the grogginess.

Whatever Malachi drugged him with still left him feeling sluggish. It felt like he took strong cold medicine before bed and then didn't get much sleep. While the fog lifted, his fingers poked and prodded the knot around his ankle. Malachi probably thought he was clever. He'd done well, but Tyler recognized it right away—a figure eight follow-through loop. It might hold many people in place.

Not the son of a retired Navy master chief.

Tyler had never been much for boats or sailing because of seasickness, but he'd known his way around popular nautical knots since he was a child. His father made sure of it. Even though Tyler himself rarely took to the water, knowing how to tie and untie ropes proved useful many times over the years. It did again this morning. He slipped his restraints in a few seconds, sat up, and rubbed his lower leg to get the blood flowing again.

Malachi left him in a small clearing with a few trees nearby and a bunch more all around. Five posts ringed the area, each with a camera mounted on top. He must be filming for his boss's benefit. Tyler wondered if any of the devices currently transmitted. None displayed any lights, but he knew a lot of the small, modern cameras didn't always give a clear indication they were recording.

His vest, phone, gun, and knife were gone. No surprises there. Tyler checked his watch—6:09 AM. He rose to unsteady feet and spent a few seconds clearing the cobwebs and getting his balance. Once he felt confident he wouldn't faceplant after a few steps, Tyler inspected the closest camera. A message displayed on its tiny screen. *Transmission set to begin at 8:00:00.* About an hour and fifty minutes. Malachi must have expected Tyler to remain unconscious the whole time . . . or at least not be able to get free if he woke early.

When he came last night, Tyler remembered seeing a small house. He didn't know his current position relative to the parking lot and trees of the prior evening. When he looked around, he spotted the structure peeking out from between two large trunks in the distance. Confident no one kept an eye on his position or movements, Tyler headed toward the building.

A sign above the door proclaimed *PARK RANGER*, and a smaller one in the main window advised the house would be closed for the foreseeable future while the park underwent renovations. The knob barely budged when he tried it. Thankfully, a large window dominated the top part of the door. Tyler didn't see any obvious sensors, so he grabbed a sturdy fallen branch nearby and smashed the glass. Another sweep cleared any remaining shards, and he reached inside to unlock the door.

He turned the knob and walked inside. No alarm wailed at his entry. He didn't spot any sensors on the interior, nor was there any kind of control box mounted on a wall. Despite the broken window, Tyler closed the door behind himself. He hustled down the hall, found a restroom, and took care of some very necessary business. The fridge was his next stop. The smell when he opened the door wrinkled his nose. Perishables must have lived up to their designation. Tyler grabbed a bottle of water from the bottom shelf and chugged it. It was perfectly cold. He plucked another and did the same. If he downed another one or two, peeing again would help clear the drugs from his system.

His stomach grumbled now, so he poked around the kitchen. There was no pantry, so Tyler opened cabinet doors until he found a jar of mixed nuts. About two-thirds of the contents remained. Tyler scooped handfuls into his mouth as he pondered what he might do until Malachi arrived. Running wasn't an option. Malachi would simply initiate a confrontation again, and he might abduct or hurt someone Tyler cared about to make it happen. Their one and only showdown needed to happen today.

Malachi was a seasoned operator . . . a former soldier and member of two elite international intelligence forces. Flanker's file pegged him for forty. Twelve years Tyler's junior and trained at least as well. It would be a tough battle. Much as he didn't want to admit it, Tyler figured he was the underdog. He could still win. A year ago, cartel enforcer Orlan Osario enjoyed every physical advantage possible, and he needed to be scraped off the walls of a processing facility by the end. Experience and treachery counted for a lot.

But would they be enough?

Tyler crunched some more mixed nuts. They were approaching the end of their freshness, but he would have eaten almost anything not rotten or molding. As he continued snacking, he explored the rest of the house. It was bigger inside than it looked from the exterior. The place was a single story with no basement and the lone bedroom. The closet didn't hold many clothes, and half of them were uniforms. Tyler wondered if anyone lived here while the park was open, or if the cottage served as a place to rest and refuel for rangers and other staff pulling long hours.

Near the bedroom and bathroom, he found a standing gun cabinet next to the stackable washer and dryer. He'd seen similar models before. It could have a shelf or two for pistols, but the height suggested rifles and shotguns. Tyler would be fine with either. Unfortunately, its electronic lock was engaged and hard to bypass with no tools. Even though the building itself lacked an alarm, the same may not be true about the gun safe. Tyler didn't need county deputies swarming the place.

Maybe he could find something else to help even the odds. He moved back through the interior. The kitchen held nothing of interest save a basic knife block. The spacious living room ended in a curtained glass door to the outside and one other which led somewhere else. It wasn't locked. Tyler found a storeroom inside. Here, the house resident or a contractor working at the park could find all manners of supplies to keep operations going.

Ropes hung from hooks along the left wall. There was the usual assortment of yard and garden tools. Tyler imagined braining Malachi with a shovel would be very satisfying but impractical. Metal spikes with circles at the top for yard signs lay on a work table. Tyler picked one up. It was light and sturdy, and the point was sharp enough to puncture hard Maryland soil . . . or the skin of an Israeli assassin.

Two stacks of cinder blocks stood against the back wall. Another table held fishing equipment on one end and yard tools like a gas-powered edger at the other. Tyler pulled the choke cord, and the edger fired up with a cloud of smoke. At least it worked. He cut the power. Ideas turned over in Tyler's mind. This room offered him plenty of ways to even the odds against Malachi and possibly seize the advantage if things went well. He looked at his watch again. Six-twenty-five. He had just over ninety minutes presuming Malachi didn't arrive early.

Might as well get started.

43

Malachi enjoyed a nice breakfast at the hotel.

He hoped it wouldn't be his last. If so, he planned to enjoy it. A perfectly toasted bagel to go along with steak, eggs, orange juice, and coffee. People needed to make time for the finer things in life. It was one of the reasons he retired from Shin Bet. He enjoyed the work—especially the violence— and the pay was good, but Malachi knew he could make more working freelance. The disadvantage came in the form of clients like Pazir, but the Israeli had a plan to deal with the wealthy trafficker.

Malachi finished breakfast and took a shower. Once out, he went through an elaborate stretching routine. As he aged through his thirties, he realized getting loose got harder every year. Soon, he would face his toughest test in quite a while. John Tyler, even at fifty-two, represented a significant challenge. The man was disciplined and well-trained, and while age takes a little from everyone, he remained quick. Understanding of movement and combat made up for any loss of speed.

Against most opponents, at least.

Once he felt limber, Malachi proceeded through some kicking and punching routines. He'd seen how Tyler fought. The older man favored defense in both encounters, but when he went on offense, his strikes were quick, hard, and designed to injure. Malachi found this a perk of fighting soldiers and trained operators. They didn't waste time. There was no dancing around. No flashy kicks. Just a series of attacks meant to wound, incapacitate, or kill.

Malachi got dressed and headed to the hotel's business center. He typed a document in Word, confirming a few facts from notes on his phone as he went. When he finished, he printed the single page, deleted his work, and signed out of the guest account. He got an envelope from a happy blonde at the front desk, folded the sheet, and placed it inside. Malachi returned to his room, packed his bag, and rode the elevator down to the lobby. He put the suitcase in the BMW's trunk and the envelope in the glove compartment.

As he drove, he realized he would arrive a few minutes late. No matter. The breakfast, shower, warm up, and final preparations were all worth it. At a traffic light, Malachi used an app to connect to the cameras and update the timer. He texted Pazir and informed the man of the late start. His benefactor sent an uncharitable reply. Malachi snorted and shook his head.

One way or another, Pazir Khayal was not going back to Afghanistan.

By now, Tyler might have come to. The second dose had been a guess. If the man were awake, he'd be tied to a tree. Malachi wondered if Tyler managed to free himself. What would he do? Would he run? No. Five of his friends were dead, and Malachi proved he could get to Alexis. Tyler would want to end this. Malachi smiled as he neared the park. If John Tyler punched his ticket today, so be it. At least he would go out clean and well fed.

The BMW surged through a yellow light. The sign telling drivers Susquehanna State Park lay five miles away zoomed past on the right.

THE SUPPLY ROOM held everything Tyler needed to seize the advantage against Malachi. Now, everything depended on making it all work.

Malachi left him in the clearing for a reason. He'd looked into the area and figured it was the best place to set up cameras for his benefactor to watch. Tyler was happy to oblige him by starting their fight there, but he wouldn't keep it there. He wondered if Malachi would grab a camera before following if Tyler moved away from the filming circle. A glance at his watch told him they would find out soon enough.

About a hundred yards beyond where he woke up, Tyler rigged a tripwire between two trees. He used a length of the fishing line and rubbed it in dirt to cut down on any sheen and make it blend in with the forest. When activated—and presuming Tyler rigged everything correctly—four things would happen. One rope would yank the edger's ripcord and fire up the motor. A distraction. Two yard sign spikes drilled through short lengths of wood for stability would swing down from the far tree. From the file, Tyler knew Malachi stood two inches taller, so he set one to swing at groin height and the other at the chest.

Even with the wood, they were unstable and might not descend with the sharp end toward their target. This was why Tyler finished preparing the ultimate trap. He'd wrapped leaves around and through a cinder block and now configured it to swing down from the near oak. This was the highest he'd been up a tree since he was a teenager. The cinder block should hit Malachi in the head. If the Israeli managed to avoid the two stakes, the concrete block should get him.

If the weapons went oh-for-three, Tyler needed to hope the collective distraction gave him the opening to kill his adversary.

He secured the rope with a better knot than Malachi tied around his ankle. Normally, Tyler would want to test his contraptions, but time ran short. It was seven-fifty-five when his feet landed on solid ground again. He jogged back to the small house, peed to try and clear more drugs from his system, and chugged a fresh bottle of water. While he still felt a little tired, the grogginess was gone. Tyler returned to the clearing and checked the nearest camera. Malachi must have updated the timer remotely. They were now set to start at ten after eight.

Even though carrying everything from the house—two trips' worth—climbing trees, and setting it all up gave him a workout, Tyler stretched to ensure his muscles were loose. He already wondered if he could take Malachi. A cramp or strain would give the Israeli a clear advantage. At five after, Tyler sat down where Malachi left him. He set the rope over his leg. It would maintain the illusion from a distance, at least. If Malachi got close enough to check, he would find out quickly.

Then, he waited.

AFTER A NIGHT OF FITFUL SLEEP, LEXI TRIED TO LOCATE HER dad again. Her grandfather hadn't heard anything. She checked his phone again. No change since last evening. It still didn't provide a location she could use. It was time to make some calls, then. At almost eight, the shop would be about to open. Either Smitty or Ortiz would be there. The latter answered the phone. "Have you heard from my dad recently?" Lexi asked before he finished the greeting.

"Lexi? I saw him yesterday before I left."

"He didn't say where he was going?"

"Not to me. I think your dad's involved in something, but he doesn't want to cut me in on it." He paused a beat. "How much do you know?"

"All of it, I think," Lexi said.

"Okay. Your father pretty much brought me up to speed. I got the feeling he was going after whoever had been killing his friends. When I offered to help, he turned me down and sent me home."

"You didn't think to stay in the area and follow him?"

"I did, actually," Ortiz said, his tone defensive. "I thought about it. Your dad is a tough man to follow. Even if I succeeded, what if the guy he's after spotted me? We don't know what would have happened."

"Yeah. You're right." Lexi sighed. "Sorry. I wasn't trying to—"

"Don't worry about it. If you hear anything, let me know, and I'll help."

"Thanks, Ortiz." Lexi ended the call and tried Sara Morrison's cell. No answer. She was probably in some secret room at the Pentagon. Lexi tried the office next, and the receptionist connected her. "I'm surprised you're not in a meeting."

"I have one soon enough," Sara said. "What's going on? Is your father all right?"

"I don't know. Are you aware of what he's caught up in?"

"I am . . . though not because he told me very much." There was an edge to her voice like she was annoyed Tyler hadn't confided in her. "I learned what happened. Your dad must have felt terrible losing friends like that."

"He did," Lexi acknowledged. "I think he figured out who the guy was. I don't know what happened, but I think my dad went after him, and now I can't find him."

"You've checked his phone?"

"No current location. It last hit a tower in Harford County, but even if he's still up there, it's way too big an area to go into blind."

"I wish I could help you, Lexi. I haven't talked to your dad in a few days. Whatever he was dealing with and working on consumed his time and probably most of his thoughts. Are you all right? No one came after you?"

"I'm just worried," Lexi said. She didn't need to tell Sara about the botched kidnapping at the apartment. "Whoever this guy is, he must be really good."

"So is your father," Sara pointed out.

"And so were the men who died." Lexi took a deep breath

to cover a sudden burst of emotion. "I'm just concerned about him." Her voice cracked a little, but she couldn't help it.

"Do you want me to call someone?" Sara asked. "I have a pretty large Rolodex. I'm sure I know someone who knows somebody else in Harford County."

"I guess, yeah." Lexi wiped her eyes. "Thanks, Sara."

"Anytime. Let me know if you hear anything."

"I will." Lexi set her phone down. She didn't know what Sara's contact would be able to do . . . if anything. The area covered by the last cell tower was a lot to search. Residential neighborhoods. Farms. A state park.

Lexi grabbed her pistol and keys. Might as well get started.

~

TIRES CRUNCHED over gravel somewhere behind Tyler. He heard the distinctive sound of a BMW inline-six before the engine cut off. Tyler's watch told him the time was 8:08. Malachi's cameras were about to kick on. They would be transmitting to his benefactor, and Tyler wondered if anyone could trace the communications. Encrypting things was easy enough these days, and many unsavory people long ago learned the benefits. Still, if he took out Malachi, it would be one avenue to pursue.

As footsteps grew closer, Tyler stretched and acted like he'd recently come to. Little advantages mattered when combatants were evenly matched. "We meet at last," an Israeli-accented voice said. Tyler turned his head, and Malachi Golan walked into the ring of cameras. He looked like his photos in Flanker's file. A little taller than Tyler, he moved with the confident ease of a man who knew many ways to kill without breaking a sweat. Malachi kept himself in good shape except for the outline of a paunch showing through his sweater. "Our association will be short, but you should know I respect you as a soldier and a fighter."

"You drug all the people you respect?" Tyler said.

Malachi smiled. "A necessity of the situation." He kept his gaze on Tyler while moving to one of the cameras, averting his eyes only long enough to check its screen. "Smile. Someone is watching." Tyler held up his middle finger. "How very American."

"Yee-haw."

Malachi cracked his knuckles and approached slowly. Tyler positioned his legs so the man wouldn't get a clear look at the rope. "Do you want to know why you're going to die today?"

"I'm more curious why you went after so many good men," Tyler said. "Plus my daughter."

"I was told to make you suffer, and the compensation was great." Malachi shrugged. "I am not a man who only gives half the effort. Five of your friends are dead." He still didn't know about Musa. If Tyler survived today, he hoped to use this to his advantage. "A year ago, you went after a man who traffics in young women."

"Durrani. Let's call them girls because almost all of them are underage."

"If you wish," Malachi said, waving a hand. "Before you killed him, he sent a message to a group of his friends. It took a while, but one of them picked up the cause and decided to take you out."

"You're an Israeli." Malachi bobbed his head. "I'm going to assume most of Durrani's friends were Arabs like him. The Seven Days War would be before your time. Still, someone must be paying you really well."

"The money certainly helps." Malachi remained out of striking distance, though he moved in an arc in front of Tyler. "I am glad you did not run."

"You've done enough damage," Tyler said. "We're ending this today." Tyler stood. A small smile flashed across Malachi's lips. He probably knew the knot was gone. While the Israeli spread his feet and raised his fists, Tyler struck. Two punches and a kick got turned away, but a right elbow caught Malachi in the cheek. He spun laterally, causing Tyler's follow-up jab to miss, and landed a punch under Tyler's ribs on the right side. Both men backed off and circled one another.

"Here I thought you favored defense," Malachi said.

"American sports. Sometimes, the best defense is a good offense."

Though a few young trees interrupted it, the area inside the cameras remained open. The shape was roughly an oval, with about as much room as a baseball diamond. Malachi came forward, and Tyler fell into a defensive rhythm. He backed toward one of the maples, hoping to use it to screen Malachi's vision and get the advantage. The Israeli proved too smart, edging rearward and wagging his finger. It would have worked against a lesser foe.

The morning breeze felt cool against the sweat on Tyler's neck. Malachi returned to offense. Tyler blunted his punches and went for a couple low kicks. Malachi blocked them, but he bent his knees to get down, making him shorter. Tyler drove his forehead between Malachi's eyes. The Israeli stumbled backwards. Tyler shook the cobwebs free for a second. When he followed up, Malachi remained on his heels but didn't go down. A thin line of blood ran down his nose, and his face twisted into a scowl. "You're better than your friends, at least," he said. Tyler shrugged. He wasn't going to take the bait. "The ones I killed barely even put up a fight."

"Should have come for me first. Your family could have buried you by now . . . if they still give a shit."

Malachi grunted and fired off three quick punches. Tyler

blocked each. He also deflected an elbow strike, but Malachi answered with a backhand which spun Tyler's head. Two hard punches landed home before Tyler brought both his arms down to knock another attack aside. He responded with a jab and cross of his own. Tyler grabbed for Malachi's hair to knee him in the face, but his foe slipped away.

Both men circled each other again, breathing harder this time. "If you want to pack it in, I'll understand," Tyler said. "Tell me who's writing your checks, and I'll kill you quickly."

"I don't think so." Malachi waded in again, this time leading with a few snap kicks. Tyler stayed out of range at first before blocking the third. His forearm deflected two left jabs. Malachi grabbed Tyler's wrist on the last one. The man's right arm snapped downward. Something silver fell into his hand, and he slashed toward Tyler, who managed to get free but not before the blade sliced him below the navel. He peeked through the tear in his shirt to see a gash already bleeding.

"Maybe you're the one who should pack it in," Malachi said.

Pain blazed along Tyler's midsection. He retreated a few steps. The stiletto didn't give Malachi much more reach, but it made any strike far more deadly. Tyler figured this would be a good opportunity to move things closer to the tripwire he'd set up earlier. Malachi called him a coward, but Tyler backpedaled steadily, leaving the area encircled by the cameras.

Veronica sipped coffee in her hotel room.

The cup shook in her hand. She set it down and let out a long, deep breath. Some maniac abducted her while she sat outside John Tyler's house. Tyler tried to warn her something was going on. A bad time to be around. She didn't listen. She wanted the story. Thankfully, her kidnapper ended up being more interested in Tyler, though the way the man eyed her a few times gave her the creeps. Then, he drove her to some state park. She ran, and the madman shifted his attention to Tyler.

Part of Veronica wanted to stay, and she realized now it was to get a resolution for her story. She would have been no help at trying to save Tyler. Instead, good sense prevailed, and she kept running. Eventually, she got far enough away to use her phone, call an Uber, and return to her rental car. The comfortable bed at her hotel did little to help her sleep. Closing her eyes just brought her abductor's face to mind, and then she would spend a few minutes wondering if Tyler were all right. He said he wouldn't show up to save her, yet there he was.

She hoped he'd managed to survive.

Regardless, she now felt conflicted. The public had a right to know Tyler's exploits. People could decide for themselves if they wanted vigilante justice when criminals acted outside the law. She knew Tyler went after those who harmed innocent people. He probably didn't see himself as a hero, and he probably wasn't one. Her readers could make the determination for themselves.

For the first time, however, she considered not revealing his identity. A nameless retired Green Beret didn't make for as good a story. The payday would be less lucrative, and her expenses mounted each day she spent in Maryland. Maybe she could sell the movie rights. Some Hollywood producer might decide to reboot the *Death Wish* franchise with her writing as the source. It would certainly make up for the diminished freelance payday she knew she'd be facing.

No, she decided she couldn't out Tyler in her story. It would be welcome news to the man himself and especially his daughter. Lexi basically handed Veronica the Sappony story. Maybe she was repaying that debt, as well. Regardless, the public would not learn the identity of John Tyler from her. She scrubbed it from her document and made sure to update her backups with the new copy.

MALACHI PROVED A WILLING PARTICIPANT. Despite the encounter heading away from his camera circle, the assassin followed Tyler, trying to work in some attacks as they moved. Tyler swatted away a punch, lunged forward, and clocked Malachi with a solid elbow across the face. It spun the Israeli's head and dropped him to one knee. Tyler snapped a kick toward his foe's face, but Malachi recovered enough to knock it aside. While Tyler regained balance, Malachi got back to vertical.

The chase was on again.

Tyler had two objectives—lure Malachi to the tripwire and not make it obvious what he was doing. The fishing line itself would be hard to spot. Tyler put enough dirt on it to get it to blend in. The tree canopy wouldn't let a lot of light through. Malachi would probably step on it. The trick for Tyler was not to make it apparent he stepped over something. Malachi needed to think a wounded adversary backed away to take the fight somewhere else or escape.

They passed the small house. Malachi tried to grab Tyler a few times, but it never worked. Each tried occasional attacks. "Where are you leading me?" Malachi wanted to know.

"Away from your cameras," Tyler said. "You want to take me on? Fine. We'll do it without your precious benefactor watching. Let the asshole wonder if he's getting his money's worth."

The fishing line stretched between two trees about 120 more feet behind Tyler. A small clearing lay past it . . . a plausible place to want to go. "He is."

"Want to go back and get a camera? Maybe I'll even be here when you return."

Malachi snorted. "Once you're dead, it'll be easy enough to get proof."

Sixty feet.

Tyler's gut still burned. He needed stitches, and continuing to exert himself didn't help with blood loss. Malachi managed to strike the gash with a short jab, and even though the punch wasn't hard, it made Tyler's vision swim. Malachi knocked him flat with a sharp kick to the chest. As the Israeli surged forward with the stiletto blade held in front, Tyler bent his knees, letting Malachi run into his feet. With his strength flagging, Tyler pushed out with his legs as he twisted to the right. Malachi landed in a thorny bramble and bit off a few curses. His predicament allowed Tyler time to stand again.

He needed to get to the tripwire. If Malachi knocked him down again, he knew it would be over.

Forty feet remained. Tyler focused on his enemy. Malachi tried body blows, probably hoping to get lucky and hit the slash wound again. In full defense mode, Tyler turned them all aside. Thirty feet. "The clearing, then?" Malachi said, his eyes flicking over Tyler's left shoulder. "How'd you know it was here?"

"I didn't," Tyler said. "Just trying for somewhere you don't have the advantage."

"Well." Malachi sneered. "No matter where you go, I'll have the advantage."

Ten feet. Tyler blocked a punch, fired off a kick to get Malachi to back up a step, and headed for the clearing. His natural stride carried him over the fishing line. He slowed a few feet beyond. Malachi approached. His face twisted into a determined sneer. His hands were balled into fists. His movements were still loose and easy like he could do this all day.

The top of his left shoe hit the wire.

Malachi looked down. Off to the right, the gas-powered edger roared to life. Malachi turned to look for the noise. One spike descended. His eyes found it, and the Israeli twisted out of the way. The second followed right after, but the skilled man managed to avoid it, too, the cruel spike slipping a couple inches past him.

His mouth opened to say something when the cinder block smashed into his head.

It came from his five-o'clock and caught him above the right ear. Malachi crashed to the ground. The stiletto fell from his grip. Blood ran from a fresh wound in his scalp. He tried to push himself up to all fours but collapsed flat again. Tyler picked up the slender dagger. "Looking for this?" Malachi didn't respond. Tyler gave him a vicious slash across the shoulder blades, raising a line of crimson and eliciting a cry of pain. He kicked Malachi hard in the side, and the man rolled over onto his back.

Tyler slashed him again with the blade, and Malachi howled in agony. He still didn't try to stand. The blow from the cinder block must have rung his bell. Tyler stood over his fallen foe, raised the weapon, and used his body weight to drive the entire length of it into Malachi's gut just below the sternum. He rocked the blade back and forth, Malachi screaming the entire time, before finally pulling it out and standing. Blood poured from the latest and most grievous wound.

Finally, Malachi broke a sweat. Most of the color drained from his face. As he lay on the forest floor bleeding all over his sweater and into the grass, he didn't look very threatening. Most people didn't in their final moments. This was Tyler's chance to get information from his foe, and he meant to do it.

46

———

Tyler watched as Malachi struggled to sit up, eventually giving up and remaining flat. "You cheated," he said, adding a chuckle which made him wince.

"Come on. You and I both know fair fights are for suckers and boxing matches."

The dying man bobbed his head. "You must have . . . been up early."

"Little after six," Tyler said. "I found the house, and it had everything I needed to lay a trap for you."

"For a man . . . without a degree, I have to . . . say you're . . . pretty cunning and intelligent. More than I . . . gave you credit for."

"You might be younger than me. You're probably stronger and faster, and I might even admit you're a little better hand-to-hand." Tyler tapped the side of his head with his index finger. "What you'll never be is smarter."

"Well played," Malachi croaked.

"You don't have time for compliments. Tell me who's writing your checks."

Malachi coughed, and blood rimmed his lips. "Why? I'm already . . . dying."

"True. If I called an ambulance, however, they might get here in time. Two hospitals are nearby." Tyler had no idea if the last part was true. Malachi probably didn't, either. He wouldn't have planned on getting hurt enough to drive to the ER afterwards.

"Fine." Malachi slid a phone out of his pocket. His fingers couldn't hold on to it, and it came to rest beside his hip. "Look in the . . . glove box." His other hand fished a set of keys out of the left front pocket of his pants. "Clean title. Keep the . . . car if you want. All you . . . need to know is . . . in there. In an envelope." His speech dissolved into coughing again. Blood continued to run from the wound below his chest. Tyler hoped moving the stiletto would nick the descending aorta. The results made him think he'd been successful.

"Good. I won't thank you all things considered."

"Ambulance?" Malachi croaked.

"You went after my daughter," Tyler said. "Twice. Piss off. I hope your death is agonizing." Tyler collected Malachi's phone and keys. The Israeli cupped a weak hand around his ankle before he could walk away.

"Soldier to soldier . . . I wouldn't make you . . . suffer."

Tyler shrugged. "You're talking about honor. Don't. You don't deserve it. You lost the right to call yourself a soldier when you went after non-combatants. Those men hadn't sniffed combat in years, and you tried to abduct my daughter twice."

"I killed five . . . of your friends. None suffered."

"Four." Malachi's brows arched long enough to convey confusion before knitting in pain again. "Musa Sadozai survived."

"I wondered. No . . . article about him."

"I talked to him recently." Malachi didn't answer. "I don't

know what else you did after you left Shin Bet, but you fell short of the mark on this job."

"You know about me," Malachi said.

"Have for a while," Tyler told him.

"How did . . . Musa survive?"

"The same way I did. He's smarter than you, too. It's a good thing you're dying because you're out of your depth."

"So much talk," Malachi said in a hoarse whisper. Blood bubbled in his mouth as he spoke. "Typical . . . American. Admit it, John Tyler. I am . . . a better man . . . than you."

"For as long as you have left, maybe you are." Malachi probably wouldn't survive the next five minutes and definitely not the next ten. Tyler shrugged. "I guess I'll console myself with the knowledge I'll outlive you." Tyler jerked his leg free from Malachi's slack grip and headed away from the dying man.

ON HIS WAY BACK, Tyler approached the original clearing carefully. He didn't want any of the cameras to pick up his movement. The trees on one side allowed him to approach two cameras without any of the other devices being able to see him. Or so he hoped at least. Once they were all down, Tyler powered them off and tossed everything into the nearest trash can. He made his way farther along.

An older BMW 5 Series sat as the lone car in the parking lot.

It was a beautiful dark blue, and while the paint had accrued a few nicks and scratches over time, the car looked really good considering it must have been twenty years old. Tyler unlocked the trunk first. A roller bag took up much of the real estate on the right. Two cardboard boxes filled the rest of the space. One contained Lexi's Glock, Tyler's vest, knife, gun, and his phone—the latter in a shielded bag. The other held a collection of assorted supplies.

Tyler took both into the car. He set them on the tan leather seat and opened the glove compartment. As Malachi promised, an envelope lay inside above the owner's manual folder, and Malachi's wallet. Tyler ripped open the envelope and read the paper inside.

John Tyler,

If you're reading this, you defeated me. Congratulations.

The first thing I want to let you know is this: it was never personal. It probably felt like it was to you, and I understand. I accepted a nice payday and what you Americans would call a fat expense account to ensure you suffered. This took the form of killing several of your friends from the Army and going after your daughter. I really don't like civilians being used as pawns in warfare, and I think I let the money help me lose sight of this.

The man who paid me is Pazir Ghayal. You've probably never heard of him, but he's heard of you. You took down a friend of his. Like Pazir, this dead man was a trafficker in things like drugs and young girls. It's all illicit, and it's all terrible. There's a small piece of paper behind this one. It's Pazir's phone number and the address where he's staying. I'm sure you'll put both to good use.

Malachi Golan

He was right—Tyler didn't know the name. He knew the type, however, and Pazir being a friend of Farzaad Durrani meant he needed to share the dead man's fate. Tyler knew exactly who he wanted to bring in on this. First, however, Malachi's benefactor would be expecting an update. Tyler used the dead Israeli's phone to text the lone contact on the list. He reviewed the conversation to learn Malachi's phrasing and syntax.

It is done.

What happened to the video?

> Tyler is a coward and fled. I chased him
> down and killed him.

Excellent. I hope he suffered greatly.

> I made sure he did. His cries were music to
> my ears.

I wish I could have heard them. Do you have
a photo? I want to see proof.

"Shit," Tyler muttered. He looked through the supply box and found a selfie stick. Maybe he could use it to help stage a couple pictures. Tyler got out of the car. The slash across his gut had mostly stopped bleeding, but there was enough crimson on his stomach to spread over his face and throat. Tyler backed up to the grass, lay flat, and held the stick out. He made sure his hand and arm weren't in the shot, closed his eyes, and snapped a photo.

There. Proof of death. He attached the photo, unsure if it would convince Pazir. Tyler didn't think it would count among his best works, but he also knew it was staged. Pazir texted back a few seconds later.

I suppose it is acceptable. I hoped for more blood and proof his last moments were miserable.

Tyler rolled his eyes and replied.

> You want me to bring his head?

Yes.

> Very well. It will be done.

Excellent. Join me when it's finished and we
can celebrate.

"I'll join you, all right," Tyler said to the empty cabin. "Doubt there will be a lot of celebrating." He checked the mirrors. No one approached. With the park closed, the odds of anyone else coming here were low, but Tyler didn't want to linger in case someone like a project manager popped by to see how things were going. He drove away from the park, found a nearby McDonald's, and pulled into an empty spot there.

It was time to bring in reinforcements.

47

―――――

Tyler's first call was to Lexi. "I'm all right," he said when she picked up.

"Oh, my god! I'm so happy to hear your voice. What happened?"

"Long story. I'll tell you more when it's done. I'm going to call a couple friends and take care of one final thing. See you later today."

"You'd better."

Tyler ended the call and dialed Fred Flanker next. He never knew whether the man was on a secure line or not, so he kept things general. "I dealt with the middle manager. Now, we need to talk to the boss."

"You want to come by the coffee shop?" Flanker asked.

"No time," Tyler said. "I'm already an hour from there, and his . . . office is another hour still. I'll send you the address. You'll need to come as soon as you can."

"I will."

"Make sure you bring enough supplies. We definitely want to close the deal."

Flanker chuckled. "Understood." He rang off. Tyler's third call went to Musa Sadozai.

"I know you're on light duty, but I'm hoping you can lend a hand."

"Name it," Musa said.

"The guy we were dealing with isn't with the company anymore." Might as well keep things non-specific. If the various police agencies across the country ever got their shit together and connected Malachi's actions, a large investigation—including the FBI—would be the result. "We need to go talk to his boss."

"You know where the main office is?"

"I do. I'll send you the address. Our colleague Freddy is going to meet us there."

"Good. Haven't worked with him in a while."

"It's about an hour from my current location. Probably about the same for you."

"I'll leave in a few minutes."

"Bring a sewing kit with you," Tyler said, hoping Musa remembered the reference. "I have a hole in my sweater."

"You all right?" Musa wanted to know.

"I'll be better once the hole is fixed. See you soon." Tyler pressed the red button and ended the call. He took the boxes —one of which was now empty—back to the trunk. On the left side, Velcroed to the carpeting, was a white first aid kit. Tyler didn't know if anything inside was still good, but he pried it loose and carried it into the cabin. The contents were pretty basic. A few alcohol swabs, bandages, gauze, medical tape, and a bottle of peroxide. Tyler pulled his ruined sweater up, opened the bottle, and poured liquid over his slash wound.

It bubbled and burned right away, and he unleashed a string of curses profane enough to make his father the career sailor blush. Once the searing pain subsided, Tyler blotted the wound with gauze. The combination of peroxide and lingering blood stained it pink. The wound was about five inches long and below his navel. It didn't look deep enough to be truly problematic, but Tyler still wanted to get it stitched. He didn't need the injury hampering him when their small team went after Pazir and whatever short-lived assholes he brought with him.

~

TYLER GRIMACED and bit down on the towel as the needle pierced his skin again.

Musa arrived before Fred Flanker. Pazir's rental was in a gated community, so they couldn't simply drive in. Both Musa and Tyler scouted the area with Google Maps. Once Flanker arrived, they could put together a plan for getting past the guard and dealing with Pazir and his men. For now, Tyler sat still and let his friend work.

"Sorry, Tippy."

"Don't quit your day job," Tyler grumbled.

"I don't remember you being so whiny back in Afghanistan."

"Once you cross fifty, you're allowed to complain a lot more."

"I'll look forward to it in a couple years, then," Musa said with a chuckle. "You act like you've never been stitched up before."

"I've usually had a local anesthetic. First time in a while, too. I forgot how much they hurt." Between the first-aid kit already in the BMW and the one Musa brought, neither contained anything to dull the pain. At least Musa's came with the supplies needed to close the wound. Once Tyler was back home, he could get it checked out by his regular doctor or visit an urgent care place.

A few minutes later, Musa finished. "There. I have some Tylenol."

"I'll take them." Tyler picked up the bottle, shook out four pills, and downed them with a gulp of water.

"I think you're only supposed to take two," Musa pointed out.

"If you don't tell, I won't."

Flanker texted and informed them he would be there in twenty minutes. Tyler dropped a pin and sent their current location. They sat in the trees off to the side of Middle River Road in Shenks Ferry, Pennsylvania. Tyler never heard of the place before today, but the large homes with their massive yards impressed him. Pazir rented a place which backed to the Susquehanna River and sat on three acres. Distance to the nearest neighbor was always a consideration when you planned on shooting up the place.

From their spot in Musa's SUV, they could look between the trunks and branches to see the entrance to Shenks Landing, the community where Pazir's rented house stood. Tyler wondered how many clauses in a normal AirBnB contract would get violated when they raided the place. He wondered if the owners employed a security system, especially one with cameras. These probably should have crossed his mind before now.

Flanker arrived at the appointed time, easing his car to a stop just behind the BMW, which sat to the rear of the 4Runner's back bumper. All three men climbed out. Musa and Flanker shook hands. "What'd you bring us?" Tyler wanted to know.

"Lot of good stuff," the CIA man said. "Weapons, vests, balaclavas. The essentials."

"Good. We know where the property is. Considering houses around here go for well into the seven figures, we should assume there's a security system. It's a rental, so I don't know about privacy and video and all."

"Probably on the outside," Musa said. "Most people wouldn't expect to be filmed indoors even if it's technically someone else's house."

"I take it we're dealing with a gated community?" Flanker asked.

"Yes," Tyler said.

"All right. We kill the guy at the gate and keep going."

"We're not killing some security guard." Tyler frowned. "The guy's just doing his job. He doesn't know who Pazir is or how he's made his money. I think we can get past him without incident."

"How?" Musa said.

"I have Malachi's wallet," Tyler said. "He has a fake ID inside, and it's clear he was coming here to meet Pazir."

Musa crossed his arms. "Let me guess. I'm going to be Malachi."

"Neither of us look enough like him," Tyler said, his hand wave covering himself and Flanker. "We can hide in the back of your SUV. There's enough room, and the windows are dark."

"All right. Let's try it." Tyler tossed him the wallet. Musa opened it, looked at the ID, and rolled his eyes. "Michael Gordon?"

"You can sell it," Flanker said, clapping Musa on the shoulder. Musa grunted but climbed into the driver's seat of the 4Runner, wincing as he stepped up. He popped the hatch, and Tyler and Flanker hunkered down inside. With each man crouched into a ball, they both fit, but Tyler hoped this part of the plan didn't take long. Musa pulled away from the curb. A minute later, he slowed for the gate.

"Who are you here for?" the guy in the shack asked.

"Pazir Khayal," Musa said, losing his accent. "He's expecting me."

Tyler couldn't see what was happening, but the guard's response wasn't immediate. "You're Mister Gordon?"

"I am."

"I was told to expect a car."

"And I was told to expect competence at the gate." Tyler grinned at Musa's barb. The man didn't lose his cool often, but it was always amusing when he did.

"Sorry, sir," the guard said. "I'll need to search your vehicle."

48

IN THE DARKNESS OF THE REAR CABIN, TYLER FELT MORE THAN saw Flanker reach for his pistol. "We're not killing this guy," Tyler whispered.

"I don't think so," Musa said.

"It's our policy to—" the guard began, but Musa cut him off.

"It's your policy to annoy the people staying here? You know I'm coming, right? I'm on your list?" Musa paused, probably for the guard to confirm with a nod. Tyler wished he could see what went on. "I thought I would come in a car, as well. There was a problem with it, however, and I'm driving this instead. Mister Ghayal is expecting me, and I don't think he would want me to be needlessly delayed."

"Mister Ghayal is not a resident, sir," the sentry said. "He's renting the property owned by the Shaw family."

"This is a public road, right?"

"Sir?"

"A public road," Musa repeated. "Paid for by the residents of this city, county, and state."

"Yes."

"Then I decline your search on Fourth Amendment grounds. Where's your warrant and probable cause?"

"What if this guy calls the cops?" Flanker whispered.

"Musa probably has his real ID on him somewhere," Tyler said. "I think it would be fine."

"Community bylaws give us the right—"the guard began.

"Look," Musa broke in. "I didn't want to do this." Another pause. "I'm a cop working a case. Yes, my name is different."

"Are you undercover?"

"I am, Rodney, and I'd appreciate you not blowing it. Now, can you let me in?"

"Sure thing."

Metal gears ground and whirred. Musa drove forward a few seconds later. After proceeding a little farther, he made a right and then pulled off. "All clear."

Tyler toggled a lever at the top of the rear seat. The back folded flat, and he climbed from the rear, wincing as the new stitches stretched a little. Once he arranged himself, he put the back up again and sat behind the empty passenger's seat. Flanker did the same, taking the spot behind Musa. "I was ready to shoot him," the Agency man said.

"Good thing we found another way," Musa said. He pointed down the road to a large house on the left. It rose two stories from the grass. "Pazir is in there. We should presume he has a few men to guard him."

"Recent satellite photos show a boat docked at the pier," Flanker added. "It's a valid avenue of escape once the shit hits the fan inside."

"Musa, I know you're still on light duty," Tyler said. "How about you cover the rear? Make sure no one gets away. Flanker and I will go in the front."

"All right." Musa nodded. "Let's find a good spot to gear up. We should have vests and weapons for everyone." Musa ended up driving the other way down Middle River Road. There, far away from the Shaw estate, the three men each put bullet-resistant vests and balaclavas on. Tyler chose a Mossberg automatic shotgun to go with his reliable Sig. Flanker, favoring rate of fire, picked an M4 carbine. Musa chose another M4 and an M11 pistol to defend the back.

"Just like old times," Flanker said.

Tyler remembered his unpleasant dreams which distorted real missions the unit undertook. Flanker was right. They'd all done this before, and Pazir's hired goons wouldn't be as capable as Taliban operatives. "Lock and load," Tyler said. "Let's roll."

"How do you want to play the cameras?" Flanker asked once the trio finished setting up their earbuds and phones.

"It's doubtful anyone in the house can monitor the feeds," Tyler said, "especially if this is a frequent rental."

"They probably farm it out to an alarm company," Musa said. "Some are better than others. Most of them say they're watching in real time, but not all of them do."

"Let's avoid suspicion, then," Tyler said. "We don't want to run up and slash the tires right away in case someone's actually keeping an eye on the place. Let's see what we're looking at in terms of device setup." Flanker tugged on his balaclava. "We can try to hide our faces and not reveal the masks. Only so much we can do. Realistically, we're in and out in a few minutes. This might be a ritzy area, but we didn't pass a police station on the way in. Response can't be fast."

"All right," Flanker concurred. "Let's hit it. Musa, give a shout when you're in position."

"Roger that."

Tyler and Flanker approached from the front. Each

slipped their balaclavas off for the approach to the house in case of any passing traffic. They didn't see any. The rented house stood a good distance apart from its nearest neighbor. Between this and the suppressors on their pistols, Tyler didn't expect the trio to attract attention. Still, they couldn't be cavalier and presume they were invisible and inaudible.

A driveway about 200 feet long stretched from the main road. It ended in a circle in front of the house. Two Cadillac Escalades—one black, the other dark gray—sat on opposite sides of the circle. Tyler scanned the area for cameras and didn't see any. Light posts stood about fifteen feet apart up the length of the driveway. Any would have been a good place for an electric eye, but there were none.

"Doorbell cam," Flanker said as they walked between the Caddies. Tyler spotted it to the right of the main entrance. "I'll block it. You take care of the tires."

"On it," Tyler said. He watched as Flanker made sure not to look at the camera as he walked up the three steps onto the wraparound porch. Once there, he blocked the device with his body. The house was a large Victorian model with dark green siding. It was wide and deep, probably over three thousand square feet inside. The window sills and shutters all looked freshly painted in bright white. The only feature the property lacked was a garage.

Tyler used his knife to puncture two tires on each Escalade. He moved around the circle, getting the driver's side pair on one and the passenger's on the other. With Flanker still screening the electric eye, Tyler joined him on the porch. "How do you want to play this?" the CIA man asked.

"Is it locked?"

"Yeah."

"Pazir's expecting someone." Tyler shrugged. "The goon

squad might know what I look like, so you should ring the bell."

Flanker nodded and rapped on the red wood while Tyler moved to the opposite side of the entryway. Tyler put his balaclava back in place and holstered his pistol in lieu of the shotgun. Flanker also covered his face and kept his M11 in hand. The door opened a few seconds later. A large man took a half step out before Flanker shot him in the head. His body crumpled into the house. Tyler took a long lateral stride to his left, stepped over the massive corpse, and walked into the house with the Mossberg leading the way.

Another giant in an ill-fitting suit emerged from the kitchen. Alarm widened the man's eyes, and he'd barely started reaching under his tight jacket when Tyler shredded his chest with a load of double-ought buckshot. A door opened somewhere past the dead man. Tyler cleared the dining room and sprinted toward the sound. A third enormous goon dashed out the rear door and across the backyard. "Musa, we got a runner."

"Copy," Musa said. "I see him."

"First floor is clear," Flanker said.

Tyler looked around the kitchen. It was at least twice the size of his, packed with stainless steel appliances, and featured enough counter space to play shuffleboard. "Pazir has to know we're here." He emerged and joined Flanker in the massive living room. Plush carpeting muted their footsteps. "The Mossberg alone would give us away. Musa, you see any activity from the house?"

"Negative. Just the guy running. He's not very fast. Not even to the pier yet."

Flanker pointed to the stairs heading to the second floor. Tyler bobbed his head and followed. Six steps led to a landing. After turning 180 degrees, the pair took the remaining seven stairs to the upper level. Tyler thought he heard a muted report, and Musa confirmed the fleeing guard was dead a few seconds later. Flanker and Tyler emerged in the middle with doors on both sides. All were closed. Tyler pointed to himself and to the right. Flanker headed left. Tyler opened the first door he came to, which turned out to be a linen closet. The next was a bathroom. Behind the third at the end of the hall, an old fat man sat on the bed.

His hair was thin and white. The man's complexion put him as hailing from the Middle East. The room surrounding him was huge and mostly empty. He sat alone on the king bed. His right hand held a pistol but lay atop the mattress. Tyler slung the shotgun over his shoulder and replaced it with his Sig. "You must be Pazir."

"John Tyler," the man said. "You defeated Malachi."

"You should have hired someone more capable. Get your hands up where I can see them."

"What if I don't?"

"You should."

"I reiterate my question."

Tyler shot Pazir in his ample stomach. He let out an agonized wail and tumbled to the floor. The gun fell from his hand somewhere along the way and ended up a few feet past him. "I'm reiterating my answer," Tyler said. "This time with force. Where's your phone?" Pazir groaned a few times but didn't provide anything coherent. Flanker walked into the room. Tyler found Pazir's cell on the nightstand. He checked for recent outgoing calls, emails, and texts and found none. "This cycle of asking some other asshole to take care of me ends with you."

"Go . . . to hell," the older man croaked.

Tyler set the phone on the floor and put a bullet through the center. He walked back to the fallen trafficker. "I hope Durrani was worth it." Pazir glared but offered no response.

Tyler shot him once in the chest, then unslung the shotgun and blew the man's head apart. Flanker spat on the corpse.

"We need to go," Tyler said.

Flanker opened the top nightstand drawer. He pulled out a wrapped stack of bills. "I think we can spend a minute relieving this prick of his money."

"Not like he needs it anymore," Tyler agreed.

49

____

Lexi didn't know what to do.

She hated feeling indecisive. She inherited the ability to make decisions quickly—and a related disdain for those who didn't—from both her parents. Sitting around and wondering what to do wasn't like her. At least her dad was all right. He'd called and talked in generalities, but she inferred both Malachi and the man who funded his campaign were dead. Her father would be home soon.

Home. Lexi missed her apartment and friends, and it was the source of her indecision. Kim had reached out twice now, and Lexi still didn't answer. She stared at the two texts.

> Hey, it's been a few days, and I feel like we should talk about everything.

> Lexi, you're not normally so quiet. What's going on?

"What's going on?" Lexi repeated at a whisper. She wished she knew. The first text read like one of those dreaded "we need to talk" messages that came before a breakup. If Emily and Kim were going to give her the boot, they should just come out and do it. Say they want to move on. Be decisive. Lexi couldn't really blame them if they did. They'd both gotten hurt because of her. The militia gunman's actions on campus left Kim self-conscious about a small scar on her forehead. Now, Emily might not feel safe in an apartment they specifically chose because of the security features.

Despite being a little over a year shy of the drinking age, Lexi grabbed a beer from the fridge. It would be easy to blame her dad for all this. The asshole gunman came to campus because his militia friends knew who her dad was and decided to go after her. The most recent attacks by Malachi were the same.

As soon as someone dangerous learned who her dad was, finding his biggest vulnerability was easy.

Lexi took a long pull of the beer and shook her head. She wasn't anyone's vulnerability, and she couldn't allow herself to think like one. Her father would never say it. He didn't go around looking for trouble, but it had a habit of finding him. When it did, he'd long proved incapable of walking away. Just like her grandpa . . . and, Lexi realized, exactly like herself. It was in all their DNA.

Maybe Kim extended an olive branch because she and Emily wanted Lexi to move back to the apartment. "You won't find out if you stay silent," Lexi reminded herself as she picked up her phone. She spent a few minutes thinking of the best way to reply and composed a message.

> Hey. It's been a rough few days. I feel guilty and terrible about what happened. I love you guys, and I'm OK with whatever you decide, but give me a couple days.

She set her cell back down, frowned at the beer, and

poured the rest out. A trip to the range would do a lot more for her.

~

VERONICA HAD BEEN KEEPING an eye on the news in Harford County, and her patience was rewarded.

She'd set a Google alert for Susquehanna State Park, and a paper out of Bel Air ran with a story. It would be making the local rounds soon enough.

BODY FOUND IN SUSQUEHANNA STATE PARK

Havre de Grace, MD—In a chilling discovery, the body of a man, believed to be around 40 years old, was found in the dense woods of Susquehanna State Park early this morning. According to Harford County authorities, the deceased, who is unidentified but appears to be of Israeli descent, was discovered by a construction worker involved in the park's renovation project.

The worker, Michael Jenkins, 34, described the grim scene. "I was clearing some underbrush when I stumbled upon . . . him," Jenkins recounted, visibly shaken by the experience. "I've never seen anything like it."

The Harford County Sheriff's Office, along with a forensic team, immediately cordoned off the area as a potential crime scene. Preliminary investigations suggest that the man died from a combination of blunt force trauma to the head and a grievous stab wound to the midsection. Sheriff's Office Spokesperson Captain Linda Harmon commented, "The nature of the injuries indicates a violent altercation. We are treating this as a homicide."

As no documents were found on or near the body, the identity of the man remains a mystery. Captain Harmon added, "Our top priority is identifying the victim. We're working with federal agencies, including the FBI, to see if he matches any missing persons reports, nationally or internationally."

Local residents are rattled by the news. Susquehanna State

Park, known for its scenic beauty and popular hiking trails, is a place many in the community hold dear. "It's shocking. You never think something like this could happen right in your backyard," said Emma Powers, a lifelong resident of Harford County.

As the story unfolds, questions abound. Who is this man, and what brought him to Susquehanna State Park? What circumstances led to this violent end? The community and law enforcement alike seek answers.

Captain Harmon urged anyone with information to come forward. "If you saw anything unusual in the park in the past few days, please contact us. You might hold the key to solving this tragic mystery."

Veronica breathed a sigh of relief. Malachi was dead. She would not be coming forward with any details, however. What she knew—or a sanitized version of it at least—would go into her story. What began as a tale of John Tyler's vigilantism now proved lighter on specifics. Still, it told the story of an anonymous retired Green Beret who meted out justice when the system failed people. If she altered or omitted a couple details, Malachi's body turning up in the park made an excellent coda for her piece.

She was also glad Tyler came out all right. When the man told Malachi to go ahead and kill her, Veronica figured all hope was lost. She would die before finishing the story—or getting married, or having children. When it mattered, however, Tyler showed up. Even though Malachi got the better of him initially, the right man won in the end.

Veronica read the article again. She mentally prepared a list of what she could use and which bits she would need to change or leave out. Once the story was finished, saved, and backed up, she would get on the road. She missed North Carolina, and her regular job was far more predictable. Sometimes, she didn't like that aspect of it. Right now, she craved it.

50

The next day, Tyler met Sara Morrison for lunch.

She picked a bistro in Ellicott City. It was in the historic part, a place Tyler always liked. All houses and shops looked like they'd been lifted straight from the early nineteenth Century. The classic architecture harkened back to a simpler time. Floods from two different major storms caused a lot of damage to this part of the town, but most of the owners stuck it out and repaired or rebuilt.

The restaurant took up the first floor of an old house. Other than a wall separating the kitchen and restroom from the dining area, the interior remained open. Simple decorations hung about. Sara sat at a table between high old-fashioned windows. She looked great—as always—in jeans and a sweater, her dark hair pulled back. Tyler sensed something was off in her demeanor right away. Her smile normally lit up the room and could be measured in gigawatts. Today, it lacked its usual wattage and didn't reach her eyes.

Still, he offered his best in return as he sat. "You been here before?" Tyler asked. He picked up the laminated one-page menu.

"A couple times," Sara said.

A waitress young enough to be one of Lexi's college class-mates emerged from the rear and took their order. Sara chose a Cobb salad. Tyler hadn't made it past the soup section yet. He scanned the sheet and opted for the fried chicken sand-wich with homemade potato chips. Both ordered iced tea to drink. As he expected, the bistro designation added at least ten percent to the prices. Tyler and Sara both returned their menus to the holder at the side of their table.

"Sounds like you finished what you needed to," Sara said.

Tyler nodded. "A little messy at times, but it's done."

"Everyone all right?"

"Musa . . . got hurt on the job earlier, but he still pitched in at the end. He'll be fine. I got a pretty nasty cut, but I'll live."

"Lexi told me you were all right." Sara's emphasis fell on the first word, admonishing him for fobbing the notification off to his daughter.

Before he could answer, the waitress returned with their teas. When she left again, Tyler said, "This was a tough one. Lexi's back at home now, and I spent last night and this morning at my easel." Both sessions saw Tyler work on the same painting. He continued to draw the dead men from his unit, but this time, they were all alive. The group stood in front of a place designed to resemble Pazir's rented house. No bodies appeared in the watercolor, but flames engulfed a small boat at the docks and popped out of several windows in the home.

"Given everything that happened, I'm sure it was chal-lenging." Sara's tone conveyed sympathy, and she gave Tyler's hand a squeeze. The server interrupted them again, this time delivering their meals. The girl could only delay what Tyler knew was coming for so long, however.

Sara started working on her salad right away. Tyler's sandwich smelled good. The chicken looked perfectly fried. It came open-faced on the plate, with bright green lettuce and a thick slice of tomato under it. Tyler closed the sandwich and took a bite. It was definitely worth the price. When Sara had finished about half her meal, she set her fork down and took a deep breath. "This isn't working for you," Tyler said when she struggled for words.

Her smile returned, and this time her eyes were soft and sympathetic. "I love you, Tyler. You understand my job and what I deal with. You don't place too many demands on my time. In countless ways, you're great. The thing is . . . I need stability. I thought you could provide it, and you do. I just need a different kind. I'm forty-eight. I've long decided I'm a career woman. Kids aren't for me. My exact duties can change with a new administration or SECDEF, but I'm still going to be a Pentagon executive. I need someone I can count on to be there."

"I understand."

"You do?"

"Yes." This time, Tyler squeezed her hand. "I love you, too. I always thought our relationship got off to a weird start. I saved you from my old boss's goon squad, they killed the man you were dating, and we . . . sort of happened." Sara chuckled. "I wish I could give you what you need and deserve, but . . . "

"You're you," Sara finished for him. "You're not going to walk away from trouble, even if it's someone else's and even if letting it go would be the safe play. It's one of the things I love about you, and it makes this really hard."

"We had a good run," Tyler said. They did. Considering the unusual genesis to their relationship, Tyler was surprised it lasted as long as it did. Still, he would miss Sara. He loved her, and he knew he would see her again in his paintings. "Does this mean I can't call you when the shit hits the fan?"

"No." Sara snickered. "I don't need to cut you out of my

life. I'd try to help if you were in a bad spot."

"I'd do the same for you."

Tyler finished his sandwich and chips. The meal was good, but the conversation with Sara, inevitable as it may have felt, dulled the taste for him.

WHEN TYLER RETURNED to the shop, Lexi sat behind his desk. "Trying to take over for me already?" he said when he walked in.

"I told a customer to piss off and gave Smitty and Ortiz raises," she said with a grin.

"You're batting five hundred. Not bad." Lexi started to stand, but Tyler put up a hand and sat in one of the guest chairs. "I just finished lunch with Sara."

Lexi must have picked up on something in his tone—maybe the way he said *finished*. She liked Sara, but his mention of her made his daughter frown. "And?"

"We've gone our separate ways."

"I'm sorry, Dad."

"Me, too, but I understand. She doesn't need someone who goes around shooting people. Plenty of them at the Pentagon already."

Lexi offered a sympathetic chuckle. "What about what you need?"

"I'll be all right. How are Emily and Kim?"

"I'm . . . not sure."

"What do you mean?"

"Kim's reached out a couple times. I don't know what to say, though. I feel terrible about what happened."

"Good place to start a conversation," Tyler said.

"They already know." Lexi sighed and pulled on her ponytail. "I'm not sure how we get past this. When that militia guy came to campus and shot up the student union, it was easy to say he was just some crazy asshole. This was different. Malachi got into the apartment. Emily was afraid for her life, and I don't blame her."

"Me, neither."

"So what do I do?" Lexi asked.

"You need to have the conversation with them. Hear them out. Don't be defensive. It wasn't your fault, but you can't lead off by washing your hands of everything. Blame me if you want. Malachi was there looking for you because he wanted to get to me. Tell Emily to go blonde, and people will stop mistaking the two of you."

Lexi flashed a small smile. "She might like a bit of humor."

"Most people do."

"I'm not ready yet." Lexi's fingers still pulled the ends of her hair. "Maybe in a couple days. I want to give them some space. I told Kim I needed a bit more time."

"You should do what you think is right." Tyler glanced at his watch. "Are you cutting class?"

"I did the work already. Professor doesn't really care about attendance as long as you keep up with assignments."

"Sounds like the best kind to have."

"Yeah, he's not bad." Lexi stood. "Thanks, Dad. You can have your chair back. See you at home."

"See you." Lexi left, and Tyler moved to his normal seat. He trusted her judgment, but he also felt she was slow-playing things with her roommates. Given enough time, people can find objections to any arrangement. The other girls needed to know what was going on. Lexi seemed resigned to the idea they were going to give her the boot. Maybe they would.

Before they did, however, Tyler wanted to talk to Emily and Kim.

51

FBI Special Agent Hope Raines stared at her burner phone.

We're a go. You know where to meet us.

It was a simple message, but it carried a lot of weight and complexity with it. She'd been hesitant about this assignment in the first place. "It's a shit job," she said to her empty motel room. Her boss used the exact same phrase when handing her the assignment. She'd be undercover with no support. Embedded in an interstate robbery ring.

Her knowledge of cars got her the gig. Now, she hoped the guys in the crew didn't discover who she really was. If they did, she only imagined what a quartet of testosterone-fueled jerks could do to the lone woman in their midst. Hope's boss's boss wanted these men caught, however, so she got the gig. The crew was ramping up operations again after being dormant for a while. Two people in different states died in earlier heists. Apart from those, the gang got in and got out cleanly.

Hope held the Android model in her trembling hand. This was her chance to get back in the good graces of her

AIC, his supervisor, and the Bureau. Her career had gone off course, and here was a chance to right it. Her fingers worked the keys.

I'm in. See you there.

It was a simple reply, but it carried significant weight. Hope would need to figure out how to make contact with her supervisor. The gang would issue her a new phone—one they could presumably track and listen in on. An idea formed in her head. The crew hired her because of her aptitude with cars, especially driving them and making them go faster. She'd done it her whole life. Making a hidden cubby in her own ride would be easy enough. An old flip phone—powered off unless she needed to use it—would fit inside.

Hope blew out a deep breath. She'd be putting it all on the line for this one. Her career for certain and maybe her life. Even if things with the gang went smoothly, who knew what the response to a robbery would be? She couldn't identify herself as a fed at the first sign of trouble. Even with a way to talk to the Bureau, the whole thing could be a mess and veer off the rails at a moment's notice.

Maybe she'd find another way out somewhere along the way. Perhaps someone might even help her, but she would need to meet someone who couldn't walk away from trouble.

Tyler parked the 442 in the lot for Plato's Parlor.

As a co-signer of the lease, parent, and emergency contact, his thumbprint opened the front entrance. He walked up the steps to the apartment and knocked on the door. Emily opened a few seconds later. She stood a couple inches shorter than Lexi—and Tyler would always say his daughter was prettier—but he understood how someone who didn't know either young woman could mistake one for the other. She wore what he now knew were yoga pants and a long-sleeved white T-shirt. "Mister Tyler," she said, smiling. "What can I do for you?"

"You've known me long enough," Tyler said. "You're an adult. Tyler is fine."

"You want to come in?"

"Please." She moved aside and swept her arm into the living room. Tyler walked through. Kim came out of the kitchen. She was the shortest of the three, slender enough to be petite, and wore her hair brushed over to hide a forehead scar. She also wore yoga pants—which Tyler used to call Spandex until Lexi upbraided him about being an old fogey —and a red Maryland hoodie. "Nice to see you, Kim."

"You, too, Mister . . . Tyler. Not mister."

"Not mister," Tyler agreed. "We're all adults."

"Does Lexi know you're here?"

"No, and she'd probably be pissed if she found out. For now, let's keep this little chat between us."

"Okay . . . for now." All three sat in the living room. The roommates took spots on the couch, so Tyler dropped onto the recliner.

"I didn't want to ask Lexi to leave," Emily said. "I really didn't. We've been wanting to live together like this for years, and then we all got into Maryland." She drew her knees up to her chest. "That man came in here, though. He thought I was Lexi. I didn't know what he was going to do to me."

Tyler put up a hand. "I understand. You don't have to defend your decision to me. Everyone should feel safe in their own place."

"What are you doing here, then?"

"I reached out to Lexi," Kim added. "We want to talk to her about everything, but I don't know if she's ready yet."

"She's not," Tyler said. "She understands why you wanted her to leave, but she's hurt. More than she'll admit to me. I think she takes it personally and feels like the whole thing was her fault."

Emily spread her hands. "Well . . . the creep was looking for her."

"Because of me."

"What?" the young woman said in stereo.

"Last year, before you all had this arrangement, you remember Lexi shooting a couple of guys on campus?"

Kim nodded. "They were trying to grab her up."

"They were. It was because of me then, too. Before my shop opened, I took a job working security for Alex Anne."

"I remember." Emily smiled. "Lexi said you could get her a ticket. We were so jealous."

"Thanks to some . . . inefficiencies in the process, kidnappers took Alex Anne. They worked for a trafficker named Farzaad Durrani. His plan was to sell her and a plane load of other girls to some rich assholes in the Middle East. Luckily, I got to the airport in time and stopped them. Durrani's nephew was supposed to grab Lexi to use as leverage against me."

After a few seconds of silence, Kim said, "That was a year ago. What about now?"

"Before Durrani died, he sent a message to a bunch of men who did the same work he did. One of them decided to get back at me recently. He hired an Israeli with an intelligence background. Before he came here to kidnap the woman he thought was my daughter, he killed four of the men I used to serve with."

"I'm sorry," Emily said, and Kim nodded in agreement.

"I don't go looking for trouble," Tyler said. "Years ago, I took out some very bad people in Afghanistan, plus Durrani last year, so this particular spot of trouble came looking for me. I never wanted anyone else to get swept up in it. In a just world, the Israeli would have come for me, and we would have settled things. Instead, he came here."

"Is he dead?" Emily asked in a quiet voice.

"Yes."

"Did he suffer?"

"Yes."

"Good," she said and then turned away as if embarrassed by her own vitriol.

"My point is . . . if you want to be mad at someone, be mad at me. Blame me. In some roundabout way, it's my fault. Malachi would never have come here if I didn't kill a trafficker at the airport last year. This isn't Lexi's fault. She loves you both, and she feels terrible about what happened. I don't want to see you take it out on her."

"You said everyone should feel safe in their own place," Kim offered.

"Yes."

"What if we don't?"

"I understand. I didn't come here to change your minds or talk you out of something you've already decided to do. I just wanted you to hear what really happened and why from me. Lexi won't tell you everything. She probably thinks she's protecting me because you'll hate me or something."

"We don't hate you," Emily said.

"Good," Tyler said. "It's even better if you don't hate Lexi."

"We could never."

"I was reaching out because we want to talk to her," Kim said. "This was always supposed to be the three of us."

"Do you want it to be again?" Both young women looked at each other and nodded. "Great. Make sure you tell Lexi, then. Just skip the part about me coming down here. She'd probably be horrified."

"I have to ask," Emily said. "I know you can't predict stuff like this, but do you think someone else might use Lexi to get at you?"

Tyler figured one of them would ask the question at some point. It was the one he didn't want to answer. "You're right. I can't know what's going to happen. I'll tell you this. Walking away from trouble isn't in my DNA. It's something Lexi gets from me. If someone sets their sights on me, I'm not a spy or anything. People can find my information, and this includes who my daughter is and where she lives. The good thing is you're in a secure building."

"What was his name? Malachi? He got in."

"Most people can't afford to hire operators in his class. I think the risk is low."

"But not zero," Emily said.

Tyler shrugged. "There's no realistic way to reduce risk to zero. Besides, even without Lexi and me, college life carries some inherent dangers . . . especially for young women. I'm sure you don't need me to tell you about shady guys on campus." They both offered resigned nods. "Now, add in the fact many of them get loaded every Friday and Saturday night, and the risk goes up." Tyler spread his hands. "There are plenty of homegrown assholes. You should worry about them before we start talking about well-paid Israeli killers. Lexi takes kickboxing classes and has a gun. I'm sure she'd be happy to introduce you to both."

Emily frowned. "Maybe we don't need to go that far."

"We can figure it out," Kim said. "What we know is we want our friend back."

"She'll be glad to hear it," Tyler said, "but I was never here."

"You were never here," Kim agreed with a smile.

52

———————

A FEW DAYS LATER, LEXI WALKED INTO TYLER'S OFFICE AT THE shop.

She'd moved back into the apartment with Emily and Kim over the weekend. He missed having her around but was happy she reconciled with her roommates. Tyler looked up from the laptop and smiled. The end of the month approached, and he needed to take time away from the service bays and tend to financials and documents. The stuff he hated. Lexi helped with this aspect. Her knowledge of Excel made things easier. "You all right, Dad?"

"I'm fine."

"How's the gash?"

"Better," Tyler said. He got it checked out at the VA hospital once the Pazir business concluded. A doctor there prescribed an antibiotic cream to guard against infection and complimented the person who did the stitches. "It'll probably leave a scar, but I'll have another to show my next girlfriend."

"Yeah." Lexi winced. "Sorry about Sara. I really liked her."

"I did, too. Still do." Desperate to change the subject, Tyler pivoted to something Lexi might be able to help with while she was here. "Did you come by for the end of the month reconciliation? I think we're a little early, but we might be able to get started. I'm sure Excel is ready."

"No, we can wait." She waved a hand. "I wanted to see how you were."

"You could have called. Or texted, knowing you. I'm happy to see you of course, but you didn't need to drive all the way here."

"Driving to or from College Park isn't so bad." She showed a knowing smile. "Is it?"

"I've done it quite a few times, so I don't really think about it unless traffic is really bad." Tyler played dumb. Both Emily and Kim said they wouldn't narc on him, and he believed them. Lexi, however, was smart enough to figure out something happened even if all parties kept their mouths shut.

"Uh-huh." She leaned back as much as the rigid guest chair would allow. "It's nice to be back in the apartment. Emily's doing a ton of laundry this weekend, so I might need to bring a load or two by the house."

"I would ask if you needed to borrow money or maybe raid my pantry for ramen, but I know you're a soup snob."

Lexi chuckled. "I might leave with a can or two."

"I have something for you, actually." Tyler unlocked the bottom left drawer of his desk and took out a small canvas bag. He set it on the desk. Lexi opened it, and her eyes went wide.

"Dad, this must be . . ."

"Six thousand dollars," he told her. "Plus your gun. Compliments of Malachi and his benefactor. They were sorry to hear the trouble they caused you, and wanted to contribute to you staying in the apartment. Should cover your share of the rent, right?"

"It'll come pretty close," Lexi said. "I'm sure the rate will go up at some point."

"Ask your boss for a raise, then."

"I get the feeling he's done some things for me recently already."

"Yes. He's handing you six thousand dollars and continuing to talk about himself in the third person."

Lexi closed the bag and set it on the floor beside her chair. "That's not what I meant."

"I only made warrant three, Lexi. I can't handle too many inferences."

"Thanks, Dad."

"Sure."

"For everything," Lexi added.

"Is there something you're thanking me for besides gifting you a few stacks of ill-gotten gains?"

"I think you know."

Tyler spread his hands. "Warrant three."

"Yeah, yeah." Lexi stood and collected the bag. "See you over the weekend, old man. Love you."

"Love you, too." Lexi left, and her Honda pulled out of the lot a moment later. She figured it out, and she didn't even get mad about it. Tyler chalked it up as a win. He'd enjoyed a few of them lately, which only served to make him wonder when his luck would take a turn.

END of Novel #7

John Tyler will return soon . . . and he'll be working with FBI agent Hope Raines, who's stuck in her bad assignment. Don't miss the adrenaline and action in the eighth Tyler novel, *Redline!*

THE END

AFTERWORD

Thanks for checking out this novel! I hope you enjoyed reading the book as much as I enjoyed writing it.

I write mysteries and thrillers with action, snark, and flawed heroes. If this sounds like something you like, you can check out my catalog below.

The John Tyler Action Thrillers

1. The Mechanic
2. White Lines
3. Lost Highway
4. Four on the Floor
5. Forced Induction
6. The Low Road
7. Backfire
8. Redline (Fall 2024)

The C.T. Ferguson Crime Novels:

1. The Reluctant Detective
2. The Unknown Devil
3. The Workers of Iniquity
4. Already Guilty
5. Daughters and Sons
6. A March from Innocence
7. Inside Cut
8. The Next Girl
9. In the Blood
10. Right as Rain
11. Dead Cat Bounce
12. Don't Say Her Name
13. Night Comes Down
14. Concrete Angels
15. Conduct Unbecoming
16. Bleeding into Winter (Summer 2024)

I generally release 3-4 new titles per year. For the most current list of books, please visit:

- https://tomfowlerbooks.com (direct sales)
- https://tomfowlerwrites.com
- https://books2read.com/tomfowler

(Notes: C.T. Ferguson appears in *White Lines*. John Tyler appears in *Don't Say Her Name*.)

While these are the suggested reading sequences, each novel is a standalone mystery or thriller, and the books can be enjoyed in whatever order you happen upon them.

Connect with me:

For the many ways of finding and reaching me online,

please visit https://tomfowlerwrites.com/contact. I'm always happy to talk to readers.

This is a work of fiction. Characters and places are either fictitious or used in a fictitious manner.

"Self-publishing" is something of a misnomer. This book would not have been possible without the contributions of many people.

- Stuart Bache for the cover design.
- My editor extraordinaire, Chase Nottingham.
- My wonderful advance reader team, the Fell Street Irregulars.